The Delta Factor

'If further titles match up to this page-turning thriller,
Lion will enjoy great success.'
Publishing News

'The Delta Factor's likable good guys, detestable
bad guys and fascinating glimpse at the world of
pharmacological research make it challenging
and entertaining.'
New Man

'The Delta Factor will appeal to lovers of good
thrillers everywhere. There is an all too plausible dose of
medical research entangled with power politics and
unscrupulous business practices, contained in a story
which will propel the reader into the cutting edge of
scientific research. It is an extremely well written book,
fast-paced and closely plotted.'
Tony Collins, Publisher of Monarch Books and
Renewal magazine

'I have read The Delta Factor straight through, at
some cost to sleep and work! I have greatly enjoyed it.
It has a beautiful fluency, a potency of language, and a
constant freshness of imagery.'
David Thistlethwaite, Program Director, UCCF

'Locke's real-life experience as a marketing manager
of a pharmaceutical companyhas left him well placed to
make a hard-hitting critique of the industry's
shortcomings.'
Church of England Newspaper

*This book is dedicated to
George Greenfield.
For the friendship, the guidance
and the challenge*

THOMAS LOCKE has resided in numerous countries over the past twenty years, with assignments in Europe, Africa and the Middle East. He pursued a highly successful business career, including a period as marketing manager of an international pharmaceutical company, before becoming a full-time writer in 1991.

Drawing on this rich experience, as well as extensive travels and research, Thomas Locke has developed a remarkable range of characters and settings. His second novel for Lion, *The Omega Network*, was published in 1994, and *The Aqaba Exchange* and To the Ends of the Earth appear in 1996. He and his wife currently live in Henley-on-Thames, Oxfordshire.

The
DELTA
FACTOR

Thomas
Locke

A LION BOOK

First edition published in the U.S.
by Bethany House Publishers

This edition published by
Lion Publishing plc
Sandy Lane West, Oxford, England
ISBN 0 7459 3177 4 (hardback)
ISBN 0 7324 3178 2 (paperback)
Albatross Books Pty Ltd
PO Box 320, Sutherland, NSW 2232, Australia
ISBN 0 7324 0890 3 (hardback)
ISBN 0 7324 0891 1 (paperback)

First US hardback edition 1994
First UK hardback edition 1995
10 9 8 7 6 5 4 3 2 1 0
First UK paperback edition 1996
10 9 8 7 6 5 4 3 2 1 0

Acknowledgments
All scripture quotations, unless indicated, are taken from
the HOLY BIBLE, NEW INTERNATIONAL VERSION.
Copyright © 1973, 1978, 1984 by International Bible Society.
Used by permission of Hodder & Stoughton, Ltd,
a member of the Hodder Headline Plc Group.
All rights reserved.

A catalogue record for this book is available
from the British Library

Printed and bound in Great Britain
by Cox & Wyman Ltd, Reading

> *"Man cannot play God and still remain sane. And the process of biology is inescapably placing in man's hands the power to play God . . . The risks of recombinant DNA techniques are historically unparalleled because the consequences of letting a new living creature loose in the world may be irreversible."*

> Dr Freeman Dyson
> *Disturbing the Universe*

1

Dr. Deborah Givens stepped from her specially fitted Jeep Cherokee, opened the back door, and pulled out her collapsible wheelchair. She was feeling all right at the moment, but there had been little warning twinges that morning, so she decided to use the chair and harbor what strength she had. But because she was nervous, and excited, and in a hurry, the wheelchair refused to unfold. It looked like it was going to be one of those days.

"Here, Debs, let me do that." A grizzled survivor of Iwo Jima shuffled up and bent over with a stifled groan.

"Thanks, Tom." She stepped back and leaned on the jeep. "I swear that thing has a mind of its own."

"All machinery does. That's the first thing they teach us in gunnery school. You scientists oughtta know that by now."

She watched him clamp the latches into place. "Good of you to help."

"Shoot. This is the only chance I get to push anybody round anymore." He held the handles while she eased herself down. "Bad day?"

"On a scale of one to ten," she replied, "I'd give it a minus five."

Tom wheezed a chuckle. "Know just how you feel, gal. The old pins just give out, and it don't matter that you still feel twenty upstairs."

"Twenty wasn't such a good year," Deborah said. "I'd prefer sixteen."

Tom wheeled her up the side entrance ramp. "You folks're about done around here, aren't you?"

Normally Deborah hated to have her chair pushed by anyone, even a hospital orderly. But Tom was different. No matter how early she arrived, he was always sitting on the front porch. He would rush down the stairs before she cut the motor. If she was walking that day, he shuffled alongside her. If she reached for the chair, Tom's age-spotted hands were usually there first. He had sort of adopted her on the first day, and Deborah had long since accepted that helping her gave definition to his lonely days. She answered, "It's a little hard to say."

"Reason I ask," Tom went on. "That young feller and the Injun, they were cooped up in there all night."

The faint tingle of excitement jangling her nerves since the early morning telephone call strengthened. "That a fact?"

"Wouldn't say it if it weren't. Took 'em a cup of coffee when the cafeteria opened. Both of 'em looked like they was sorta running on reserve. But excited just the same."

They pushed through the entrance. The halls were already filling with patients, mostly old, mostly men. The only feature Dr. Deborah Givens had in common with these patients was her wheelchair. That and the clinical trials which had brought her here twenty-two days ago.

It was a typical veterans hospital, a rundown building in a grim inner-city Norfolk, Virginia neighborhood. The cheerless architecture was worsened by coils of razor-wire crowning the chain link fence. The interior was no better. Walls were plastered with government-issue green paint. The patients wore identical striped bathrobes, which left them looking like prisoners. The air conditioning was a feeble, smelly joke. Old-fashioned metal-frame beds lined long wards like weary soldiers on parade. Sounds echoed back from miles and years away.

The majority of patients were old and male and poor and lonely. Many bore the scars of a rough life. Almost half of those Deborah had selected for her clinical study were cachectic—overly thin, anemic, sunken eyes and cheeks—signs that often indicated long-term alcohol abuse.

Yet despite it all, they possessed a burning gleam of patriotic pride and rock-hard dignity, the result of having fought wars for a country they loved. The fact that the country had long since forgotten their battles was accepted along with all of life's other injustices.

After twenty-two days of working with the patients at the Norfolk Veterans Hospital, Deborah Givens thought them to be some of the finest men on earth.

Tom stopped at the lab entrance, walked around, and pushed open the doors. "Promise you'll come back when you find a cure for old age?"

"You'll be the first to know," she assured him, and wheeled herself inside.

She found her two best men, as she called them, so deep in concentration that they did not notice her arrival.

There was no chance of anyone's ever getting the pair mixed up. Kenny Griffyn was a techie, a nerd's nerd, all bony angles and bottle-bottom glasses and speech that was lifted from a computer magazine. Cochise was an entirely different matter. He stood six feet ten inches tall, had hands the size of breakfast skillets, and outweighed Kenny by at least two hundred pounds.

Cochise was a Carolina east-coast Indian, which meant he was five generations and half a continent removed from the warrior who had first used the name. He bore the lines and grimness of a hard life, even though he was only thirty-three years old. Deborah knew his real name was John Windover only because she had seen it when registering his social security number. He had been dubbed Cochise in some long-forgotten bar, he had explained with the blank-faced take-it-or-leave-it attitude he used whenever talking about himself, and had never seen any reason to change back. Deborah thought him the find of the century, the best lab assistant she had ever worked with. The fact that the remainder of the

9

Pharmacon staff found him tremendously frightening disturbed her not at all.

She wheeled up beside the pair and demanded, "So what is so all-fired urgent that it couldn't wait two days?"

As usual, when anyone else was there and willing to take on the burden of speaking, Cochise remained mute. "We have some good news," Kenny announced. The techie's eyes were glazed as marbles, a clear signal of no sleep, excitement, and continuous infusions of coffee that had been cooking all night. "Very, very good news."

Deborah responded as she usually did when others threatened to go off the deep end. She retreated into skepticism. "You want to quantify that?"

"How high do you feel like flying?" Kenny Griffyn demanded, refusing to give in this time. "Interplanetary orbit? Beyond Jupiter? We're talking major news here."

Deborah glanced at Cochise. The massive, fatigue-smudged features were blank as ever. "I'm already sitting down," she replied. "So hit me."

"Okay, the control group." Continuous sheets of computer graphics were unfolded and slapped down on the cluttered desk before her.

Deborah studied them and declared, "No change."

"Zip. Across the board." Kenny began stabbing a finger at individual patients, identified only by numbers. "Stable, stable, uh-oh, here's a bad one. Another stable. Roller-coaster downslide on this one. Stable, stable, stable, look here, free fall from twenty thousand feet. No parachute, either."

"These are people we're talking about," Deborah reminded him sharply. "People in pain. Sick people."

"Right. Exactly." The techie tossed the control data aside. He was taut as an electric power cable. "Now check this out." A second graph was accordioned out with a flourish.

Deborah bent over the tables, squinted her eyes, felt her own nerves start humming. She leaned back, took a

10

couple of deep breaths, rubbed her eyes, then checked the figures a second time. "You've made a mistake."

"Uh-uh. No way."

"You goofed."

"This is the third time we've run the figures. Want to see the others? Carbon copies."

She looked at him, her heart rate zinging up to maximum velocity. "No patient showed a decline in condition? Not one?"

"Not one. And three remissions. Three. Count 'em." He grabbed two handfuls of his hair and tried to pull it out by the roots. "Want to tell me the odds of that happening? In twenty-two days?"

"Three remissions?"

"Take a look out the window. We got two meningitis patients out there with less than a week to live dealing blackjack."

"They've cleaned half the night shift outta next week's pay," Cochise rumbled, speaking for the first time since her arrival that morning. As always, his voice sounded like a bear growling from the back end of a very deep cave.

"I was right, wasn't I?" the techie insisted. "Major."

"I've got—" Deborah broke off as a strange pucka-pucka-pucka sound droned through the window, growing louder by the second. She wheeled herself over, searched the sky, then demanded, "Did either of you order the company helicopter?"

"Me?" Kenny's eyes widened. "Since when did I rate perks like that?"

The lab door opened for the duty nurse, who announced, "Dr. Cofield just called."

Kenny and Cochise chimed in with groans.

"The message was for you, Dr. Givens. He says there's an emergency. He needs you to leave immediately for Edenton."

"Thank you," Deborah said, folding up the printouts.

"Tell the pilot I'll be right there."

"Just like I said, we're talking major league here," Kenny told her as she started for the door. "So big the word's getting out by osmosis."

"One of you will have to drive my car back," Deborah told them. "I hereby order you to keep four wheels on the road at all times."

Deborah wheeled herself outside, then allowed the pilot to push her chair up to the chopper's passenger door and help her alight. She kept her countenance composed throughout. It was only when they were airborne that she leaned back in her seat and gave in to the one luxury she had refused herself for seven long years.

Hope.

Tom shuffled out the veterans hospital's doors and made his slow way down the drive. The guard at the main entrance, almost as old as Tom, gave him a friendly wave. Tom did not return it because he did not see it. His eyes remained fixed upon the road at his feet.

The car was parked right where it had been the last time. It was one of those foreign jobs, low to the ground and built without any corners. The windows were almost as dark as the black metallic paint. Tom steeled himself and kept going.

The window powered down as he approached. "Well?"

"First things first." Tom stuck out his hand.

"Tell me," the man inside the car insisted.

"Look, bud. I don't like doing this one bit. The only thing that's keeping me standing here 'stead of running for the cops is I'm broke as a sharecropper in a ten-year drought. So if you want what I got, hand it over."

A longish pause, then an envelope slid through the window. "What do you have?"

"They found it," Tom replied, tearing open the envelope and ruffling the bills.

"Found what?"

"Whatever it is they been looking for," Tom snapped. "You're bound to know that much, or you wouldn't be wasting time around a dump like this."

"You're sure?"

"Sure as sure can be. Them lab fellers was holed up in there all night. Took 'em coffee at dawn, and they was all but dancing round their computer. Then Dr. Debs arrives in a roar of dust and takes off twenty minutes later by copter." Tom nodded in solid certainty. "Yep, whatever it is they was after, they got it."

As the window powered back up, the man inside said, "We never met."

"Been through two wars and more'n seventy years," Tom crabbed at the departing car. "Never met a foreigner I'd care to remember a second longer'n I had to. And that includes you, mister."

Deborah Givens hated going into what the scientists and techies called the Tombs. The Pharmacon executive office suites were connected to the labs by a plushly carpeted, domed hallway whose air conditioning sucked up every sound as soon as it was emitted. Deborah's colleagues insisted the effect was intentional.

The scientists were always nervous around the bean counters, which led to adolescent jokes and overloud laughter. The execs loathed levity almost as much as they did the scientists' casual dress code. The execs could not insist that their lab rats wear ties and shirts with collars, but they could try for what they called "proper decorum" and the lab rats described as a mental vacuum. The techies said the bean counters couldn't gain respect through scientific knowledge since they didn't have any. So the suits demanded deference by making the lab rats grovel for every research dime and by dragging them down to the Tombs from time to time.

Rare was the senior bean counter who ever made his way into the labs. Conferences were limited to the Tombs, or as some techies called it, the Tower of Money. Summonses were issued via junior bean counters who could not be arm-twisted while in alien territory to opening up the corporate wallet.

One of the few positive sides to her illness, as far as Deborah was concerned, was that her visits to the Tombs had grown few and far between. As the illness progressed, she had been released from duties as chief researcher on one of the firm's major projects. The execs had been understandably terrified of investing sizable chunks of corporate dough in a project their top scientist might be unable to finish.

Deborah had allowed herself to be replaced, but for a price. In return for going peacefully, she had forced the bean counters to grant her lab space and funding. She had decided to check out a possibility that Deborah called intriguing and the bean counters considered far beyond left field.

She wheeled herself into the outer office and stopped before the desk belonging to Blair Collins, newly appointed secretary to the vice president for research and development. "Is his highness in?"

Blair made a face. "Unfortunately. So is Whitehurst."

"Do you know what this is all about?"

"Nobody tells me anything." Graceful fingers pulled honey-colored hair behind her ear.

It still amazed Deborah that she and Blair were becoming pals. Looks like Blair's were normally synonymous with hostility from both sides. "Maybe somebody lost a bean."

Blair nodded. "You found a place for me yet?"

"You're asking the wrong person, sister. I've got to rely on the grand high poobah in there for funding." She spun her chair toward the doors leading to the inner sanctum. "Besides, moving you downstairs would cause riots and mayhem. Best to let my overheated techies dream from afar."

"I'll wear sackcloth and ashes," Blair offered.

"In your case it wouldn't help," Deborah replied, and opened the door.

"Deborah!" Angrily Dr. Harvey Cofield raised both hands over his head. "Where on earth have you been?"

"Exploring the outer reaches of science," she answered. "Good morning, all."

Deborah's boss was a sleek-suited tyrant. At some point in the distant past he had collected several degrees and still considered himself to be a capable scientist, although he had not spent quality lab time in years. These days, the only journals Dr. Cofield opened contained stock tips and money-market trends. Dr. Cofield considered himself to be an extremely capable administrator. His staff considered him an overpaid clown.

Dr. Cofield loved toys. He loved perks. He loved power. He loved everything that bore the scent of success. He drove a Lexus with leather interior and a bumper sticker that read, "My other car is a Lear."

If Dr. Cofield did anything well, it was play the corporate game. His talent for infighting was legendary. He swam through the murky waters of company politics and scientific credit-grabbing like a hungry shark.

Dr. Cofield demanded, "Is it too much to expect my staff to check in from time to time?"

"Let's see. Today is Friday, right?" Deborah said crossly. "Since you were the one who sent me to the Philadelphia conference for the past four days, I assumed you might know where I was. Then this morning—"

"Never mind," Dr. Cofield snapped. "There's been a leak. Somebody on your team must have opened their big yap."

"Now just a doggone minute, Harvey," Deborah started.

15

"What Dr. Cofield meant to say," Pharmacon's executive vice president, James Whitehurst, interrupted smoothly, "was that we have been forced to play our hand sooner than we would otherwise have liked."

"Nobody from my staff talked," Deborah fumed. "Not a soul, not a word."

"Be that as it may," Whitehurst continued, pouring corporate oil on the stormy waters, "we have ourselves a problem that will not go away of its own accord and which will require us all to pull together as a team."

Deborah subsided, dispatching a baleful glare in Cofield's direction. "I'm listening."

"Rumors have begun appearing in the most unlikely places."

"What sort of rumors?"

"The worst kind," Harvey Cofield snapped, irritated as always when his scapegoating was not going as planned. "Ones with a shred of truth."

"It appears that some members of the press have been led to believe we are further along in our process than is the case."

"We are," Deborah announced smugly.

"We are what?"

"Further along," Deborah replied. "That's where I was this morning. It looks like—"

"Never mind," Whitehurst interrupted. He disliked anyone else speaking once he began. Whitehurst considered himself to be a prime example of urbane leadership. Deborah had not yet formed a final conclusion, but she was tending to think that the new exec VP most resembled an eel—slippery and hard to pin down, but dangerous when cornered.

Whitehurst had assumed the executive vice-president role at their Edenton facility scarcely two months before. The former ranking exec's wife, a born and bred New Yorker, had loathed North Carolina and commonly referred to the little bayside community as a time warp

16

to Tobaccoville. The exec had taken early retirement and moved back to their Fifth Avenue condo, leaving Pharmacon's new Edenton labs to be run by Whitehurst.

Pharmacon was considered a second-tier ethical pharmaceutical firm. Ethical because it did original research into new drugs. Second-tier because it was far outranked in both size and research potency by the giants—Squibb, Pfizer, Merck, Bayer, and the others.

Back in the seventies, Pharmacon had come up with the vanguard treatment for heart attack and stroke victims, also used in lesser doses for treatment of high blood pressure. The incoming revenue had quickly swollen Pharmacon's coffers to the bursting point. But instead of enabling new research breakthroughs, success had turned Pharmacon into a corporate pachyderm—slow and ponderous and unwieldy. Occasional modifications and add-ons to existing products, as well as aggressive advertising campaigns for its over-the-counter drugs, managed to keep Pharmacon financially afloat. But for industry watchers and those in the know, Pharmacon was a company going nowhere fast.

Three years earlier, Pharmacon's aging board had finally agreed that something radical was required to resuscitate the firm. Something bold. Something that would shake the company from its complacent slumber.

The Edenton facility had been that bold new step.

As far as the New York City-based board was concerned, Edenton, North Carolina was only a half step away from the Third World. Tucked snugly along a little bay in the backwaters of Albemarle Sound, it did not even have a decent airport. Anyone visiting from headquarters had to copter over from either Norfolk or Raleigh. This was exactly what the board had wanted. By selecting a site next to a village of some six thousand people, it had hoped to discourage most of the New York staff from coming within a hundred miles of the new factory.

They had succeeded almost too well. The only way top administrators like Cofield and Whitehurst had been enticed to sacrifice a New York lifestyle for Edenton was with promises of untold wealth and power and eventual returns to civilization. But scientists, Deborah Givens among them, had been far more willing to go where called on the promise of sparkling new labs. The research staff had been given a relatively free rein and encouraged to tackle new problems. Promising initial developments had been made in several directions. The reports filtering north had been sufficiently positive to frighten some of the New York staff into actually getting some work done—another hoped-for result.

But no one, neither in New York nor in Edenton, had ever expected the payoff to come so soon. Or from the direction it did.

"We have no choice," Whitehurst told them. "We have been forced to call a press conference."

Deborah sat up straight. This was serious damage control. "We've barely started the FDA approval process."

"You let me handle that," Dr. Harvey Cofield replied smugly.

"Allow *us* to handle it," Whitehurst corrected.

"Whatever."

Deborah swung her gaze from one man to the other. "What are you two talking about?"

"Perhaps you don't understand the significance of what we are dealing with," Whitehurst said.

"I should," Deborah countered. "I discovered it."

"Yes, well, there is a tremendous latent demand for your discovery."

"Not to mention a tidal wave of political pressure once this thing gets out," Cofield added with evident satisfaction.

"This already *is* out," Whitehurst replied.

"From which source no longer matters. What we must

now do is make sure we are able to state the facts clearly and precisely before the rumors are printed as fact and this whole affair is blown completely out of proportion."

Deborah kept her eyes on Cofield. "You're planning to pull some political strings, aren't you. Do an end run around the FDA."

"Not in the least," Whitehurst demurred. "We simply intend to speed things up a bit. In the interest of all the patients who shall benefit from your marvelous discovery, my dear."

Eel, Deborah decided. Definitely an eel. "So when do we put on the song-and-dance act?"

"In," Whitehurst glanced at his watch, "precisely one hour and eleven minutes."

"What?" Deborah gaped. "I don't have anything prepared. No press kits, no data, no—"

"Save it," Cofield ordered. "This is the prelim only. We go out, say we're working on the drug, close up shop."

"There shouldn't be more than a handful of media hounds," Whitehurst soothed. "We kept the invitations to a very few people only."

"Hard to say how many exactly," Cofield warned. "Things like this tend to spread through the press like wildfire."

"A dozen at most," Whitehurst assured her, and rose to his feet. "What say we meet back here and go down together?"

There were two fist fights and a dozen bruised egos before the higher-ups admitted the conference room was too small. The press conference was delayed an hour for the auditorium to be prepared, for tempers to be cooled, and coffee to be served.

Dr. Cofield opened and directed his address specifically to the scientific journalists, which meant he talked over the heads of the popular press. Whitehurst watched in horror as the initial hostility returned in force. He sat there and visualized the kind of coverage that would be generated.

Finally he could bear it no longer. He stood and moved up beside Cofield, and said into the microphone, "Thank you very much, Dr. Harvey Cofield, for that most engaging introduction. Now perhaps we should allow Dr. Deborah Givens to proceed."

Deborah jerked in surprise. She had not expected to speak at all. Feeding piranha would normally be easier to disengage than Harvey Cofield from a microphone.

Whitehurst realized he had just made a major gaff by the venomous look Cofield shot him. But it was too late to turn back. "After all," he said, smiling nervously. "It was Dr. Givens who made this discovery."

Deborah hid her grin by lowering her head. Another glorious blooper. Cofield would be fit to be tied.

"Dr. Givens?"

Deborah pushed herself erect and walked toward the microphone. She had left her wheelchair to one side of the stage, but now she wondered if that had been such a good idea. She was feeling increasingly weary. But no time to worry about that now. Deborah rubbed her nose hard to cover her smile as Cofield spat a little venom her way on his way back to his chair.

She approached the microphone, smiled briefly, and said, "Good morning."

"For several generations," she went on, "Central Europeans have been taking a root extract called echiniacin—"

"How do you spell that?" someone called out.

She did so, then went on, "Echiniacin was said to strengthen the immune system. Some doctors scoffed at it, while others swore by it. The reasons are obvious."

"Maybe to you," muttered someone in the front row.

Deborah kept her cool. "We have well-established lab methods for measuring how well a particular substance acts in fighting a particular illness once the ailment has been identified. There is no way, however, for us to prove that a solution might *prevent* a certain individual from contracting a specific disease. None whatsoever."

"Can you explain that?" called a voice from the back.

Whitehurst rose from his chair to call for order. Deborah stopped him with an upraised hand. When the exec had subsided, she said, "Okay. Let's say for example that from a thousand healthy people, an average of seventy-five will suffer from one form of cancer or another within a twenty-year period. Any test of a preventative medicine would be inconclusive, even if we found a thousand people willing to report to our lab every morning for twenty years so that a technician could give them a dose and record the data. Remember, these would all have to be *healthy* people, so there would be no illness as an impetus to their being willing subjects. No, strike that, there would have to be two thousand. We would need a control group taking a placebo to ensure reliability."

"A what?" called an impatient voice.

"Placebo," Deborah repeated. "Usually a water-sugar solution, something to make sure that the medicine itself and not the act of taking a medicine has made the difference. For instance, having to show up every day at a lab may make the subjects more conscious of their health, so they might stop smoking and drinking and eat a more balanced diet. That sort of thing. As I was saying, though, even if we *could* do this type of study, the results would be inconclusive."

"Why?"

She shrugged and felt a sudden wave of fatigue rise with the movement. "Because we would have no way of knowing who out of that thousand would have developed the illness *without* the drug. Maybe we chose the wrong segment of the population. Maybe a hundred different reasons. The only way to be sure that a group *might* have become cancerous would be by starting the experiment with all participants already ill. And then, of course, we

21

would no longer be studying prevention."

There was a pause, then someone asked, "So what did you do in your testing?"

"Instead of trying to study how to keep healthy people healthy, we studied the drug's effect on viruses. We restricted our initial studies to infected patients."

"And?"

"We managed to identify several potentially active ingredients within the echin root," Deborah replied. "And by recombinant DNA experimentation we raised their potency through growing new strains of the plant."

Deborah shifted to ease the growing ache in the back of her neck. She knew she had lost some of the journalists on that last stretch, but she did not have the energy to explain herself. "Our initial findings indicate that the concentrated solution retards the growth of virus-related illnesses."

There was a moment's stunned silence, then a roar of demanding queries.

"*All* viruses?"

"We have only worked on about a dozen viruses so far," Deborah answered, struggling to keep her voice steady. "And not all subjects have been healed. But the natural progression of the virus-related illness appears to have been curtailed, or perhaps even stopped."

"Does this mean you've found a cure for the common cold?"

"No cures," she said. "Remember, we are talking about prevention here."

"What about AIDS?"

"No evidence on that one yet." Suddenly Deborah visualized all her remaining energy being sucked down an open drain. "All we can say at the moment is that if a person were to take this solution on a regular basis, it appears that they would be much less likely—"

Suddenly Whitehurst was there at her elbow. "I believe we should wait to discuss our specific findings once all the results are in," he said, forcing the words around a pasted-on smile.

Deborah was only too happy to relinquish the podium. "Thank you," she said to the mike, then walked on faltering legs toward her wheelchair. Camera flashes lit her way like a flickering strobe.

If Hank Aaron Jones' daddy could see his land now, he would keel over and die a second time. For certain and for sure.

The thought gave Hank pause from time to time, but not for very long. As far as Hank Aaron Jones was concerned, the best thing that had ever happened to his family's land was having Pharmacon move in as a neighbor.

Hank Aaron Jones had been named after his daddy's number one hero, and he hated his name almost as much as he loved his farm. The Jones family had toiled their land for eleven generations, through three colonial governors and every president since Washington refused to become king of the new United States. They had lost family to every war except the one with Mexico. They had even known the misery of losing great-great-uncles to both sides of the War Between the States. The Jones family was American to the core, and they had bought the right to stand tall through the sweat of their brow and the blood of their kin.

News of Hank Aaron Jones' new neighbor, the one who had purchased the derelict farm on the other side of the forest, the one between him and the new bypass, had come by way of a stranger. The man in his city suit and big polished car had pulled up unannounced three years ago, and offered Hank so much money for his east forty that Hank's wife, Mildred, had been forced to go lie down. Hank had figured the man for a big talker with more mouth than sense, until another group had showed up three days later and doubled the first offer.

Hank Aaron Jones was not selling. Not then, not now. His boy was up studying modern agriculture at the state university in Raleigh, preparing for a future that fair boggled Hank's mind. There was not a thing Hank Aaron Jones wanted doing, nor a place he wanted seeing, that lay outside Chowan County, North Carolina. But Hank was a forward-looking fellow, and he felt in his bones that Pharmacon's arrival was good for the area and good for the farm.

Not that it had all been easy street. Pharmacon's arrival had meant a revaluation of his property. That had brought on higher taxes, right when the federal government had looked ready to slice a chunk out of tobacco price subsidies. But before Hank Aaron Jones had reached the point where he needed to approach the bank for another loan, Pharmacon had come to his rescue. In a very big way.

Two scientists had stopped by and asked if he would be willing to set aside some of his acreage and grow some plants for them. That would depend, Hank had replied, on what they were willing to pay. They asked, how much was he making from his tobacco and soybean crops? Hank Aaron Jones' daddy hadn't raised no fool for a son. Hank had picked the amount he'd made from his very finest year, set his face in rock-solid lines, and lofted the sum skyward. Without even batting an eye, the scientists had offered him twice again as much.

Now Hank Aaron Jones stood on his back porch, looked out over his fields, and respectfully asked his daddy's memory to shut up. If those scientists were willing to pay good money for him to grow weeds, then so be it.

Mildred was busy in the kitchen with the breakfast dishes. Through the window over the sink, she spotted a plume of dust rising from their dirt road and said, "Trouble's a'coming."

"Naw it ain't," Hank replied. The only person who'd

come by that early was their neighbor to the southwest, Jude Taylor. Jude wasn't more trouble than any other neighbor. Jude was just Jude.

The old Ford pickup did a four-point turn in their swept front yard, scattering chickens and dust in every direction. Through the open window a beefy, red-faced man called, "What you know, Hank?"

"Morning, Jude."

"Got to run into town for some feed. I swear I got me a heap of prize hogs in the making. You need anything?"

Hank swiveled about and called back, "We need anything from town, Mildred?"

His wife answered by clattering the dishes as hard as she could without breaking them. She would just as soon have walked around the block than given Jude Taylor the time of day.

Hank hid his smile behind a swig of coffee. Jude was a buddy from high school, and goodness knows there weren't many of those still around. He was lazy and he drank and word was he wasn't any easier on his wife than he was on his truck. But Hank found reason to forgive Jude much by remembering the good old days. "Looks like we're set, Jude. Thanks for stopping by."

"Ain't no problem. What you been up to?"

"Been going like a ten-mule team in a mudhole since spring."

"That a fact?"

Hank nodded. "Them scientists fellers, they got me running in seventeen directions at once. Come by three weeks ago, told me to plow back thirty acres of soybeans I've been sweating over since April. Want me to put in some more weeds. You believe that?"

"They figure on having a crop come up, planting in July?"

"Ain't interested in holding to the season," Hank answered. "They say it's a perennial, brought it all the way from Hungary, I think I got that right. This is the

25

second crop of it I put in for them. All they want is the roots."

"Roots?"

"That's what they said. Aim on making a potion from the roots. Strange thing, too. Them new plants are already bigger'n the ones I planted back in June." Hank stretched and looked out to where Jude's distant fields blazed yellow, like an earthbound sunrise. "How're your crops doing?"

Jude's gaze turned shifty. "Don't hardly know. Ain't been down there in almost two weeks."

"How's that?"

Jude started to say something, then stopped. There was a moment where his mind seemed bent on following two different tracks, then he said, "Aw, ain't much to it. Stick the seed in and stand back is all I gotta do."

Hank knew that for a fact. One of the local seed-oil companies had contracted with Jude to raise a crop of rapeweed, which didn't hardly seem like farming at all. This suited Jude down to the ground, as it left him with enough time on his hands to hang around pestering his neighbors. Hank asked, "You like a coffee?"

"Naw. Gotta get going." But Jude stayed as he was, beady eyes peering through fleshy folds like deeply embedded marbles. "Them scientists pay good money, I hear."

Hank flipped the dregs of his cup over Mildred's rose bed. "I get by."

"Think maybe you could mention my name to them folks?" A dirt-encrusted forearm emerged from the truck's interior to lean on the sill. "I got all kinds of acres I'd be willing to plow over, they give me the right price."

"You already asked me that, Jude." The man had been pestering him all year. "And I done told you, I've talked to them until I'm blue in the face."

"And?"

26

"And nothing." Hank set his face in no-nonsense lines. There was nothing to be gained from telling his neighbor that the scientists had looked over his land and decided they wouldn't touch him with a cane pole. Them scientists were nothing if not cautious. They checked things out real careful and were always hanging around, taking soil samples and just generally being nosy. They gave him pages and pages of instructions and expected them to be followed to the letter. If they said irrigate thoroughly and use only their special fertilizers and weed by hand, that was exactly what they meant. They paid good, but they expected him to keep his side of the bargain. "It's their decision, not mine."

Jude started his motor. "Yeah, well, you get a chance, you just remember your old buddy Jude."

"You got it," Hank said and waved with his coffee cup as the truck belched smoke and roared back down the drive.

Only then did Mildred emerge. "I declare, that man is nine-tenths lazy and five parts fool."

"Jude's all right."

Mildred humphed her disagreement. "His land's so weary it's amazing it don't snore."

Hank handed her his cup. "I ain't got time to listen to this."

"We'd all be a lot better off if that man didn't ever set foot on our land again."

Hank did the only thing he could to stop that conversation, which was walk over and start his tractor. He swung the heavy machine around and waved down at his wife, who was still going on at him.

He started down through his southern acreage, all of which was growing strange-looking crops for the scientists at Pharmacon. A faint breeze was blowing straight from the south, and there wasn't a cloud in the sky. The day was going to be a scorcher.

He followed the track on a ways, it being his habit to start each day by circling the fields he would work, just checking things over, getting the tasks straight in his mind. He paused where his fields met the road, which was little more than a gravel track and used only by the two families. Hank looked across to Jude's rapeweed fields. The golden blossoms stretched out as far as he could see, a truly glorious sight. Their smell was captivating this early in the morning. Hank took a deep breath, then started back up to where he had unhooked the fertilizer tank the evening before.

It was just about then that the first plant opened its eyes and waved up at him.

Hank Aaron Jones yanked on the hand brake, held on tight as the tractor shuddered to a stop, then rubbed his eyes. Hard.

Tendrils the color of a neon rainbow suddenly popped from the earth and started winding their way up both sides of his tractor. But Hank found it hard to be afraid. More and more of the little plants were opening their eyes, and they all looked so *friendly*.

The tendrils were fanning out, completely enveloping the tractor. The most beautiful flowers he had ever seen began to emerge, all rose-tinted, with long graceful stems of deepest violet. Bright yellow butterflies gushed forth as each flower opened its face, their wings brushing his face as they formed a cloud over his head.

Hank fumbled for the switch to cut the motor. He could scarcely see his hands, there were so many of those glorious little butterflies. Then a parting formed, and he looked down. The flowers were pulling up their roots, walking over, gathering around the tractor.

And they were singing the most beautiful song.

Mildred Jones came back out on her porch, drawn by the strangest sound. Yes, there it was again. She pushed through the screen door, and realized the tractor had stopped halfway through the fields. The motor was no longer running.

She called out, "Hank?"

She watched her husband clamber down from the tractor, his gait unsteady. Then she heard the sound again. He was laughing.

"Hank Aaron Jones," she yelled shrilly. "If you are fooling around with me, I'm going to give you what for!"

Her husband replied by falling down and disappearing amidst the wavering plants.

"Hank!" Mildred scrambled across the yard and down the path as fast as her legs would carry her. In her panic, she failed to notice Jude Taylor's truck parked at the end of their drive.

The big man watched her race toward her husband. He waited until she had half-walked, half-carried Hank back into the house before driving slowly away.

2

Cliff Devon closed the door on the organized clutter of his office and said to his secretary, "I won't be in this afternoon."

"I know," Madge answered, her voice filed to a raspy edge by heavy doses of cigarettes and city life. The ruling that ended all smoking in federal buildings had been a tough one on old Madge, but she wasn't a quitter. Her desk bore a massive five-year calendar, which she was halfway through on the way to winning her very own thirty-year pension. She asked, "You get the okay from Sandra?"

"Yes." Sandra was his boss and the scourge of Cliff's existence, an overly ambitious climber of the federal power ladder.

"Let's see, that Pharmacon facility is in Edenton, right?"

Cliff nodded. "Have you ever been there?"

"Don't need to." Madge could sneer better than anyone Cliff knew. "You seen one dull little Southern town, you've seen them all. It hasn't changed a bit since the Civil War and has the population of a small petting zoo. The inhabitants all bear striking resemblances to each other."

"You're always such a ray of sunshine," Cliff said.

"No mall, no nightlife, no liquor by the drink. A Baptist's idea of heaven." Madge gave him her smug little smirk and added, "Enjoy."

Just outside his doorway, Cliff ran into Ralph Summers, Sandra's boss and the head of the Food and Drug Administration's division dealing with applications for new drugs. "Sandra tells me you're off to see a friend at Pharmacon this weekend."

"That's right." Cliff was hardly surprised to hear that Sandra had checked with the higher-ups before giving her okay. Sandra checked the political winds before blowing her nose.

"I assume you have run it by their coordinator down there. Who is it, by the way?"

"Cofield," Cliff replied. "Harvey Cofield. He's supposedly their research director, but this discovery caught everybody by surprise. He's handling the application personally. I guess the new facility doesn't have its coordinating team in place, and something this big he wanted to cook at home."

All the major pharmaceutical companies, Pharmacon included, had teams whose sole purpose was to steer new drug applications through the FDA maze. Cliff had met Cofield on several occasions and decided Harvey Cofield was a true control freak.

Ralph Summers asked, "Who is this friend of yours?"

"Dr. Deborah Givens. We met when I was in college. She's one of Pharmacon's top researchers."

Summers scrunched his forehead in concentration. "Haven't I seen her name somewhere lately?"

Cliff could not help but be impressed. The man dealt with more than two hundred drug-approval applications per year, most listing as many as sixty researchers as co-discoverers. "Her team came up with that immune-system strengthener they've got undergoing clinical trials in Norfolk."

"That's it. You're handling that application, aren't you?"

"Yes."

"And Cofield is letting you traipse around on your own?"

Cliff grinned. "I think Debs can handle Cofield."

"Well, just be sure you don't let them host you in any

way that might look questionable under scrutiny."

"Don't worry." Cliff genuinely liked Ralph Summers. He was a political appointee, but one who tried hard to do his job well and keep his cumbersome operation moving ahead as swiftly as any federal operation possibly could. "I'll pay for everything out of my own pocket. I've already talked to Deborah about that."

"Fine." Summers gave him a friendly nod. "You should have an enjoyable weekend. From what I hear, that new Pharmacon facility is really something else."

The Food and Drug Administration occupied one large portion of the federal rabbit warren in Rockville, Maryland, situated about an hour's drive north of Washington, D.C. The building housed various agencies of Health and Human Services of which the FDA was one. Almost six thousand people worked in the concrete beehive. His first week on the job, Cliff had gotten lost between the main entrance and his office, then again between his office and the cafeteria—even finding the restroom had been a major feat. The FDA building was about as user-friendly as a tax form.

The elevator doors were closing when a munchkin-sized co-worker squeaked inside. "Made it!"

"I've been meaning to ask you," Cliff said. "Where do you buy those ties?"

Horace Tweedie touched his trademark red bow tie. "State secret."

Cliff nodded amiably. Horace held some job in filing—he forgot exactly what. He had a reputation as a purebred grouch, but Cliff managed to get along with him fairly well. Cliff was able to get along with about anyone. Except, that is, with his boss. "Got big plans for the weekend, Horace?"

The little man ran a hand over his graying crewcut. "Plan to work in my garden if the weather stays nice. You off on your trip? Where was it you're going?"

"Edenton, North Carolina," Cliff replied, no longer

amazed at the trivia passed along in federal gossip. There was an invisible network akin to jungle drums that somebody had forgotten to teach him during his indoctrination. "I have a friend who works at Pharmacon's new facility."

"Take it easy," Horace told him as the doors opened on the ground floor. "I don't envy you, out in Friday afternoon traffic."

"That's why I'm leaving now." Cliff gave him a friendly smile and headed for the front door. He faltered momentarily when the backside of a familiar head appeared at the coffee shop's counter. He then speeded up as fast as humanly possible without actually breaking into a run.

He almost made the main doors before a voice called out, "Oh, Cliff."

He heaved a silent groan and swung around. "Hello, Sandra."

A meticulously made-up woman tap-tapped her high heels down the corridor toward him. Sandra Walters was a dedicated soldier in the endless battle with middle age. She swore by every diet book that hit the New York Times bestseller list. She owned every exercise machine known to modern science and used them all. She biked, she jogged, she rowed, she climbed stairs, all without leaving the comfort of her basement. Cliff knew this because she bragged every morning about just how far she had not gone.

To Cliff's mind, Sandra Walters represented everything that was wrong with the federal government. Her hours were filled with schemes and plots and intrigues, none of which had anything to do with serving the people who paid her salary. She saw everyone with whom she worked from the standpoint of what they could do for her. Big names got the big hellos, potentially useful up-and-comers got the schmooze, peons got the heel of her high-powered pumps. She made a big production out of everything. Cliff thought she was meant for the stage.

She stopped in front of him. "I see you are leaving early."

"Just like I said," he agreed. "Three different times."

"Be sure and dock the extra hours from your vacation time."

"I already did."

"Oh, I meant to tell you." A blood-red fingernail adjusted one earring. "Ralph finally approved your going down this weekend. I really had to twist his arm on this. He was incredibly opposed to the whole idea, but I eventually talked him into seeing things my way. You owe me big time on this one."

"Funny," Cliff replied. "I just spoke with Ralph, and he didn't seem the least bit bothered by my trip."

Anger flared at being caught out. "You talked with Ralph directly?"

"I'm a big boy, Sandra. I can talk with whoever I like."

"You'll go through proper channels like everyone else, mister, or you'll wind up in hot water. Again." She wheeled around and tap-tapped away.

Cliff gave her back a little two-finger wave and called out, "I hope you have a nice weekend too, Sandra."

He started for the doors once again, not bothering to hide his smile. A solid base hit for the home team.

A sliver of light pierced the darkness. "Debs?"

She worked her way up through several layers of sleep. "Yes?"

"Can I turn on the light?"

Deborah struggled to sit upright. "Go ahead."

The light showed a very concerned Blair. She looked into the basement chamber which the techies had furnished with thrift-shop furniture and claimed as a sort of unofficial parlor, away from the bean counters' prying eyes. "Are you all right?"

Deborah did a swift internal inventory and was delighted to reply, "I am now. What time is it?"

"Almost two. Are you hungry?"

"Starved. Haven't you eaten?"

Blair shook her head. "They had a load of work for me to do, all of it urgent. Most of them are all huddled together discussing the future of your project. Don't you think you'd better be up there keeping the bean counters in order?"

"Not hardly. And you better watch it," Deborah said, rising to her feet from the battered old sofa. "You're beginning to sound like a techie."

"Do you need your wheelchair?"

"No, it looks like the attack has really and truly passed." She followed Blair into the hallway. "Where do you want to go?"

"How about the usual?"

"Sounds good. I'll drive."

Dr. Cofield's new secretary was the talk of the entire laboratory section, especially among the males. Initially Deborah had assumed with the others that Harvey Cofield had offered the position to Blair precisely two and one-half seconds after she had opened his outer office door.

Women who had the ability to reduce men to drooling idiots had long aroused Deborah's deepest suspicions. But the week before, after Blair had been on the job for ten days, Deborah had found herself facing an impossible deadline. Cofield had been off at some conference, Deborah's own secretary had been sick, the files had been lost, and things had been generally coming apart at the seams. In panic she had asked Blair for help, and Blair had proved to be as efficient as she was beautiful. She typed well over a hundred words a minute, had a memory like a mainframe, and relished challenges. She also brooked no nonsense whatsoever from any of the men who ventured near her office. Beneath that honey-coated Tidewater accent rested a perception as keen as a surgeon's scalpel and a patience as thin as piano wire.

Since the deadline scramble, Deborah and Blair had made it out for a lunch and a dinner together. To their mutual surprise and pleasure, a friendship appeared to be in the making.

"I don't understand your illness at all," Blair confessed.

"Join the club," Deborah said. She wheeled the jeep into a parking lot beside an antebellum mansion. "Multiple sclerosis isn't something anyone understands. You just endure it."

The Peterby Country Cafe was a hidden surprise in the countryside near Edenton. A Chicago couple had fallen in love with the scenery surrounding Carolina's Inland Waterway and opened a city-style eatery in the mansion's two front rooms. Blair had heard about it from her aunt, with whom she lived in Edenton. She and Deborah had tried it for the first time together and immediately claimed it as their own.

As they walked toward the entrance, Blair said, "I just feel like a friend ought to have a better handle on something this important."

Deborah smiled her thanks. "The best description I can give you is in a name they gave MS a while back. They called it the invisible disease. There are no symptoms that anyone can see, and even the internal symptoms vary so widely that experts cannot always pinpoint the cause."

Once they were seated, Deborah said, "Mind if I ask you something?"

"Of course not."

"Why don't you go on for a higher degree? Quite frankly, you've got ten times the smarts of some of the people on my staff."

"I've thought about it." Blair used long fingers to draw back her long, honey-colored hair. "But I decided I would be doing it for other people and not for myself."

"Come again?"

"Don't get me wrong, I admire you and what you've

done with your life. But having a profession and rising up in the world just never has interested me all that much." She turned anxious. "Does that sound just awful?"

"I'm not sure." Deborah watched the waiter set down their iced teas and sipped before asking, "So what is it you want out of life?"

"All the old-fashioned things," Blair answered briskly. "A home, a good husband, lots of kids, some dogs, maybe a couple of horses if we can afford them. I know this will probably cost you your appetite, but there's not a thing I'd like more in the world than to be a good mom."

"Why are you here?"

"You mean, why am I sitting here a single woman, or why am I working for Pharmacon?"

"Both, I suppose."

"I've had my share of maybes." Her face took on a pinched look. "They never worked out. At least, they didn't the way I was hoping. I may be asking too much, but I sure would like to find myself a settling-down kind of man who doesn't treat the good-old-boy macho creed as something handed down from on high."

"How long have you been out of school?"

"Four long years. And let me tell you, sister, I'm getting awful tired of looking."

"There doesn't appear to be a whole lot of single-male ground to cover out here in Edenton," Deborah pointed out.

"I know. But I couldn't stand the strain of staying in Norfolk." She gave a weary smile. "That town is filled with good-time boys and all that goes with them. Like temptations too strong for this girl."

"At least you're not too far away."

"Yeah, going home is a real treat. My brothers are always on the lookout for marriage material. It's gotten so I spend all my weekends listening to sales pitches for whichever buddy of theirs has just broken up or just gotten out of the service or something. I feel like I'm being shuttled around a used-car lot."

"You going home this weekend?"

"I'd thought about it, but I'm not sure I'm up to it. Why?"

"Just wondering." Deborah played it as casual as she could. "I've got a friend coming down from Washington I thought you might like to meet."

"That might be nice," Blair said neutrally. "So what about you, Debs? Do you have a score of lovers stashed away somewhere?"

"Not hardly. I'm just not a romantic person, I guess. I don't think I ever have been. When I was growing up, I couldn't understand what all the fuss was about, with makeup and clothes and boys. I remember going to Zeffirelli's *Romeo and Juliet*, did you ever see the movie?"

Blair nodded. "On video. Seven times. Cried my eyes out."

"Once was more than enough for me. I went with some girlfriends right after it came out. They all sat there and bawled. I thought it was silly. Not the movie, it was really well done. The way they carried on, though, I never could understand that."

Blair cocked her head to one side as though trying to study something that remained just slightly out of focus. "Don't you ever get lonely?"

"The million-dollar question. Sometimes, yes. I wish I had a good friend. Especially now, when there are bad days, I wish..." She shrugged. "But my wishes aren't ever for a lover, not in the way you want a husband. Not that I think you're wrong for wanting that. I just never have." Debs smiled. "I find comfort where comfort is offered these days. And I have my cats."

"Cats, plural?"

"Two. Cassandra and Rapunzel. They are as spoiled as cats can be. Himalayan. Probably the most expensive cat you can buy. Bred for looks, not brains."

"I think Himalayans are adorable."

"Thank you. Cliff used to call them my walking decorative items."

"Cliff?"

"My friend, the one who's coming down this weekend. He also referred to them as the pillows that pee."

"And you stayed friends?"

"Cliff is a darling man who has a sort of skewed perspective on just about everything. I used to call him my perpetual challenge. He is very handsome, or at least I think he is. Maybe a year or two older than you. Blond and big and freckled, sort of like an overgrown kid. He is one of the most good-natured men I have ever met, which used to drive me crazy at times."

"What do you mean by a skewed perspective?"

"Oh, Cliff is the kind of guy who thinks the world ought to run along the track of what is right and good. I used to think he would have been better off being born in the days of chivalry, when he could go riding off on a white charger to rescue the damsel in distress. If Cliff had his way, he would spend his days righting wrong. As it is, I'm afraid that the system is just going to beat him down. He works for the FDA, and nobody was ever less suited for the cynical government environment. I tried to get him to take a job in the private sector, but he wouldn't listen. He has this idea that maybe someday he'll be able to do something to make the system better."

Blair's look carried a timeless wisdom. "Maybe bringing us together wouldn't be that good an idea after all."

"There is nothing between Cliff and me romantically," Deborah said, understanding her perfectly. "And there never has been."

"No?" Blair said doubtfully.

"Cliff is, well, *was* my best friend." Her gaze took on a wounded distance. "I hope he still is. We haven't seen each other in a year and a half. Longer."

"Why was that?"

"A long story." Debs forced a smile for the waiter who deposited their food. "Saved by the bell. Let's reserve that story for later and just enjoy the meal, okay?"

Horace Tweedie had a nervous, fawning air that irritated almost everyone at the office. His graying crewcut revealed an oblong and bumpy head. His glasses were dark and square as his speech. He wore white, polyester, button-down shirts, short-sleeved in summer or winter, and no one knew if he owned two or two dozen, for he never altered his dress. Every day it was a white shirt, a tiny red bow tie, dark trousers, and dark lace-up shoes.

Had Horace been brilliant, his habits would have been forgiven and laughed over. But Horace was a plodder, just one step above dull. Instructions more than three sentences long had to be repeated to the point that superiors wished they had simply done the job themselves. Horace had long since been shunted into the filing department, where the work was boringly repetitious and nobody had to force feed him new instructions.

But Horace Tweedie didn't see himself as a plodder. He considered himself to be anything but dull. And he deeply resented not being recognized and rewarded for his gifts and his efforts. He had watched younger people rise within the FDA hierarchy while he remained stationary, plodding toward an early pension. The older Horace grew, the more bitter and angry he had become. As his retirement date approached, Horace's entire department had begun keeping a calendar, counting down the days until they could finally see the back of Horace Tweedie.

But Horace had plans for revenge.

After watching Cliff Devon speak with his boss and then depart through the main doors, Horace returned to his windowless cubbyhole and switched on his computer. Being in files had its advantages. Horace Tweedie had access to all sorts of fascinating data.

Horace worked quietly and intensely through the remainder of the afternoon, certain that in the long-honored tradition of Federalville most people would spend their Friday either preparing for, discussing, or getting an early start on their weekends. His work was not disturbed.

Long after the others in his department had left, Horace switched off his console and massaged the cramped muscles in his neck. He punched out the disk from his computer, slid it into his pocket, grabbed his coat, and made for the door.

The black car was exactly where it was supposed to be, parked on a backroad halfway between the FDA and Horace's Metro stop. He recognized the vehicle as a brand-new Infiniti, and for a moment he wondered if he shouldn't perhaps use some of the money to buy a car like that for himself. Why not? For the first time in his utterly frustrating life, Horace Tweedie was almost within grasping distance of just about anything he could name.

The window glided down as Horace approached. "Well?"

"I have it," Horace said, and waited.

An impressively thick packet emerged through the window. Horace could not refrain from a tentative fondle before sliding it into his shapeless leather satchel—another item on the replacement list. He then plucked the disk from his pocket and handed it over. "It has everything you asked for. Initial trials, formula, doses, the works."

Despite the heat, the hand that reached for the disk wore an Italian driving glove. "We need more information from you."

Horace made his face as blank as he possibly could. He had known this was coming. He had spent a dozen sleepless nights working out what to say when the man with the dark liquid eyes and slicked-down black hair made the request. Horace knew the man was foreign. His heavy accent and aquiline features and languid gestures were unmistakably alien. Horace had decided the man was Spanish. He asked, "What else?"

"We need the exact method by which the drug was prepared. A step-by-step explanation of the production process."

Horace swallowed. "We don't have that on file. The team's microbiologist keeps that separately. With the final application, sure. But not now."

"Can you get it?"

He pretended to think. "I have a friend in the patent office, a guy I play poker with. When a new drug is patented, the compound is usually listed both by molecular structure and process."

"How much?"

His bow tie was suddenly as tight as a noose. "Twice as much as this time," he replied. "There will be two of us to pay."

A long moment passed while the blank-faced foreigner almost melted Horace with his inspection, then a single nod. "I must have it immediately."

"Next Wednesday. Same time. Here."

The window powered up. Horace stood and watched the car move off and moved his lips silently, working to commit the license plate to memory. All of this was going down in writing, to be kept in a safe place. There was never enough insurance when dealing with people like this. Horace turned and started down the street on rubbery legs.

Another five days, and he could thumb his nose at the whole shooting match.

Five days, and he would finally be a free man.

3

Cliff Devon crossed the Carolina border a very happy and a very heartsore young man.

He was happy for two reasons. First and foremost, because he was finally going down to see his best friend in all the world. Second, because he was doing so alone.

His reasons for the deep-down case of heartache were exactly the same.

Deborah had been less than fully healthy for as long as he had known her, which had been since his sophomore year in college. It had been at that point that a brilliant researcher and part-time lecturer had taken pity on a bumbling student, coached him through biology, and refused to take payment for her services. A deep and abiding friendship had resulted.

At that point, Deborah's illness had been characterized by frequent bouts of flu and severe migraine headaches. His senior year, she had felt tingling sensations in her limbs. His first year with the FDA, she began to experience extensive numbness for no apparent reason.

And all the while she had refused to go in for a medical checkup.

The worse her condition became, the harder it had been for Cliff to stand by without knowing what was happening.

Deborah, on the other hand, was a virologist. She had understood that a diagnosis would probably make no difference. For virtually every suspected cause of her symptoms, she had known there was no cure. Or at least that is what she had told him. And the knowledge had not helped him cope.

Gripped with the fervor of watching a dear friend decline, Cliff had argued with a force that had wounded them both. She had turned understandably stubborn. He had stormed out, promising not to return until she came to terms with her illness. Deborah had shouted at his back that he was the one who couldn't accept it.

That had been exactly twenty-one months ago.

During the ensuing period, Cliff had not forgotten her. Far from it. Deborah remained with him everywhere, that and the pride which had kept him from calling and trying to patch things up. He cursed his own pride almost as often as he did her stubbornness.

Two months ago, she had called. Since then, their renewed contact had come in gradual stages. They had exchanged letters. They had talked on the phone. They had tested the waters, speaking about everything except what was most important.

Then, this past week, she had asked him to come.

It never occurred to him not to accept.

Cliff made the trip in what he called his hobby car. The day was far too hot for open-air driving, but as the car had no air conditioning and little insulation between the engine and cockpit, the choice was either drive with the top down or bake.

His final year in high school, Cliff had come across a '67 Jaguar E-type sportster in absolutely wretched shape. A succession of uncaring owners had reduced the once-proud auto to little more than a rusted hulk. Cliff had spent the entire four years of college and every nickel he could earn or scrounge restoring the Jag to its former glory. He knew every screw, every coil, every stitch along its entire length by name.

The Jag was long and low and ridiculously cramped for his six-foot-three frame. His feet rested on pedals a scarce eight inches behind the rumbling engine. From where he sat, the cowling ran on for miles. The car was hideously impractical, had more quirks than an old maid, and was so loud passengers had to shout to be heard. Cliff loved it to distraction.

The body was a dark ivory, the color of milk with a dash of coffee. It shone with the rich luster of eleven coats of paint and weekly waxing. The canvas top and leather interior were matching saddle-brown. The chrome-and-wood dash shone like new, as did the wire-spoke wheels. The car turned heads everywhere it went.

Cliff entered the Edenton city limits and purred his way down tree-lined streets. Deborah's faxed instructions rested on the seat beside him. He was too distracted to notice much about the town, except that it seemed both quiet and picturesque. Then he spotted her waving from the veranda of a well-kept home. He steadied his nerves and wheeled into the parking lot.

The first thing she said when he cut the motor was, "Still driving the old clunker?"

"Nice to know your tongue hasn't lost its edge," he said, pushing open his door.

"Don't ever gain weight," she added, watching him swing himself to his feet. "You do, they'll need a crowbar and a can of grease to pry you free."

Cliff stretched, played at casual, looked at the vast white house behind her. "Impressive. Is it yours?"

"Hardly. This is the town's nicest guesthouse. There is no hotel. It's called the Granville Queen and was built a year or so before the Revolutionary War."

Cliff nodded at the news. "I'll have to pay for everything out of my own pocket."

"I've already been through this with the bean counters, who would just as soon treat you to a free weekend in Vegas and a real car. I did get you the company rate here, I hope that doesn't stretch your ethics too far."

45

"Long as I pay." Cliff dropped his gaze and inspected her.

She looked old. And tired.

Her hair was chopped short, as always. As long as he had known her, Deborah had treated her hair as a sort of curious biological accessory that had no modern purpose—sort of like an external appendix. But there was a lot of gray interrupting the mouse brown now, much more than there should have been for someone her age.

Her face was drawn into sharper angles than he recalled. Fatigue lines traced their way out from her eyes.

Her eyes, her brilliant probing eyes. Her eyes looked weary. Yet immensely happy.

"I knew it was going to be great to see you again," she said, taking both his hands with hers. "But not this great."

In all the days that had come before, he never missed her as much as he did in that moment. "Oh, Debs."

"Straighten up, Junior," she said softly. "I didn't ask you down here for pity."

"Sorry." He struggled to recover.

"That's better. Now, then. We will get the worst part over and done with, all right?" She took a breath. "You were right to be angry with me."

"No I wasn't."

"Just shush up for a minute, please. I was fooling myself, thinking that if I ignored it everything would somehow go back to normal, or at least back to the way it was before. I hid behind a lot of scientific gobbledy-gook because that's the way I am. And you were the only one who cared enough to make me see the truth."

"Debs, please." Her words were tearing at his heart. "You don't have to say this."

"Yes I do. I have MS, Cliff. Multiple sclerosis. It's certain now. I really went through the wringer, though, before I could get it confirmed. I had tests done that curdle the blood just thinking about them. The results

46

were confusing. I heard diagnoses for everything from leukemia to sleeping sickness to a severe psychological disorder. Finally I went to a specialist up in Minneapolis, and he did a couple of MRIs—that's magnetic resonance imaging to the uninitiated."

"I know what it is," he said quietly.

"Sorry. I've grown accustomed to talking with people who would just as soon play deaf and dumb when it comes to things like this. Not that I can blame them. Anyway, they detected scar tissue on the brain, and that was that."

"I'm sorry," he said, and could only feel the futility in his words. "I'm sorry for everything. Most of all, I'm sorry I wasn't here for you."

"You're here now, and that's what matters most," she replied. "I need you, you see. If you had not forced me to look at myself like this, by being absent, I would have probably kept my own head in the sand for another couple of years. As it is, I have really grown a lot."

"I can see that," he said, and he did.

"Yes, and it's all thanks to you, in a way." She took his arm. "But we'll have time for that later. You must be tired."

He allowed himself to be led up the sidewalk. "I'm okay. How about you?"

"There are good days and not-so-good days, and then every once in a while a really bad day," she said crisply. "Today started off bad, but now it is a good day."

"I'm glad to hear it."

"Yes, so am I. There is also a major storm blowing up at work, but I'll tell you about that later, too. If it's okay, we'll check you in, then rush back and let the bean counters make a fuss over you before they take off for wherever bean counters go on weekends. Is that all right?"

"Sure, Debs. Whatever."

She grinned. "I may just have a surprise for you this weekend, too."

"You know I've never been much for surprises."

"This one you'll like, I promise. Sort of a welcome-home present."

"What is it?"

"You'll see."

Cliff settled his long frame into her Cherokee, winced at the sight of the wheelchair in the backseat, and said, "How old is this vehicle? Five years, maybe six?"

"Don't start," she warned. "I happen to be very attached to this rolling junk heap."

"I thought all successful researchers with the biggies drove late-model cars that most of us peons have never even heard of."

"Not this researcher."

"How come?"

"Long story." She returned the wave of two men crossing the street. "So how is the young lady you wrote me about in your first letter? What was her name?"

"Andrea Davenport," Cliff answered. "Andrea and I are no longer an item, as they say."

"Should I be sorry?"

"According to my friends, yes. According to my heart, no."

"You want to tell me about it?"

Cliff sighed. "Andrea was pretty in a willowy sort of way. She was also rich and well connected. Her daddy owned Davenport Motors, the largest Chevrolet dealership in the Richmond area. That's how we met—her dad is a bigger nut for old Jags than I am. She had a great smile, she could make polite conversation with a wall, and she would have been great for my career."

"That was your friends talking," Deborah said. "Now let's hear from Cliff."

"Andrea was a William and Mary graduate in art history,"

Cliff replied. "She minored in the Southern dress code. She alone has kept the Izod knit shirt company from going bust. Everything she owned was either green or pink. She loved long pleated shorts and wore them with one of her sixteen alligator belts, all bearing gold buckles."

"Nothing the matter with liking clothes," Deborah said.

"I swear she must use a dozen clips in her hair," Cliff persisted, "all of them tortoiseshell. I think she looks forward to growing old and needing glasses so she can have matching frames and hang them around her neck by a gold chain."

"Let's get to the nitty-gritty," Deborah directed.

"That's what I'm trying to tell you," Cliff said. "There wasn't any. She was about as substantial as cotton candy. Andrea lived to shop and spend her daddy's money. Period. She wouldn't know an original thought if it reached up and grabbed her by her gold Rolex."

The road leading out of town was a bright green tunnel. Ancient trees rose up on either side, their lofty branches forming a solid cover overhead. The houses lining the street were clearly very old, their porches and roofs trimmed with fussy Victorian woodwork. Most had been carefully restored, and many still possessed original touches such as wavy lead-paned windows.

"These places look great," Cliff decided. "Which one is yours?"

"None of them," she replied. "I'll show you around town tomorrow before it gets too hot, then take you out to my place." She was quiet for a time, then said quietly, "I've come to really love living here."

"I can understand it," Cliff said. "What I've seen is really beautiful."

"It's a small town, and small towns are best seen on foot. But I think it is beautiful too." She smiled at him. "I do believe I'm putting down roots."

"Everybody needs roots, Debs."

"Even you, right?"

"That's what I thought when I met Andrea. But you've spoiled me. I need somebody I can *talk* with. Somebody who's got something to say. Sure would be nice to find somebody who could be a friend as well as a girlfriend." He turned and said, "Now it's my turn."

She nodded. "Fire away."

"Tell me about it," he said.

Deborah did not need to ask what he was speaking of. "Don't worry, I will. But not all at once. Experience has taught me that some things are better taken in small bites. It keeps you from being overwhelmed."

"I already am."

She patted his knee. "For most people who have MS, myself included, the worst part of the disease was not knowing what it was. Once the diagnosis was confirmed, I was able to identify a symptom as just that, a symptom. And symptoms pass, Cliff, at least in this stage of the disease. And there is always hope that the disease will not grow any worse. For most people, it doesn't. And for some, there is even hope of recovery."

"So what *is* it?"

"Multiple sclerosis is a disease of the central nervous system," she explained, her matter-of-fact tone belied by the tragic depths to her eyes and the weary lines that creased her face. "It hits the brain and spinal cord. The nerves there are surrounded by myelin, a sort of fatty insulation. With MS, this myelin sheath breaks down, a process called demyelination. The myelin is replaced by scar tissue, which is not such a good insulation, so the tiny electronic nerve pulses that control everything in the body can be impaired. Sort of a biological short-circuit."

His heart was so sore he reached one hand up to grip his chest. "It sounds awful."

"Don't look so sad. My symptoms are not too bad, and believe me, some of the symptoms can be pretty horrid. Paresthesia, or pins-and-needles all over the body. Lhermitte's sign, which is like lightning surges through limbs. Spasticity, a fancy name for rigidity and stiffness. Diplopia, eye muscle weakness. Ataxia, disturbances of balance and coordination. Dysarthria, slurring of speech. Myokymia—"

"Stop," he said quietly. "Please."

"What I personally feel most is tired," she went on. "That's the worst part for somebody as hyperactive as I've always been. And achy. Lots of little pains. I've had to watch it with the doctor on that. He would drug me to death if I let him. Prozac, Darvocet, Baclofen, Beta Seron, you name it. If I asked for it, he'd probably prescribe it."

"That sounds dangerous, Debs."

"I've learned to live with a certain amount of pain in my life. Now I sort of know my limits, and I know when it's time to give in to the drugs. But the worst thing has been the fatigue."

"It's there all the time?"

"No. On the good days it's sort of there but not there, like a dark cloud on the horizon. On the bad days it's a dark hole as big as the universe, and I can't help but fall inside."

"Is there any hope you might get better?"

"A little. Myelin repairs itself, and given time it will replace the scar tissue. So if the disease can be checked, then there is a chance—a *chance*—for a complete recovery. They have also identified several retroviruses that might be either primary or secondary causes, most particularly one known as the human T-cell lymphotropic virus I, or the HTLV-I. A couple of new drugs have been effective in treating some cases. Not mine, unfortunately." Deborah hesitated a moment, then said, "And now there is another drug. Or there might be."

Something in her tone caused him to sit upright. "What new drug?"

Deborah kept her eyes on the road ahead. "We collated some new results on the echiniacin tests just this morning."

"And?"

"They were promising, Cliff. Very, very promising." She swung the jeep onto the bypass. "But I'd like to wait and lay everything out for you tomorrow at the lab, if that's okay. It's just too important, having you here and sharing this new work with you, to rush things. That's one of the lessons I've had to learn. To pace myself."

He looked over at her, said, "It's good to see you again. Very good."

She responded with a single nod. "I almost lost it the first few times the fatigue overwhelmed me. And you weren't there to help me find my way out."

"I can't tell you how sorry—"

"Don't," she said softly, her gaze remaining on the gathering dusk. "Strangely enough, there was a purpose to that as well. I learned to seek help where help was waiting to be found."

She stopped at a light and turned to face him, showing the familiar strong gaze, the chopped-off hair, the determined set of her chin. "I might be healed some day, I might not. I hope for it. But for now, I have been given peace. Even in the darkest moments, I have found peace."

Their way took them several miles down the bypass, past picturesque farms and carefully tended fields. They drove in the comfort of friends who did not need to fill the air with words. That silence remained until Cliff broke it by leaning forward in his seat and asking, "What is *that*?"

"That," Deborah answered, "is my corporate home sweet home."

Cliff swiveled to keep his gaze fixed on the building as Deborah turned in and parked. "Promise it won't take off while we're inside?"

"It's pretty well fixed to the earth," she assured him. "Come along, Junior, the suits are waiting."

The Pharmacon facility was a series of three enormous

geodesic domes, each showing as many glittering facets as an insect's eye. The mirror-glass glinted bronze and proud in the late afternoon sunlight. Translucent metal-and-glass tunnels connected the domes, and carefully sculpted gardens surrounded the entire structure.

"They really tried to blend in with the area, didn't they?" Cliff said.

"This is what is known as making a statement," Deborah replied.

The doors were heavy polarized glass, a full inch thick and operated by a pneumatic suspension. They slid smoothly open, then locked behind them with a well-oiled click. Inside the air sighed softly through an unseen vent; otherwise there was no sound. A reception guard inspected them from behind bulletproof glass. His voice came over the intercom, "Afternoon, Doctor."

"Jim, this is Cliff Devon," Deborah replied. "He'll be needing a pass. Labs and all."

"Sure, I got him down on the list. How long?"

"Three days should do it."

The guard said to Cliff, "Just put your right hand down on the stand, please."

"Do I have to?"

"Yes." Deborah pointed him to the waist-high metal column standing to one side of the reception booth. Cliff did as he was told. The column emitted a warm hum as his hand was scanned. The screen embedded in the wall at eye-level lit up to reveal a single sentence. The guard said, "Please read what it says, sir."

"My name is Cliff Devon," Cliff complied. "My voice is my passport."

"Again, please."

Cliff repeated the sentence. This time a chime sounded. The guard watched a monitor on his side of the glass, then took a plastic card that emerged from a slot on his desk and passed it through. "You'll show him the ropes, won't you, Doc?"

"Sure, Jim. Thanks." Deborah handed over the featureless white plastic card and said in all seriousness, "Don't you dare lose this."

"Right," Cliff agreed, thoroughly cowed. He followed her through the second set of heavy glass doors and down a long, carpeted corridor. The hall was domed and soundless and so oppressive it felt hard to breathe. "Where are you taking me?"

"The Tombs."

They took the elevator to the third floor, then walked down yet another hallway. The elevator bell sounded again behind them, and Cliff jumped involuntarily.

"It's gotten to you, has it?"

"I feel like I've been vetted for Fort Knox."

Deborah shook her head as she led him into a wood-lined outer office. "Our security is much tighter."

A vision.

That was all Cliff could think of as he stared down at the woman behind the desk. She was undoubtedly one of the most beautiful women he had ever seen.

Deborah grinned at his reaction, "Cliff, I'd like you to meet Blair Collins. Blair, this is the friend I've been telling you about."

"Nice to meet you," Blair said, her tone flat, her eyes neutral. Giving nothing away. Clearly used to being stared at.

"Likewise." Cliff turned to Deborah's smirk and said, "It's great knowing I can entertain you."

"Sorry," Deborah said. "I guess maybe I should have given fair warning."

"Yeah, maybe so." Cliff turned back to Blair. "Do you get used to having guys stumble over their tongues?"

"Long, long ago," she replied, a glint of something else appearing in her eyes. Humor? "How did you like the entrance routine?"

"If they had an X-ray machine and matched Dobermans,

it might have been a little eerier. But that tunnel was perfect."

"You should try having to walk it every morning," Blair said. "Sometimes I feel like stripping off my clothes and running up and down screaming my head off."

"If you ever decide to really do it," Cliff replied, "be sure and let me know. I'll make a special trip down for that."

Deborah interrupted with, "Are they ready for us?"

"I'm supposed to make this big production of calling ahead, you know, give them time to huddle. But I guess we can dispense with the nonsense for once. Besides, it's almost quitting time."

"Fine with me," Deborah agreed, and said to Cliff, "Come along, Junior. It's showtime."

As they pushed through the double doors, Cliff muttered, "Is she for real?"

"That's for you to decide," Deborah whispered back.

"Deborah, great to see you!" A silver fox in a gray suit rose from the conference table extending down from the massive desk. "And this must be Cliff Devon."

"Must be," Cliff agreed, and barely avoided Deborah's elbow.

"I'm James Whitehurst. So very, very glad to meet you. You of course already know Dr. Harvey Cofield, head of our R&D section and currently acting as our FDA representative."

"Dr. Cofield," Cliff said, accepting the hand.

"Cliff, great to see you," he exuded with complete falseness.

"Right," Cliff responded, deciding to give the circus ten minutes max.

"Here, take this seat right here beside me," Whitehurst said. "Deborah has told us so much about the young man who is responsible for the echin drug approval study."

"This trip is purely for pleasure," Cliff replied.

"Of course, of course." Whitehurst beamed at all and sundry. "Still, we are just delighted to have the FDA coordinator down for a visit, official or not."

"I've prepared a complete dossier of our latest clinical trials," Cofield informed him, hefting a massive notebook and extending it his way. "I thought you might like to take a look at it this weekend."

"Absolutely," Cliff agreed. Four years in federal government had given him a lot of practice at keeping his face blank.

"We were intending to put you up in the company cottage, give you the red-carpet treatment," Whitehurst said around his smile. "But no, our Debs said that just wasn't on."

"The department has a pretty strict policy on such things," Cliff said.

"Sure they do. But if there's anything you need, anything at all, you won't hesitate to call, now, will you?"

"Not for an instant," Cliff agreed.

"We're expecting a pretty strong reaction to the press conference we called today," Dr. Cofield said.

"You held a press conference today?" Cliff looked from him to Debs and back again. "About what?"

"Remember the storm I was telling you about?" Deborah replied.

"Rumors were getting out about the echin compound," Cofield asserted. "We decided to go public with what we know."

"What you *think*," Cliff said, struggling to keep a grip on his temper. "The clinical trials have just gotten started."

"Yes, but what we've seen so far has been incredible," Cofield ground on. "Incredible enough for us to decide we'll probably need to report the findings to our friends in Washington next week."

"My director will be delighted to hear this," Cliff said, knowing Ralph Summers had about as much time for political pressure as he did. Cliff leaned forward and said with all the force he could muster, "And I expect your application for product approval to proceed exactly according to proper schedule."

"We'll see about that," Cofield snapped.

"We certainly shall," Cliff agreed, and decided he had just about had enough. He rose to his feet. "Anything else?"

"Well, it certainly has been delightful to meet you, Mr. Devon," Whitehurst said, rising with the others. "Now don't you forget—anything you need, anything at all. Debs knows where to reach me night or day."

Cliff allowed Deborah to usher him out. When the doors were shut behind them, he stood and fumed, "You know those lower life forms you use in the labs? I think some of them escaped."

To his surprise, it was Blair Collins who responded. "He'll do," she announced to Deborah. "Okay for tomorrow night at seven?"

"Perfect," Deborah replied, and took his arm. "Come along, dear. You're steaming up the windows."

Daylight was just beginning to wane when Horace Tweedie showed up in front of the U.S. Patent Office headquarters in Washington. The air still smelled of its city imprisonment, hot and muggy and acrid. Ted Kelley was outside waiting for him, nervous as a new recruit arriving at boot camp. As soon as Horace's car pulled up, Ted raced over and tried to crawl in through the side window. "What took you so long?" he hissed, dancing in place. "You're almost half an hour late."

"Friday rush-hour traffic," Horace replied, rolling toward a curbside parking place. He climbed from the car, clapped a hand on Ted's shoulder, grinned broadly, and said in a quiet voice, "Calm down. You don't want anybody to get suspicious, do you?"

"I don't know if I want to do this at all."

"That's okay," Horace said amiably, knowing the guy

had to be nursed. His poker buddy was a gambler, mostly small stakes, but a lot of them. And he lost. Almost always. Like many gamblers, Ted gambled to reinforce his own self-hatred, something best accomplished by placing bets that had almost no chance of succeeding.

Horace hated playing poker with Kelley. He didn't like watching him gradually melt into a sweaty little puddle as he overbet and lost hand after hand, trying time and time again to fill inside straights and flushes missing two cards. The guy rarely lost more than a couple hundred, but for him it was almost a nightly ritual. Not to mention the football pools and the basketball and the golf and the hockey and anything else he could find to bet on.

Needless to say, Kelley was perpetually in debt. And to the wrong sort of creditors. Ones who insisted on being paid. Insisted in the strongest possible terms.

So Horace played it cool like he was still at the poker table with this guy. "It was just an idea. They really don't need the information right now, and I'll have it on file myself in a month or so."

Then he started back toward the car, his heart tripping a frantic beat.

"No, wait." Ted's hand was on his elbow.

Horace breathed a silent sigh and allowed himself to be turned back. "Yeah?"

"I guess it's okay." The furtive glance up and down the street, then, "You got the money?"

"Of course."

Shoulders hunched even further. "Can't you ask for more? You know it's worth a lot."

Horace made a worried pout. "They're not the type you can ask for much of anything."

"But a lousy thousand bucks. That's—"

"A thousand more than you have now," Horace pointed out.

Kelley slumped in defeat. Probably thinking about the goons breathing down his neck. "Yeah, okay. Come on, let's get it over with," he muttered as he led the way toward the entrance.

As soon as pharmaceutical companies began work on a new compound, and long before any positive or negative effect could be identified, a patent was applied for. The patent office did not require information as to what effect the product would have. That was the job of the FDA, and as many as five years might pass before final FDA approval was granted. But the only requirement for filing a patent was demonstrating that the product or the process was new.

With new compounds being designed almost continually by pharmaceutical companies and independent laboratories, a U.S. patent was granted on the basis of two different types of information. The first was the molecular formula of the compound itself. The second was the *process* of how the compound was produced.

For all molecular patents, this second type of information was essential because the compound itself was too small to be seen—and in some cases, when the application was made, only a microscopic amount might have been produced. So the production methods had to be spelled out in careful detail. The rule of thumb used by the patent office was, make the explanations so complete that a nonexpert would understand.

Kelley pasted on a totally false smile as he approached the night-duty guard, an overweight black man engrossed in his crossword puzzle. "Can you believe it? Of all the luck, the boss has got me working Friday night."

"Tough," the bored guard said, not even glancing up.

Horace signed a false name in the book and felt only disgust for the guy and his nervous chatter. Small-time losers, he thought. I'm surrounded by small-time losers. When Ted wouldn't shut up, Horace turned and started for the elevators on his own.

In the elevator, Kelley wiped off the grin with the sweat beading his face. Silently they waited while the floors pinged away, then walked together down the hallway to Ted's office. The hallway was completely silent. That was why Horace had taken the risk of going ahead and arranging this meeting before talking with the foreigner earlier that day. On Friday afternoons, downtown Washington was a ghost town.

Kelley had to use both hands to get his key in the door, his hands were shaking so bad. Horace rolled his eyes as the guy did a final up-and-down-the-hall search before waving him inside. Talk about telegraphing the message to the world.

"Okay," Ted whispered, sweating so hard his shirt was matting to his back. He pointed a trembling hand at the top file on his desk and said, "I gotta go do something down the hall. I'll be back in a couple of minutes."

"No problem," Horace said, surprised at how calm he felt. Maybe Kelley's nerves didn't leave any room for his own. "I'll leave the envelope in the file," he said in a low voice.

"The what?"

"Envelope," Horace said, drawing out the word.

"Oh. Yeah. Right. Well, I'm off."

"See ya." When the door was shut once more, Horace slipped the miniature camera from his pocket. The camera had cost almost as much as the bribe. Small time, Horace thought as he opened the file, arranged the desk lamp for maximum lighting, and began shooting pictures of each page. He would soon be leaving these small-time losers behind for good.

4

On Saturday morning, Deborah drove at a slow, steady pace through peaceful Edenton streets. She did not speak much, but allowed Cliff to take in the town bit by bit. Occasionally she would draw his attention to special sights: a pre-Revolutionary home with double balconies large enough to accommodate the entire family on hot nights. A blooming magnolia more than two hundred years old, its branches encompassing almost a quarter of an acre. An entire street of crepe myrtle trees frothing with pink blossoms. A Victorian house whose ground floor boasted seven great windows, each framed in a stained-glass pattern of flowering vines. An old stone house so overgrown with creeping wisteria vines that it looked from a distance to be painted green. Earlier in the spring, Deborah informed him, the whole house bloomed lavender.

Everything moved slower here. Even the car's blinkers ticked more deliberately in this small, hot town. There were so few automobiles that drivers greeted each other as they passed. The dogs saluted cars with their waving tails, lapping up the heat with lolling tongues.

The trees had long since grown high and broad enough to create living canopies over all of Edenton's streets. Deborah took him down the bayside road under a veil of sun-dappled green. The points of land jutting into the bay were anchored by houses older than the nation that claimed them.

Deborah drove back inland several blocks and stopped before a solid, red-brick church building. She turned off the engine, sat back in her seat, and sighed softly.

"What's wrong?"

"I had so hoped this weekend would be okay," she murmured.

"You're not feeling well?"

"I don't know yet." She gave her head a tired shake. "Stress can set off attacks, and there's been a lot of that recently. Plus I was looking forward to your coming and sort of staying up nights thinking of everything I wanted to tell you."

"Do you need to rest?"

"Maybe in a little while. First I need to wait and see what's happening." She turned to him. "I'm sorry, Cliff."

"Don't be."

"But there was so much I still wanted to show you. The lab, my house, these latest trial results."

"This won't be my only trip down, Debs."

"Promise?"

"Absolutely."

She let out a breath. "Okay, then we'll just take this one step at a time. I want to show you around here a little more. I know that may sound silly, but it's important to me. This little town is sort of becoming the center of my world."

"It doesn't sound silly at all," Cliff said. "I think the place is beautiful."

"You're not just saying that?"

"This is a great place, Debs. I could learn to love it here. I know it already." He looked around. "I just can't help but think, though, that it's a strange place to be making scientific history."

"We may actually be doing that, you know." She slid from the car with visible effort. "Come on, let me show you the church."

She led him across the street at a slow but steady pace. "Scientific revolutions occur when paradigms, the frameworks we use to study the universe, are overthrown.

The discovery of penicillin did this in medicine. A spiritual revolution occurs the same way, but one person at a time."

"That's what has happened to you?" Cliff asked. "A spiritual revolution?"

She made a noncommittal humming sound, and changed the subject, as they passed through ancient wrought-iron gates and entered an old cemetery. "We know for a fact that more than two thousand people are buried here, but we can only account for four hundred graves."

"We?" Cliff smiled, deciding to let her set the pace of conversation. "You were born a million light years from this town."

"Call me a recent transplant." Deborah continued down the path. "The church was built over older graves, and there are people buried on top of other people—not hard to do when wooden tombstones had rotted and people fighting an epidemic didn't have time to bother with records."

She stopped before a series of flat markers. "Three of these belong to colonial governors who ruled in the king's name before independence. Charles Eden, the man this town was named after, was one of them. The first tombstone over there belonged to Mrs. Pollock, wife of another colonial governor. When she died, the governor told the engraver what he wanted written over his wife's grave. After the tombstone was laid, he came back out to pay his respects, took one look at what the engraver had written, and blew his stack. The engraver had gone into a lot of intimate detail about Mrs. Pollock, things only her husband should have known. The governor decided that while his wife was living she had come to know the engraver a lot better than she should have. So he took a gravedigger's pick and dug out all the parts he didn't want anybody else to see. That's why it's all cracked like that."

"You've gotten to know this area pretty well."

"Just tapping at the surface," she said, and led him toward the church. "This is the second oldest church in the state, and it took thirty years to build. Finished in 1766. There was an early law requiring churchgoers to tie their horses at least three hundred feet from the church door. If they didn't, they were barred from ever holding public office."

She pushed open the ancient portal and stepped inside. "In the colonial era, each family would bring a footwarmer to church with them, something like a lidded shovel that held hot coals. The mother and father would place their feet on it, with the children spread down the pew. That was the building's only heat."

Deborah unlatched one of the little gates blocking the pews and ushered Cliff into a seat. "A family would buy a pew and pass it down from generation to generation. The upstairs galleries were sectioned off. They held the servants, transients, and families too poor to afford a family pew. There were a lot of transients here, Edenton being a big port city."

"I've never been much for history," Cliff confessed. "But somehow you make this stuff live for me."

"Too often people look at history and see only *things*. I've learned to look and see what my own world has lost. They are after a claim for themselves or their family; I am after values that never die. This town is full of people determined to justify their quirks and failings by finding refuge in the past. But there are a few here and there who acknowledge the past because it holds things they wish to keep for today. Blair's aunt is a good example—I just met her a few days ago. When I discover someone like her, I feel like I've uncovered a special treasure."

Cliff inspected his friend's profile and declared, "You've changed, Debs. A lot."

She did not deny it. "I was born with a restless spirit. And I've never minded that in the least. It has driven me to go and hunt and find and do." She combed fingers through her close-cropped hair, then rubbed her neck. "I'm tired now, Cliff. My mind tells me it's the disease. But my spirit stays restless. Questing, searching, and now condemning. I am so hard on myself and my weaknesses."

"You shouldn't be."

"But I am. I am so ashamed of myself and everything I'm leaving undone."

"You can't help it."

"That doesn't matter. I want so much to keep working my twenty-hour days. But I can't. My restless spirit pushes me hard as ever, but my body stays still and simply says no, I won't, not any more. The storm threatens to tear me apart sometimes."

"Debs—"

"Wait, let me finish. But something is happening to me. As though all this storm has had a purpose. It has forced me to look beyond myself, beyond the world I have spent my entire life studying and analyzing and trying to control. Now control is lost. Now the power of analysis is gone. And what is left is *vision*."

Cliff shifted uncomfortably in his seat.

"I know. I know. The whole idea is alien. To me, too. I've been trained to hold everything at arm's length, to tie everything down by the empirical method. But I can't deny the power of my realization. No matter how hard I try."

Cliff tried for diplomacy. "It sounds like you've found a good source of strength."

"Yes, I have. And a reassuring knowledge of being accepted." Her eyes held a gentle light of seeing beyond the church's confines. "Warts and restlessness and MS and all."

Of the luxury hotels lining New York's Central Park, the Ritz-Carlton was the smallest and least ostentatious. The same was true for its restaurant, the Jockey Club. It looked like the paneled study of an old manor house, and attracted a conservative wealthy clientele. On any given night, at least half the tables were occupied by patrons with paintings on loan to the Guggenheim, the National Gallery, or the MOMA. Conversations were quiet, the service swift and discreet, the prices staggering. The Jockey Club was the sort of place where to ask the price meant not belonging.

They met there because the chairman of Pharmacon lived in a Central Park triplex just up the street. Owen MacKenzie was a regular and was greeted with discreet murmurs and bows from the maitre d'. He had ordered the meeting when Whitehurst had called to report on the press conference.

Whitehurst watched as Cofield took in the surroundings and added them to the list of goodies he wanted for himself. Whitehurst had only contempt for Cofield and his size-fourteen ego. But a man as vain as this one was a man easily controlled, and Whitehurst needed a research director whom he could control. So he put up with the man's insufferable vanity and his unbridled lust for perks and his drive to remain in the limelight. And he waited. One day his own power would be cemented, and then he could bring out the knife he kept hidden behind his smile.

Owen MacKenzie wore his face like a comfortable old shoe, well-worn and long broken in. His clothes fitted his face. His suit cost two thousand dollars, yet looked slept in. His tie was canted at a forty degree angle. He continually spilled cigar ash over his sparkling white shirt. His shoes were hand-sewn, yet had never been polished and were scuffed down to the leather.

Owen MacKenzie knew next to nothing about the pharmaceutical industry. He liked to say that before being offered this job, his only contact with the drug business had been taking two aspirin for a cold. But he was an expert at turning around sluggish companies. His

66

last two employers had been a maker of spark plugs and the nation's largest producer of tin cans. Then the Pharmacon board had brought him in to inject new life into the company. And Owen MacKenzie had responded by setting up Pharmacon's new North Carolina facility.

As was his habit, he kept the conversation light throughout their meal. Only when the plates were cleared away and the snifters of amber liquid set before each gentleman did his face settle into somber lines. "So how did the press conference go?" he demanded.

"Fairly well," Whitehurst responded, not looking at his companion. Cofield still had a short fuse on that one. "We managed to excite quite a bit of interest within the general press."

"Excellent. Nothing like a few journalistic fires to get the FDA into high gear. Especially if there's any hint that Joe Public is missing out on a major new relief because of bureaucratic holdups."

"As a matter of fact," Whitehurst interjected, "it appears we are actually on the brink of just that."

"Just what?"

"A major new relief," Whitehurst replied.

Owen MacKenzie's gaze took on a keener focus. "How major?"

"According to the latest trial results, as big as Zantac," Whitehurst predicted. "Maybe bigger."

Zantac was an industry byword for success, the most prescribed drug in the world. The ulcer medicine had chalked up 1993 sales of over four billion dollars.

The chairman fiddled with his napkin. "I didn't cancel my other engagement to endure a sales pitch that wouldn't impress a new GP."

"He's not kidding," Cofield said. "This could be really big."

Owen MacKenzie glanced from one man to the next. "All right. I'm listening."

Cofield said, "One of our chief researchers is a woman by the name of Deborah Givens. She was originally brought in to head up research into new monoclonar antibodies, but it turns out she has an illness that could get worse at any moment."

"Which one?"

"MS," Whitehurst answered. "We didn't know it at the time of hiring her, of course."

"Right," Cofield said, recovering the ball. "So we decided to take her off the main research, replace her with somebody who didn't have this risk of not being around to finish the job."

"We were planning to let her coast for a couple of years," Whitehurst explained, "then give her the boot. Use her lack of productivity as the reason."

"Good thinking," the chairman agreed. "No need to attract any unnecessary litigation."

"So she comes up with this idea to look into some natural medicines used behind the Iron Curtain," Cofield went on. "Or what used to be the Iron Curtain. Tradition still plays a strong role in medicine over there. From what I hear, they're still using roots and herbs from the Middle Ages. We thought, what the heck, it wouldn't cost much, and who knows, she might actually turn up something."

Owen MacKenzie nodded his understanding. A number of key medicines had been discovered in just such studies of natural healing elements. Digitalis, used for heart failure, came from the foxglove plant. Taxol, a new drug used in the treatment of ovarian cancer, had been recently isolated from the bark and needles of the Pacific yew tree.

"We kept her under a tight rein," Cofield said. "She's got the smallest lab section in the company, a grand total of five lab technicians, one of which is the biggest man ever created. All of her people are a little odd. Her lab's been sort of the deposit for techies nobody else wanted to touch. So what happens but she strikes gold. And I mean gold."

"In what field?" the chairman demanded.

"That's just it," Cofield said, growing excited. His hands refused to stay still. They were everywhere, dancing across the table, touching his tie, rubbing the side of his face, patting down his wire-brush hair. "We still don't know exactly how far we can go with this one."

"Deborah was looking at a root extract that was claimed to help strengthen the immune system against viral attacks," Whitehurst explained. "She isolated half a dozen molecules that had not been previously identified."

"All of them complex as they come," Cofield broke in. "One of them is like a mile and a half long. She started her lab trials then and found that the single compounds alone didn't have near as much effect as using them all together. Something about the combination appears to stimulate immune system activity."

The chairman demanded, "And side effects?"

"The extract has been in use in Europe for decades," Whitehurst replied. "Some doctors swear by it, others swear at it. But no one has ever, as far as we have been able to ascertain, accused it of having any harmful contra-indications."

"A general immune strengthener without side effects," Owen MacKenzie mused. "A pity it is already in such general use. We would probably find it impossible to patent."

"We already have," Whitehurst announced smugly.

MacKenzie's gaze turned hard as diamonds. "What's that?"

"Debs started fooling around with the molecules," Cofield explained. He was growing impatient with all these interruptions and the need to share center stage. "It appeared that the compounds had a direct effect on the T-cells and that how they combined depended on what disease the system was fighting. So she decided to try and add marker molecules to each of the compounds."

"Now, just hold on a doggone second," Owen MacKenzie groused. "You think maybe you could bring this discussion back down to earth?"

"I had to do some research on that one as well," Whitehurst said soothingly. The chairman hated to be placed in a situation where he had to admit not knowing something. "It appears that T-cells, which fight viral and fungal infections, are in the lymphocyte family of immune cells. They have molecules on their surfaces called receptors, which are used to identify invading infections. They identify these by what are called marker molecules, sort of like red flags waved in a bull's face."

"Right," Cofield barked, determined to grab the spotlight again. "Debs figured that maybe what the compounds she had isolated did was strengthen the immune system. Not toward anything specific, just alert it in general. So she wondered if maybe by attaching marker molecules she would cause the T-cells to pick them up more swiftly and specifically. Sort of homing in on them, collecting them, and pushing the immune system into super-high gear."

"Fascinating," the chairman murmured. "And it worked?"

"That's why we're here," Whitehurst replied smugly. "It worked incredibly well."

"And in the process," the chairman went on, "we've created a group of new compounds that are patentable."

"Already done," Whitehurst confirmed.

"Not to mention exclusively ours to manufacture."

"Ah," Whitehurst cautioned. "Not exactly."

"Yeah, like I said," Cofield agreed, "these compounds are more than complex. We haven't come up with a way to produce them synthetically. They've got to be grown naturally, for the moment, anyway. But this is a temporary thing. I'm working on the production process personally."

Which would mean a ten-year delay, Whitehurst thought to himself, but he kept his face blank. "Deborah came up with a means to both increase the plant's growth rate and to force the plants to change the compounds naturally."

"And just how did she accomplish that?"

Cofield's smile made his face look like a vulture homing in on a carcass. "You'll like this one," he replied. "You really will."

5

Cliff arrived at Blair's house ten minutes late. He would never have thought it possible to get so lost in a town this small. Put it down to first-date nerves.

Deborah had returned him to the guesthouse after the visit to the church. He had not argued. The rising fatigue had given her features a grayish pallor.

"So much I wanted to do today," she sighed. "So many plans."

"There's always tomorrow."

"For you, maybe."

He knew a peal of real alarm.

"You think it might get worse?"

"I don't *know*. Not knowing is worse than anything, almost." She rubbed an angry hand across her forehead. "I've got to be going, Cliff. Have a nice time. Behave yourself tonight, all right? Blair is a friend."

"What's her story, anyway?"

"That you'll have to ask her." She slid behind the wheel of her Cherokee, and immediately Cliff understood why she had purchased the jeep. There was no need to lower herself to get in or raise up to get out.

"Do you want me to drive you home?"

"No." Definite about that, at least. "I want to be able to show you my home when I am able to enjoy it with you."

She shut her door, the effort costing her, and asked through the window, "Do you understand?"

"No, but it doesn't matter."

"Yes, it does matter. That's why I want to wait." She

forced out a tired smile. "Until tomorrow. I hope."

He finally found Blair Collins's house on a tree-lined street directly across from the bay. As he hurried up the walk, an old woman seated in one of the rockers called out, "Would your name happen to be Cliff?"

"Yes, ma'am."

"Come up here and have a seat, young man. I'm afraid Blair is running a tad late this evening, so you'll have to put up with me for a while."

He mounted the stairs and said, "It would be a pleasure."

"Thank you kindly." She patted the rocker beside her. "My name is Sadie Atkins, but you may call me Miss Sadie. All the rest of the world does, and there's no need to make an exception for you, now is there?"

"I'm pleased to meet you."

"The honor is mine. I'm not near as pretty as my niece, I'll be the first to admit that. But I have had a nodding acquaintance with life for quite some time now. Never can tell, it might even make for an interesting chat. Would you care for something cool to drink?"

The rocker creaked a welcome as it accepted his weight. "No, thank you, I'm fine."

"Blair is late because she volunteered to take a neighbor of mine to the dentist. The old dear was to have another tooth extracted and be fitted with dentures. But it appears the tooth was not consulted in the matter, and proved unwilling to depart without a rather lengthy struggle."

"I'm sorry to hear that."

"That is kind of you, young man, but don't be. Mrs. Simpkins suffers from the ailment of many old folks who don't have pretty nieces to liven up their world. It's commonly referred to as boredom, although how one small word could hope to hold all that discomfort is beyond me."

73

"It ought to be twelve syllables long," Cliff agreed. "Begin with 'acute' and end in 'itis.' "

The old lady gave him an assessing glance. She nodded once, as though approving what she saw, then turned back to the sunset and continued, "In any case, Mrs. Simpkins had the most memorable afternoon of her entire summer and was left with sufficient fuel to fire simply hours of gossip."

Light footsteps traced their way across a hardwood floor. Cliff was on his feet in time to watch Blair emerge through the screen door and say, "Good evening, Cliff."

"Hello, Blair," he replied. He wanted to say more, but he couldn't. The words simply were not there.

She wore a simple white linen skirt, a midnight blue blouse with matching pumps, and a single strand of pearls. The effect was simple and unpretentious and maybe even a little bit severe, with her blouse buttoned up to her neck. It matched the cautious warning in her eyes. Blair stepped toward him, holding a thin black purse with both hands, everything about her shouting for him to keep his distance.

Still, she was beautiful. Her dark blond hair spilled in lustrous waves over her shoulders. She walked erect and poised, with a natural grace that dancers struggle for years to achieve. Her hands were slender, her fingers unusually long. Her eyes were the color of wet jade. Her figure was heart-stopping.

Miss Sadie looked from one to the other and said approvingly, "Why, I do believe you two would make an attractive couple."

A faint flush appeared on Blair's cheeks. "I'm sorry to have kept you waiting."

"No problem," Cliff replied. "How was Mrs. Simpkins?"

"Well, would you look here?" Miss Sadie said. "He even remembered the poor dear's name. Young man, there might indeed be hope for you."

"We're off, auntie." Blair stooped and bussed the old lady's cheek. "Don't wait up."

"Now why on earth would I do a silly thing like that?" She winked at Cliff. "I do happen to own a mirror, you know. I realize full well how much I need my beauty sleep."

As they walked down the steps, Blair said quietly, "That woman irritates people easier than most folks draw breath."

"I like her," Cliff declared.

Blair inspected him for any hint of derision. When none was found, she said, "Then maybe she was right."

But when he stopped beside the Jaguar, she said, "I take it back."

"You don't like my car?"

"It's not a question of liking or disliking it. I just don't like what it stands for."

"And just what is that supposed to mean?"

She took in the car with one sweeping hand. "Status. Pride. Everything that money can buy."

Cliff turned hot. "I bought that car ten years ago for two thousand dollars and overpaid."

Again there was the frank examination. "You rebuilt this yourself?"

"From the pavement up."

"How long did it take?"

"The four longest years of my life."

The Southern accent was stronger when she said, "Then I truly love your car, Cliff."

"You're not just saying that?"

"It is indeed a work of art," she replied, her eyes on the car, not him. "This lady would dearly like to be taken for a drive. Would you do me the kindness of helping me in?"

Blair accepted Cliff's explanation of Deborah's fatigue with calm understanding. Once they were seated in the restaurant Deborah had suggested, she asked, "How did you two become friends?"

"Debs was my tutor. Well, not in the normal sense. I didn't pay her anything. Not with money, anyway. We played racquetball together."

"Come again?"

"Debs wouldn't play with girls. And most guys didn't like to play her because they didn't like losing to a lady." He smiled at the memory. "She had this forehand shot that almost drilled the ball through the wall. On her good days, that is."

"What did she teach you?"

"Biology first, then pharmacology." He looked back over the years. "She was working on her Ph.D. and lecturing in biology. I enrolled because I thought I wanted to be a doctor. I was on the verge of flunking when Debs took me under her wing. She coached me through the entire year, pushed me hard, really hard. I ended up with two B's, but man, she made me work for them."

"And you became friends."

"Debs was the most intelligent person I'd ever met. Not just smart. *Intense*. She would focus on you, and it felt like two lasers pinning you to the spot."

"You admire her a lot."

"I do. She's everything I'm not. Focused, directed, driven, determined." He shrugged. "I guess I've always taken an easier road. I know I've enjoyed life a lot more than she has, but when I see what she's done, despite everything, I'm not sure it matters all that much."

There was a pause for ordering, and when the waiter had departed Blair asked, "So what is it you want out of life?"

She used her questions both to probe and keep a distance—that much was clear, as was the fact that if he switched and asked about her, she would draw away. Yet he found himself not minding this one-sidedness. There was something at work here, opening him up more than a dozen dates with another woman could. He looked across the table and knew with hidden wisdom that now was a time for honesty.

Cliff answered, "Sometimes I feel like I've spent my whole life waiting."

"Waiting for what?"

"That's just it. I don't know. I just feel like," Cliff tried to capture the invisible within his fist. "Like maybe one day I'd look at something and just *know*."

"Like it had struck a chord in you," she said, her guarded gaze unwavering.

"Yeah, that's it. That's it exactly. Like all of a sudden it all made sense. Like there's a *reason*. Why I'm here, what I'm going to do with my life, everything."

"Like suddenly your life was given the meaning it lacked."

"It sounds crazy, I know."

"Not to me." A pause, then, "Have you found it?"

He replied slowly, "I don't know. Sometimes lately I feel like I have, like I'm looking right at it and can't see it. Other times..."

"How do you feel when that happens?"

"Sort of excited. Sort of stupid, too, like maybe I'm kidding myself to think it might really come off."

Blair leaned both elbows on the table. "You know what I think?"

"What?"

"I think you better keep your eyes open and your ears turned to high."

He smiled. "Yeah?"

She nodded, all seriousness. "Have you ever watched how a hawk goes hunting in the wild?"

"I don't know. Maybe."

"He hovers high overhead, poised and waiting, all his attention focused down on this point on the earth. He doesn't see his prize. But he *thinks* it might be there. So he just hangs there in midair and waits. It is hard, though. Probably the hardest thing he does in his entire life. But he hovers there. He waits. And then when the prize appears, he is *ready*."

Cliff felt as though he could dive into her jade-green eyes and lose himself completely. "You really think this might be it?"

She leaned back. "You're the one who's hunting. It's your prize. All I'm saying is, if you think this might be the one, you've got to be ready to *commit*."

Fernando Aristide Montoya de Cunhor surveyed his kingdom with a very disapproving gaze. A frown sharpened his aquiline features. He was actually very pleased, but Fernando de Cunhor had long ago learned that people moved much faster if they feared his wrath.

De Cunhor's kingdom of some seven thousand souls lay in the heart of Sao Paulo, a city that came second in any number of categories. The industrial center of Brazil, Sao Paulo was second only to Poland's "Triangle of Death" in air and water pollution. It was second only to the turbulent native townships outside Johannesburg in nightly murders. It was second to Medellin, the world's capital of cocaine production, in street battles between armed gangs. It was second to its more temperate neighbor to the north, Rio de Janiero, in the number of homeless street kids under the age of nine.

Sao Paulo was home to more than ten million people, eighty percent of whom were considered by United Nations' standards to live below the poverty line. Shanty towns crawled about the hills surrounding the city's industrial complexes like rapidly growing cancers. Entire families lived in one-room hovels constructed from corrugated metal and plastic sheeting. The unpaved streets were constantly awash with sewage, so that from a distance the rubble-strewn lanes looked like bleeding veins.

Sao Paulo proper was a city of walls. Factories and homes and crumbling apartment buildings were all lined by high concrete battlements topped with barbed wire and shards of glass. The walls acted as dikes against the rising flood of crime. The city's newspapers were daily full of warnings against the problem. The issue was constantly on everyone's lips.

Fernando de Cunhor also hated crime. He had a security staff of one hundred armed men and fifty attack dogs to protect his factories and his family and his three private villas. He traveled everywhere in a bulletproof limousine, accompanied by three bodyguards. He worried constantly that he or a member of his family might be kidnapped. He paid protection money every month to the local mob.

Yes, Fernando de Cunhor hated crime as much as any of his countrymen. But he did not mind the poverty. Not at all. Fernando de Cunhor loved the freedom and the flexibility that a city of poverty gave to a man of wealth.

To the developed world, Fernando de Cunhor would have been known by his title of Chairman and Managing Director of the Medyka Pharmaceutical Company. But to the seven thousand people who relied on him for their daily bread, Fernando de Cunhor was known simply as *Padron*. The boss. Or more accurately, the king, for his was literally a life-and-death power over his employees and their families.

With an unemployment rate approaching thirty percent, a man or woman fired from Medyka stood little chance of finding a job elsewhere. And with a national social-security system swamped by an inflation rate of more than 600 percent per year, life without a job meant a daily threat of starvation.

Rare was the man or woman who dared cross or question Fernando de Cunhor. He was accustomed to being obeyed.

Now he turned his dark gaze from the window and focused upon the young man standing before his desk. "You say the information is valid?"

"Yes, Padron. The scientist we hired in Washington

has checked it carefully and says that it all fits together well."

"And the FDA man is to obtain the production specifications for you next week?"

"On Wednesday, Padron."

Fernando de Cunhor permitted himself a thin-lipped smile. "You have done well, Luis."

The young man gave a stiff little bow. "Thank you, Padron."

Fernando de Cunhor studied the young man standing before his desk. He had initially had great reservations about taking Luis on. The young man was a distant relative, a nephew several times removed, from a branch of the family that had previously produced nothing but troublemakers and spendthrifts. But the request had come from de Cunhor's aging mother. Blood is blood, the old woman had said. And the young man has studied in America. How often I have heard you wish for someone trustworthy who knew that country? Just see him, talk with him. Is that too much for a mother to ask?

For the sake of peace, he had reluctantly agreed. But at their first meeting, Fernando de Cunhor had detected something unusual in the young man. Something familiar. A hint of the same ruthless drive that had propelled a druggist's son to become the ruler of the nation's third largest pharmaceutical empire.

Yes. The young man had promise.

De Cunhor asked, "What else did our scientist tell you?"

"That whatever the process, it will be very difficult to produce these compounds. Some of the molecular chains are extremely complex."

Fernando de Cunhor nodded. It was to be expected. Those American scientists were clever. "We must begin on the paperwork immediately."

"I will initiate the process before my return," his nephew agreed.

De Cunhor and his colleagues in the Brazilian pharmaceuticals industry were no respecters of international patents. They did not ignore U.S. patent laws, however; the United States was too strong a political and economic force for them to publicly flaunt their disregard. Instead, they maneuvered around the laws in a uniquely Brazilian manner.

Every major Brazilian drug manufacturer had at least one government patent official on their payroll. For suitable sums, that official would be most willing not only to backdate an application, but also to "lose" the international paperwork that notified other countries. A new Brazilian drug could thus be copied from an existing one, the production process begun, and the market penetrated before an official protest from the United States could be lodged. Legal challenges to such abuses of patent infringement were expensive and often futile. International tribunals were slow to take action, and Brazilian courts moved on such complaints at the pace of arthritic snails. In many instances, by the time the case was actually tried, the patent's validity had already expired.

Most of the American pharmaceutical giants responded to this threat by establishing their own Brazilian factories, protecting themselves and their patents by operating within the same corrupt system. The Brazilian drug companies thus focused their search-and-copy missions to second-tier companies that did not produce in their market.

Pharmacon was a perfect target.

Fernando de Cunhor inspected his manicured hands. He wore a heavy gold ring bearing the family crest and a gold watch with the same crest emblazoned upon the face with diamonds. He asked, "You return to America when?"

"Monday, Padron."

"We will have to find some way to slow this Pharmacon down."

The subordinate nodded. He had thought of the same thing. "I have an idea."

Fernando de Cunhor looked up. "Yes?"

Luis explained his concept. The chairman heard him out, thought it over for a long moment, then nodded. "It solves our problem. See that it is done." He inspected the young man and said, "Your efforts will be properly rewarded, Luis."

Again the slight bow. "Thank you, Padron."

The hand motioned a dismissal. As his nephew turned for the door, de Cunhor added as in afterthought, "There must be no tongues left to wag."

"I shall see to it, Padron. Personally."

Fernando de Cunhor watched as the young man quietly closed the door behind him. The Padron nodded his satisfaction. Great promise indeed.

6

Cliff Devon walked the halls of the FDA on Wednesday morning, and reflected that he was one lucky CSO.

His FDA drug review team worked exceptionally well together. In a federal organization, especially one staffed primarily with brains, such synergy was nothing short of miraculous.

Cliff's actual title was Consumer Safety Officer for the team. In truth, Cliff functioned as chief grunt. The others were all specialists—a chemist, a pharmacologist, a physician, a bio-statistician, and a microbiologist. Cliff had majored in business at college and taken only those biology courses that Deborah had taught. That unusual mixture, however, had proven ideal for his work as CSO. Cliff learned early on that his duties consisted of everything that nobody else wanted to do.

Cliff worked with all the drug companies' representatives, kept up with all the incoming documents, moved all applications through the process, fielded all complaints and demands for more speed in processing, and made all requests for more information from the applicants. In other words, Cliff was the team's chief go-between, facilitator, and wheel-greaser.

The fact that Cliff did not mind dealing with federal administrivia was one reason their team ran so smoothly. He recognized his own limitations. He admired the others for their talents. And they in turn were delighted to have an administrator who was neither bitter nor bored.

Cliff's team looked to him for guidance. They trusted his word. As a result, they granted him more freedom to maneuver than any other CSO within the organization—a fact that Sandra Walters positively loathed.

It had taken until Wednesday for Cliff to bring the team together to discuss the situation at Pharmacon. Arranging a full-level team meeting on such short notice meant canceling half a day's work on other urgent matters. At any one time, each team member worked on up to a dozen drug applications. Each new drug application contained several hundred thousand pages of reports and trial data through which they had to sift. Such unscheduled team meetings meant pressing matters being pushed aside. Still, they did it for him.

Cliff's chief ally on the team was a no-nonsense physician named Dana Browning. Dana was a pediatric oncologist, a childhood cancer specialist, attempting to recover from an advanced case of burnout. Two years before, worn down by the regular experience of watching children die, she had taken a leave of absence from her regular work and buried herself in the comparative safety of new drug applications. She had insisted on working with a drug review team that had as little as possible to do with children, and this had landed her on Cliff's team. He considered her a treasure.

As was his habit, Cliff arrived early at the conference room. Granting the rest of the team status through knowing he had waited for them. Counting their time as more important than his own. Taking the extra moments to review what needed to be covered. Thinking back to the weekend before.

Sunday had been a disappointment. Deborah had called his guesthouse while he was still in bed to tell him, "I had a great dream. I was in my favorite opera, *La Bohème*. I gave Mimi a pill, and she recovered."

Cliff rolled over and rubbed his face. "I think coffee would help me make sense of that one."

"I guess you had to be there."

He swung his feet to the floor. "I always wished Bogie

had gotten on the plane with Ilsa and left Casablanca for good."

"Okay, okay."

"Or maybe tonight you could walk into *Love Story* and convince Ryan O'Neil to fall in love with somebody who doesn't die. Instead, she gets fat and has nine kids and makes pot roast every night."

"Can we please change the subject?"

"Sure. When are you coming over?"

"I'm not. This day looks like a nonstarter. Sorry, Junior."

"Don't be. Do you need anything?"

"To be alone. To get better. To have this medicine work on me as well as it has on some of the others. To be given a miracle healing." She paused, then went on, "Have I forgotten anything? No, I guess that pretty well sums things up."

"I just wish I could do something."

"You can," she said. "Come back down again soon."

"How about next weekend?"

"That would be great. Would you really?"

"I was thinking about it. That friend of yours sure is a handful."

"Had a nice time last night, did we?"

"A beauty, but a handful. She gave me a lot to think about."

"How nice for you." Deborah's smile came over the telephone. "Well, I want you to come stay with me this time. There's no need for you to spend money on a guesthouse when I've got a perfectly good spare room going to waste."

On his way out of town, Cliff had driven by to see Blair. This time, instead of hurrying up on the porch, he stopped and savored the picture the old house presented.

The houses to either side were much more impressive. To the left was a staid Jacobean manor, standing white and strict and proper, granted stodgy support by four external brick chimneys. To the right was a Victorian house, glorious in cream and ivory, lavishly embellished with peaks and trellises.

Miss Sadie's house stood between them but farther back from the road, as though it were a tad bashful to stand between such fine examples of the builder's craft. The carved wooden posts supporting her double balcony were in dire need of painting. The front steps sagged a trifle under their weight of years and feet and memories. The trio of front-porch rockers looked scarred and worn and humble. Yet the trellises climbing both side walls were heavy with bougainvillea. The front yard was crowded with ancient magnolia and blooming crepe myrtle trees. Twining roses clambered for space on the porch handrails. Nesting birds sang the glory of a warm welcome.

"What on earth are you doing out there, young man?" Miss Sadie called out from her place on the porch. "Ladies with proper upbringing do not appear unless the young man comes up the steps and asks for her."

Cliff climbed from his car and walked up to the house. "I've been looking for a home like this all my life."

"My goodness, this house is falling down around my ears," Miss Sadie retorted, easing herself back into the rocker. "But I reckon it will last as long as I do. Care to set a spell?"

"Thank you." He sat and looked out across the street to where the placid waters of Edenton Bay joined with the morning mists. The bay's shores were heavily forested, the nearby waters adorned with tiny islands just large enough to support half a dozen cypress trees. "This is beautiful."

"Yes, I would have to agree that God has spared us much and granted us even more." She smiled. "But you did not come here to have an old lady bend your ear, now, did you."

"I was on my way back to Washington," he replied. "And I just wanted to say goodbye to Blair."

"I am sure she will be pleased to see you," Miss Sadie said. "She has been walking around this morning with a most bemused expression. If I were you, young man, I would take that as a good sign."

"That's more than enough, auntie," Blair said sharply, appearing in the doorway. Then more calmly, "Hello, Cliff."

He was instantly on his feet. "I hope I'm not disturbing you."

"An attractive man with manners," Miss Sadie said, her rocker creaking agreement. "I do believe I would hang on to this one, dear."

"Let me walk you to your car," Blair said, a bright flush painting her cheeks. When they were out of range, she said, "Look at me. I haven't blushed since I was sixteen."

"You should do it more often, then," he said, refusing to give in to the urge to walk a half-pace behind her. Blair wore a faded blue cotton workshirt bunched and knotted at midwaist, a pair of ancient cut-offs, and sneakers. There was a lot to watch.

She tossed her ponytail. "Auntie has always had the ability to get under my skin."

"Maybe because she tells things the way they are," Cliff offered.

When they arrived at his car, Blair stopped and turned to face him. "I would like to thank you for a nice evening, Mister Devon."

"I'd like to do it again," Cliff said.

"Well, if your big-city ways ever wind down again in the direction of our little town, do be sure to call."

Cliff took in the cool gaze, the nonchalant voice, and felt a sudden surge of insight. The perception broke through her shell, granting him the ability to both see and understand how past pains had created Blair's cautious distance. "How about next weekend?"

A flicker of hope, of almost painful eagerness, and

then all was locked up tight again. "You're planning another trip?"

"If you'll see me," he said, his voice as steady as his gaze.

"I believe I might be free," she said, giving nothing away.

"I'll call you," he told her.

"I don't take kindly to people who make promises and don't keep them," she warned.

"You can rest assured," Cliff said solemnly, climbing into his car. "If I don't call you, I'm dead."

Dana Browning entered the conference room last and slammed her notebooks down on the table. "If I see another application for an analogue I am going to tear my hair out by the roots."

That earned sympathetic nods around the table. An analogue drug was one in which a minute change had been made to an already licensed medicine. In some few cases, the change of one molecule in a complex drug erased a whole host of bad side effects. But in the majority of applications, the analogue was a smoke-screen.

Some pharmaceutical companies used analogues to renew aging patents; they would make minor alterations and then claim that a new drug had been discovered. Other companies used them to skirt around patent-protected medicines, claiming to have come out with something newer, better, stronger. Analogues were headaches from the onset, primarily because the drug companies did everything in their power to cloak their own hidden agendas behind a veil of data and gobbledy-gook.

"This one you'll like," Cliff assured her, and began passing around copies of the information he had brought back with him.

"Pharmacon?" Ben Travers, the microbiologist, was a

very small man. Cliff had privately decided his size helped him concentrate on the invisibly tiny. "They're not scheduled for another hearing for, how long is it?"

"Six months," Cliff answered. "But I was down there visiting a friend this past weekend, and she passed this information on to me. It's the results for their first set of Phase Two trials."

"Over how long a period?" Dana asked impatiently.

"Three weeks," Cliff said, and held up his hand to hold off her outburst. "Just take a look, Dana. You know I don't make it a practice to waste your time."

They read in silence for almost half an hour. Cliff watched as each went through the entire study, then returned to the segments of particular interest to their specialty. Marybeth Schuler, their statistician, checked the figures and the math. Martin Corelli, their chemist, studied the complex molecular formulas. Ben Travers flipped back to the summary of drug indications. And Dana Browning, still a physician at heart, concentrated on the individual case-study reports.

As usual, she was first to finish. "This isn't some figment of a hyperactive imagination?"

"I've known Debs since my sophomore year at college," Cliff replied. "She's as solid as they come."

"If the study continues as it's started," Ben proclaimed, "we've got a major development on our hands. And I do mean major."

Dana leaned back, stripped off her glasses, and rubbed the bruise marks on either side of her nose. "That explains it, then."

"Explains what?"

"The pressure I've been getting. Crazy. Yesterday I was called by one of our friends over on Capitol Hill."

"Larson?" Martin asked. Congressman Larson of Utah was a perpetual nuisance.

"No, it was another of the members of Larson's committee. A congressman from New York."

"Pharmacon's headquarters is in the Big Apple," Cliff pointed out.

"Yes, it's making a lot more sense now. The guy couldn't even pronounce the drug's name. And I had no idea what he was talking about, which made him certain I was stalling. We got into a shouting match you could have heard in Manhattan."

"It's a little early to start having the political thumb-screws applied," the chemist said.

Ben snapped his fingers. "Now I remember. Something's been jiggling in my memory since I started reading. There was an article in the Post Saturday morning about a new possible miracle drug. You know, stuck on page sixteen instead of the story about a six-headed dog born in upper Mongolia. I paid it about as much attention as I would have the dog. The only reason I remember it at all was because the claim was supposedly made at a Pharmacon press conference."

"The press conference was last Friday," Cliff said. "I heard about it when I got down there. No advance word from Cofield, which was a surprise."

"You'd have thought he would have used it for a three-day trip up here," Dana agreed. "Drop an expense account bundle on a suite and some nice meals. Camp out in our offices, pass on another thousand pages of data."

"Cofield apparently had less than a week's notice," Cliff replied. "Debs told me there had been a spate of rumors circulating, and the execs decided to get their own version out. Have any of you heard about these rumors?"

A chorus of head shakes rounded the table.

"Sounds like it's time to batten down the hatches," Dana said.

"You'll need to pass this by the director," Cliff pointed out. "Sandra won't let me within a mile of Summers's office."

"I hate these pressure tactics," Dana muttered. "Can anybody tell me why I took this job in the first place?"

"You wanted to serve the public," Martin Corelli replied. "Didn't I read that somewhere?"

"Okay," Dana said, flapping her study closed. "We better stay on top of this. Next week, same time, same place."

"I'm going back down there this weekend," Cliff said, and a sudden thought of Blair sent his heart rate up a notch. He hoped it didn't show.

"Maybe you better point out to the suits that the FDA does not appreciate being railroaded," Dana said. "Not by the press, and not by Capitol Hill."

"Nix on that one," Cliff replied. "I've already traded broadsides with Cofield and their new executive VP, a guy by the name of James Whitehurst."

"From the look on your face," Ben said, "it appears that we do not have an ally in either."

"Harvey Cofield looks like a hungry vulture. And Whitehurst's heart wouldn't power a snake."

"But he's probably very nice to his mother," Ben said, rising to his feet along with Dana.

"Doubtful," Cliff said, following them from the room. "Extremely doubtful."

Dana stopped him in the hall. "On the level, Cliff. Does this stuff really do what they say?"

"My friend Debs says it's the real thing," Cliff said. "She also says this study was checked from every possible angle, given the time available. I've always found that I can take Debs' word as solid gold."

Dana sighed. "You know what that means, don't you?"

"We're in for a storm, aren't we?"

"What was the name of the typhoon that just gave Japan a close shave?" She replaced her glasses and peered at him through the thick lenses. "This is going to make their storm look like a cloudburst on a pretty summer day."

Horace Tweedie approached the car lathered in sweat.

So close. Closer than he had ever come in his entire life. Too close for everything to be going so smoothly.

He had spent the past three sleepless nights terrified there might be a double-cross. He had tossed and turned and sweated through visions of being tricked, hoodwinked, kidnapped, disappeared. But every time he turned on the light and stared at the suitcase already packed and waiting, he stopped, held by the thought of the money he had been promised. The money he might get. No, *would* get.

The Infiniti's darkened window lowered at his approach. A sudden mental picture of a long-barreled silencer sliding out left Horace so weak-kneed he could barely stand. His bow tie felt tight as a noose. Horace stood half a dozen paces away and died a dozen deaths until the stranger poked his head through the window and impatiently motioned Horace closer.

The stranger wore what he had always worn, from the first time Horace had met him in the Circular File, a local bar frequented by FDA employees—cream-colored suit, white-on-white shirt, muted pastel tie. Horace could not see, but he assumed the man still wore those strange pale shoes. The shoes had fascinated Horace at their several meetings in the bar. They had looked thin and supple enough to be rolled up like socks. The man had worn them with ultra-thin yellow silk socks like Horace's grandfather used to wear.

Everything about the man, from the shoes up, had seemed slightly effeminate to Horace. He had very slender, almost delicate features and dark eyes so large they would have been better suited to a woman. But the way he looked at the cocktail waitresses, and the way they looked back, had left no doubt in Horace's mind where the stranger's interests lay.

"Well?" the stranger demanded.

"I have it," Horace squeaked. He swallowed and tried again. "The money?"

The stranger slipped a thick manila envelope out through the window.

This time the man would just have to wait. This time Horace had to be sure. He tore at the envelope with fingers that trembled so badly he could scarcely work the paper. When the stacks of hundred-dollar bills came into view, Horace knew a surge of adrenaline so strong he wanted to shout, laugh, dance, run screaming down the street.

Instead he found himself calming. *Free.* The word was there so big in his mind there was no longer room for nerves. *Free.*

Horace slid a hand inside his pocket and handed over the three rolls of film. "It's all there. I photographed each page twice to be sure." *Free.*

Silently the man accepted the rolls. He turned his head away from the window as he stashed the film, then searched for something.

A gun. Horace felt the world drop away with his stomach. The man was going for a gun. Horace wanted to run, flee, hustle for cover, but his legs wouldn't have carried him to the other side of the street.

But when the stranger turned back to the window, he held only another envelope. It was twice as big as the one he had just handed over. Which was twice as big as the one Horace had received the week before. The stranger asked, "How would you like to earn this?"

Horace's heart could not possibly have beat faster without exploding. A roller-coaster ride was swooping him along, out of control. Nights of terror, a moment of freedom, panic-horror again, and now this. More money.

His mind screamed *run!* His gut, though, his gut saw the envelope and hungered.

Horace reached.

The envelope was withdrawn. "I need more information."

Horace licked dry lips. "I don't have—"

93

"The review team," the man said in his strange fluid accent. "I want information on them. What is the status of the study? How far are they from approval?"

"Information," Horace repeated weakly. His mind screamed the constant frantic cadence, *run*. But his eyes were glued to the envelope in the stranger's hand. It was as fat as a square balloon.

"Weaknesses," the stranger told him. "I want to slow things down. Find me a lever."

The stranger hefted the envelope. "Do so, and this is yours."

7

Cliff was less preoccupied on the second trip south to Edenton and more aware of his surroundings. This time he took pleasurable note as his way carried him through gradual stages of countrification.

The Washington metropolitan area barely gasped its last shopping-mall breath before the interstate broadened to enter Richmond. From there it was two traffic-clogged hours across Virginia to Portsmouth and Norfolk. Once the North Carolina line had been passed, however, the road and the surrounding life took a soft and gentle curve to bygone days. The way straightened, the landscape flattened, and suddenly the breeze was laden with the perfumes of a country summer.

Untouched pine forests sent out fragrant invitations to slow down, sit back, forget the city hassles, and just rest a spell. Well-kept farmhouses sported cool-looking front porches and a host of hickory rockers. Butterflies and dragonflies coasted in lazy circles alongside the road. Cars kept to the speed limit not because they had to, but because fifty-five was simply fast enough.

He passed a final pine grove, and suddenly the Pharmacon facility loomed up like a burnished copper space station. He pulled into the parking lot, unfolded himself from the Jag, and stretched before walking up to the entrance. When the first set of bulletproof doors glided shut behind him, the only sound he could hear was the air conditioning's constant sigh and the reception guard's metallic voice through the speaker system. The outside world was suddenly a thousand miles away.

Cliff gave his name and was pointed toward a leather bench running down the hall's opposite side. He declined to wait there and asked instead to be let back outside. The doors glided open and he escaped into the brilliant afternoon sunlight. He much preferred to bake outdoors than feel he was seated in a carpet-lined petri dish.

Deborah came out and greeted him with a hug and the words, "Hot enough for you?"

"Better than sitting in there under the gun."

"Yeah," she agreed, taking him by the arm, "but you should see what the treatment does for salesmen. An hour of waiting out there, and they'll agree to just about any deal."

He allowed her to lead him over to her jeep. "Where are we headed?"

"I want to stop by and check on something," she said, "then we'll swing back and collect your car. I'm cooking dinner for you at home tonight. I invited Blair, but she's got some family emergency and has to drive to Norfolk. So it'll just be you and me."

"Sounds great," Cliff said, trying to hide his disappointment.

Deborah patted his arm. "She said to tell you she's sorry and she'll be back tomorrow. Brace up, Junior. She was as broke up about it as you are. More."

"Really?" The thought cheered him.

Deborah started the Cherokee and gave Cliff her lopsided grin. "Not falling off the deep end, are we?"

They drove along a pretzel of narrow country roads. "The distance we're covering is only a mile or so as the crow flies," Deborah explained, "but to get there we've got to cover about five times that. You get off the main roads in this area and you're entering a time warp. Nobody's in enough of a hurry to feel the road's got to go in a straight line."

"What's that?" Cliff pointed to smoke scarring the otherwise blue sky up ahead.

"I'm not sure." Deborah searched through the windshield. "It looks like Hank is burning some fields. They better not be ours."

"Hank works for you?"

"Hank Aaron Jones is a local farmer. If you'll take some friendly advice, don't ask him about his name. And yes, he works for us. In a way. He grows crops under our direction."

"*The* crop?"

Deborah nodded distractedly, her concentration focused on the blackened field. "What on earth is that man doing? That's not even his land."

As they approached, Cliff saw that Hank Aaron Jones wore a heavy towel wrapped tightly around his mouth and nose. He spotted Deborah's Cherokee and waved them toward his own drive. The fire was almost out. Hank stumped across the smoldering field, crossed the road, and stepped up to the jeep. "Morning, Miss Debs."

"Hank, what in the world?"

"Bought me some more land. You said you wanted me to put in another fifty acres."

"Yes, but not for another month or so."

Hank shrugged. "Feller was ready to sell. I bought."

"But those fields look ready to harvest." She shielded her eyes and looked out at the golden acres. "What is that, rapeweed?"

Hank nodded. "It was, yes ma'am."

"You bought the field closest to your own a few weeks before harvest and burned up the crop? Why?"

Cliff pointed out beyond the still-standing fields to where a group of people milled about. The sound of rock music drifted in the still air. "What are all those tents over there?"

"Oh, excuse me," Deborah said. "Hank, I'd like you to meet a friend of mine, Cliff Devon."

"Howdy."

Cliff accepted a hand as firm as aged teak. The man

smelled of smoke and hard work. "Your neighbor having a party over there?"

"You'll have to go ask him about that."

Deborah's confusion deepened. "I thought you told me you and your neighbor were old friends. Isn't that the one you asked if we could use some of his fields?"

"Times change," Hank Aaron Jones replied, biting off the words. "Right now, ma'am, the only thing Jude Taylor and me got in common is a prevailing wind. You had something special you wanted to talk about?"

"No, I just wanted to show Cliff what we're growing here."

Hank lifted his face as though tasting the air. "I guess that'll be okay. Y'all excuse me, I gotta make sure the fire stays out."

They watched him fit the towel back over his face and stride away. Deborah asked, "What was that all about?"

"If I didn't know better, I'd have said he was testing the wind," Cliff answered. "He reminds me of how a sailor looks when he's worried about a storm."

She watched the farmer stamp around his smoldering new field. "This doesn't make any sense. None at all."

Cliff followed Deborah's jeep a long winding route away from Edenton. Each turning led them onto a narrower, more rural road. Eventually she pulled onto a small graveled track and stopped. She stepped out as he pulled up beside her and said, "I'd like you to see my place for the first time on foot."

"Fine with me." He looked around as they crunched down the gravel. Here and there small country houses emerged from the pine groves. Small front gardens shone like new pennies in the afternoon light. "Why out here, Debs?"

"Cash," she replied simply. "Same as the car. I wanted a place, my own place, with a view that would stay good and fresh for all my remaining days. And I needed it bought and paid for."

"I think I see," he said slowly.

"I can't afford the risk of loans. I need everything I own to be free and clear of any debt. Just in case."

"Hey there, Miss Deborah." An elderly black man with a face as seamed as a freshly plowed field walked over. "How you doing?"

"Fine, Reuben. Is that daughter of yours feeling better today?"

"Yes ma'am. She's had herself a right peaceful night. Looks like that fever's done broke for good."

"You be sure and let me know if you see any of those symptoms I told you about."

"Surely will, Miss Deborah. Can't thank you enough for all you done."

"It was good to have a chance and repay you, at least in part."

"Shoot. Ain't done nothing 'cept be a neighbor."

She smiled. "I'd like to introduce an old friend of mine, Cliff Devon. Cliff, this is Reuben Haskins. He lives down the road a ways."

"Nice to meet you."

The old man nodded briefly in Cliff's direction but kept his gaze on Deborah. "Anything you need, Miss Deborah, you know where to come."

"Thank you, Reuben. Give my best to Hannah."

"Surely will. You take care, now."

Deborah watched him amble away and said, "That man defines what a giver should be."

"He didn't have much time for me," Cliff observed.

"Black people in these parts don't pay much attention to their first impressions of a white person."

"Are all your neighbors black?"

She pointed away from the direction Reuben was walking. "Down that side road is pure country. A couple of fishermen, two brothers who own a local gas station, some I haven't met yet. You learn that out here. Some people just want to keep to themselves, and it's best to let them be." Her eyes remained on the elderly black man in his well-worn overalls. "Some of the black families won't have anything to do with me. But most of them are coming to be good friends. You know what brought about the biggest change?"

"I can't imagine."

Deborah returned the waves of three children carrying poles and scampering down the road on muddy feet. Two were black, the other a tow-headed white boy. "I had a bad attack a few months back. First time my legs ever gave out completely. Couldn't get up my three front stairs. Reuben's sister happened by and found me sprawled on the ground. She managed to carry me inside and settle me in my chair. The next day Reuben came over and built me a ramp."

She squinted and looked into the sunlight. "These people understand tragedy. I've discovered that since coming to live here. The good sorts of country people have a deep understanding of suffering, and they respond to it in others."

"It sounds like you've made a home for yourself, Debs."

"I'm working at it. I'm still the outsider, and there are still a lot of invisible fences. But I'm in no hurry. I've got time to learn their ways." She grasped his hand and led him forward. "Let me show you around."

Immediately beyond the windbreak of pine, the water fanned out on two sides. "This is Edenton Bay," she explained. "Same as in town. It opens into Albemarle Sound, part of the Inland Waterway."

The house rested on a point shaded by cypress and pine and elm. Wisteria climbed in untrimmed abandon over the pumphouse and other outbuildings. The loudest noises were the wind and the katydids and the birds. The town of Edenton was the only break in the forest lining the distant banks.

"This is fantastic," Cliff breathed.

"Locals call this a shotgun house," she said. "One room opens directly into the next. It was built by a fisherman back in the twenties."

"How did you find it?"

"I bought it from his daughter, who wanted to move into the city. She's a nurse at the hospital where I go for treatment."

"Treatment?"

"They take my blood pressure, thump my chest, give me a shot of vitamins, and let me know they are there if ever I need them." She walked toward the stairs, whose sides were now sloped for her wheelchair. "Come on, I want to show you inside."

The house was a long wooden tunnel separated into five rooms—kitchen, parlor, bath, and two bedrooms. Each room shared walls with its neighbors. The outer shell was nothing more than plywood and big windows. A broad screened porch, as large in floor space as the entire house, formed a generous "L" around two sides. The porch had two daybeds to sleep on when the nights were balmy, and a large hickory-slat swing cushioned by a riot of floral-print pillows.

Cliff walked into Deborah's bedroom, spotted the bed's occupant, and cried, "Hairball! Is it you?"

"Now don't you start," Deborah warned.

But Cliff was already down on his knees, stroking the cat. "I tell you, Debs, this animal has a terminal case of the warm-and-fuzzies. Might be nearing time to put it out of its misery."

"I happen to be very attached to my pets."

"A matched pair of neutered powder puffs," Cliff said, smiling as the cat started purring like a tiny outboard motor. "Overweight, declawed, lazy, and dumb. This how you like your men?"

"You should know," she said, walking out. Over her shoulder she said, "You can take the back bedroom."

Dinner that night was a comfortable affair. Music was

supplied by a serenade of cicada tenors and full bass bullfrogs. The wind sighed through the pines like an orchestra of strings, and the waves counted time upon the bulkhead.

Cliff sighed his contentment, declared, "That was a fantastic meal, Debs."

She beamed. "It really is nice to have the chance to cook for you. I'm sorry it didn't work out last weekend."

"Me too." He laid the cutlery out in very neat lines, deliberate motions matching the line of his thoughts. "Can I ask you something?"

"Anything." Somber now. Sensing what was to come.

He took a breath, asked, "Are you taking Pharmacon's new experimental drug yourself?"

"Yes." Simple as that. Despite the fact that doing so was professionally unethical. Between them, there were no secrets.

"And you haven't noticed any difference?"

"It's not like that with MS," she replied. "First of all, nobody is absolutely positive that a virus is the cause. It may be a virus that attaches itself only to those who are genetically disposed, or the disease may be entirely genetic. Even if we had proved it is a virus, which is my guess, there's still no way of telling what course the disease would have taken with me if I wasn't on the drug."

"I think I see."

"Maybe I would have already slipped into the more extreme disabilities. Maybe I would be completely bedridden. There's just no way of telling. But if you're asking why I haven't had a complete remission, I don't have an answer for you." She stood and began gathering plates. "Why don't you go sit on the swing. I'll put the coffee on and join you."

"Can I help?"

"Tomorrow, yes. We'll work out a system. But for tonight, you're my guest, so go make yourself comfortable."

When Deborah returned she served coffee, then set a high-back chair where she could watch both him and the dwindling sunset. Together they watched the gold-streaked glory fade to ever gentler pastels, the day content with its work and bidding this corner of the world a fond farewell.

"I've sat out here captured by sunsets that ended two hours earlier," she said quietly, "and listened to a thousand angels sing a hymn to the passing day."

Cliff searched the dark, trying to fathom how she could speak with such peace. "Don't you ever grow angry at how life's treated you?"

"Less and less often," Deborah replied. "I don't like plugging up the eyes and ears of my heart any more than I absolutely have to. Anger is too expensive an indulgence when you've learned what beauty the moment can hold."

"Maybe for you," Cliff said. "If something like that happened to me, I'd have lost it completely."

"I almost did," she admitted. "Anger comes in various stages. I learned that in my dark days. That's what I call them now, how I remember them. They were filled with the worst kind of anger—helpless, endless silent screams. There's no kind of fury worse than hopeless rage."

She shook herself, forcing away an unwelcome chill. "Enough of that. It looks like I'm going to be up your way this week."

"Hey, that's great, Debs."

"You may not think so when you hear the reason."

"Politics?"

There was just enough light for him to see her nod. "They've made it out like I need to be up there—or Whitehurst has. I get the distinct impression that Cofield would rather I didn't show up at all, so he can play the prima donna. But Whitehurst has been after me on a daily basis, you know, like the inventor is the only one who can really explain what it's all about. The real reason

103

is he wants to put me on display. You know how Washington's all caught up in this health care thing."

"You're telling me."

"Anyway, he wants to put me on a pedestal, the Pharmacon woman scientist, hit the feminists and the equal-rights people. Nothing would make Whitehurst happier than for me to show up in my wheelchair."

"You're kidding."

"I wish I was. Whitehurst keeps asking if maybe the trip wouldn't be too much of a strain for me to walk everywhere. Washington's such a big place, there will be so much going on, blah, blah, blah."

"It's strange how I haven't heard anything about this through the official channels."

"I know. I get the impression this has been pushed into high gear by the top bean counters."

"You mean Whitehurst?"

"No, I think it's gone beyond that, right up to the board of directors. I'll find out in Washington, I suppose."

"Whatever is happening officially," Cliff mused, "the Washington rumor mill has really gotten its teeth into your drug. The *Post* did a little article on the press conference last weekend, then followed up on Thursday with a longer piece about the new antiviral wonder drug."

"I saw it."

"That was like poking a stick in the hornet's nest." Cliff smiled at the memory. "Pretty much everybody at the FDA knows by now that I'm coordinating the application. I had people I've never even seen before stop to speak with me. Then there's this little guy by the name of Tweedie, believe it or not. Horace Tweedie. He looks like his name. Wears these red bow ties, sort of his trademark. These past couple of days he's been all over me like glue, always asking questions."

He shifted on the swing, rearranged the pillows so he

could lounge more comfortably. "I've seen it happen to others before me, you know. Something comes up and suddenly they're the flavor of the month. The gossips make a sort of competition of who knows the most the soonest."

"Must bug you."

"Not really. I mean, if you could only see this guy Tweedie. He's really kind of odd. I think he's just lonely." Cliff was silent, then pondered aloud, "Still, it's really weird how Pharmacon's turning up the pressure when the second phase of tests has only just been started. I wonder what's going on."

"You and me both. Right now I feel like a puppet on a string." Deborah rose with a sigh. "It's time to put these bones to bed. Stay up as long as you like, Junior. There's a wall of books at the back of your room if you feel like reading."

"'Night, Debs. Thanks for everything."

"Pleasure to have you. I mean that from the heart." She reached over and tousled his hair. "See you in the morning."

8

Tuesday morning Cliff shrugged on his jacket, closed his office door, and said to Madge, "I'm off to play political football."

"Sandra wants to see you before you go," Madge replied.

He shook his head in denial. "You forgot to tell me."

"That's right, I did. Such a lousy memory, me." She motioned him over. "Come to Madge. Your tie needs straightening."

He bent over her desk. "Did you hear from Deborah?"

"For the eleventh time this morning, no." She fitted the knot up snug to his collar. "I'm sure she would have gotten word to you if anything had changed." Madge patted his arm. "Go be a good boy."

"I always am."

"You know, I almost believe you." She gave him what passed for a smile. "More's the pity."

Cliff turned to the door just as Ralph Summers came in. "Cliff, got a minute?"

"Barely."

Summers nodded. "Headed over to Capitol Hill?"

"That's right."

"Any idea what they've got going on?"

"Only what I told you yesterday. One of the chief lobbyists for the pharmaceutical industry pulled some strings and got Pharmacon time today before some congressional subcommittee hearing."

"There's a lot of them around," Summers said. "Subcommittee hearings, I mean. The number exploded when the health care bills first came out, and now they're all scrambling for something to keep them in the headlines. I'm glad you're keeping an eye on this."

"I wish you'd tell Sandra that."

"Sandra doesn't think you should be going," Summers said. "She's been by twice to ask that I block your attending."

"If she had her way, I'd be locked in a closet," Cliff said bitterly.

Summers inspected him, then with a pat on the back led Cliff through the door and out into the hall. He pulled Cliff over to one side and asked quietly, "Is there something going on here I should know about?"

It almost came out then. Cliff was tempted, very tempted, to tell the man what was really behind their feud. But he couldn't. "I guess she doesn't think much of my friendship with Deborah."

"I don't believe I've ever met Dr. Givens." Summers crossed his arms and leaned against the wall. "She's never been married?"

"Only to her work."

"And she's handicapped?"

"Don't you let her hear you say that," he warned.

"So she's sensitive about her illness, is she?"

"It's not like that at all," Cliff said stoutly. "She's the strongest person I've ever met. Her MS is something she's come to terms with, in her own way."

"What way is that?"

"She's not handicapped at all. Not in her own eyes, and not in mine," Cliff replied. "Becoming ill has just sort of balanced her out with the rest of the world. Before, she was maybe a little too superior to the rest of humanity."

"You obviously think a lot of her," Summers said.

"Debs is one of the finest people I've ever met," Cliff replied.

"Sandra seems to feel this session today is going to

turn into a real FDA bashing, which we shouldn't dignify with our presence."

"Not with Debs," Cliff said confidently. "About the other guys, I can't say." He related his confrontation in Cofield's office. "They're pushing hard, but for what I can't figure out. It's way too early for them to be wheeling out the big guns."

"Well, I can't see any reason for not allowing you to attend," Summers decided. "I'm away the rest of today and all of tomorrow and Thursday. But I want to meet with you first thing Friday morning."

"I will. Thanks."

"And if there's anything we need to discuss, about Sandra or anything else, my door is always open."

The desire to unload welled up again, but he couldn't get out the words. "I guess we just don't get along," he said weakly, and left.

Deborah found people's responses to her wheelchair a never-ending study in human nature. Her scientist's mind continually catalogued the reactions she observed.

The majority watched furtively, turning away if she looked in their direction. She saw this as motivated by shame and fear—shame that they could walk and she could not, fear that if it had happened to her it could happen to them.

Then there were the ones who strove not to see the chair at all. Having a conversation with them was like leading a recently reformed drunk past an open saloon; both ended up raw-nerved and exhausted.

Others reacted with pity, still others with pain, a few with condescending superiority. These talked slow and loud, as though being chairbound also left her deaf and demented.

A few, many of them scientists, showed surprise at first, gave the chair an open inspection, then dismissed it. They treated it as they would a personal idiosyncrasy, like a penchant for wearing purple headbands. They were concerned with what lay beneath the surface and had little time for vagaries of the human condition. When she met such a person, Deborah felt as though a special perfume had been sprayed on her day.

But very few such people surrounded her in Washington's corridors of power. None, in fact.

Their chief lobbyist left them in the hall outside the Congressional hearing room and went off to determine if the program was running to schedule. Whitehurst remained in deep discussion with Owen MacKenzie. The chairman of Pharmacon had flown down for the hearing.

She sat in her wheelchair surrounded by power-players. Congressmen and aides hustled by, occasionally snagged by lobbyists and herded over. They came because doing so was the fastest way out. They smiled and shook hands and spoke words by rote and hustled off. Deborah doubted they saw her at all.

Tiring of the charade, she moved her chair to the hall's other side. Cofield took the opportunity to walk over and hiss, "This is neither the time nor the place to have your boyfriend drop by."

"If you say that one more time," Deborah snapped back, "I am going to wheel myself out of here."

The expression flittering across Cofield's features confirmed what she had thought—that he did not want her here at all. She wondered what pressure Whitehurst and the chairman had exerted to have him relinquish the spotlight. And why.

Cofield seethed, "No FDA busybody is any friend of ours. Especially now."

She looked up at him in consternation. "What's gotten into you, Harvey? Since when is the FDA on your hit list?"

"Not here," Whitehurst said, sidling over with his number one smile firmly in place. "We must present a united front."

109

Cofield snorted and stomped off. Deborah turned to Whitehurst and demanded, "Is there something going on I don't know about?"

"Of course not," he soothed. "Now, you're sure you know what to do."

"Give them an overview of my research," she said impatiently. "Keep it short and sweet. But what—"

"Later," Whitehurst said and returned to the chairman.

Deborah sighed in exasperation and debated going over to them. She had news. Important news. Twice since joining them in Washington she had tried to break in on their discussion, but they had brushed her aside, their attention focused on the hearing. Deborah stayed where she was and vowed they would not pass her off so easily once the circus was behind them.

She checked her watch. Still a half hour to go before Cliff was scheduled to arrive. She should have made it for earlier. Deborah wheeled farther away from the milling crowds of lobbyists, journalists, congressional aides, and sensation seekers. She looked out a window at a sky of washed-out blue and wondered why she had allowed herself to be goaded into coming at all. She was tired and wanted this over with. It was not a good day. Not a good week, for that matter, and today was only Tuesday. She escaped farther from the worst of the noise, moving around the hall's nearest corner, and thought back over the previous day.

Monday afternoon she had returned to the Norfolk Veterans Hospital, dozing fitfully through the trip as Cochise drove her jeep. The big man had scarcely been able to fit behind the wheel, and upon their arrival he had taken several minutes to pry himself loose.

Once free, Cochise had asked, "Want me to unload the chair?"

Deborah searched the forecourt for Tom. Where was the old man? "I suppose so."

Once seated, she propelled herself up the side ramp. Cochise knew better than to push her. When she came through the front doors, she spotted Tom seated in the main hall. He had pulled his chair away from the others, and was staring blindly out the side window.

Deborah rolled herself over. "I missed you today."

He started, turned, and shrunk inside himself. "It's you."

"What's the matter, Tom?"

He sighed and rubbed an age-spotted hand down one side of his face. "Ain't been sleeping so good."

She reached out and grasped his arm, her chest hurting for him. Relapse. It had to be. Of all the people here, why old Tom? "Do you want to tell me about it?"

The old man lowered his head and inspected her hand. "You always been good to me, Dr. Debs."

"Of course I have," she said tenderly. "We're friends, aren't we?"

Another sigh. He lifted his head, spotted Cochise waiting patiently behind them, and said, "Get rid of the Injun. I got something to tell you."

Deborah turned and said, "I'll meet you in the lab." Once Cochise had ambled off, she said, "Tell me what it is, Tom."

"Let's go outside," the old man replied and pushed himself from the chair.

The air was blistering hot, the humidity bordering on 100 percent. Deborah followed Tom over to the shaded alcove by the entrance ramp and waited while the old man settled himself. He appeared in no hurry to speak. Despite her cloud of fatigue and the sweat that was already plastering the blouse to her skin, she forced herself to be patient.

"Done something I ain't proud of," Tom said finally.

She tried to make light of it. "Making mistakes is what keeps us human, Tom."

But he wasn't having any of it. "You 'member the last time you was here? Went flying off in a chopper."

"Of course I remember. You helped me with my chair."

Tom squared his shoulders. "I took money from a feller. I'm broke, plain and simple. Owe money to just about everybody. Ain't no way to grow old, sick and broke. This feller showed up and offered me money, and I took it, and that's all there is to it."

Deborah searched the old man's face, a knot growing in her gut. "I don't understand, Tom. What was it they were after?"

"Was a him, not a them. One man. Foreign feller. Don't ask me where from, 'cause I don't know. Never had much time for any of 'em. Wisht I hadn't of this time. But what's done is done." The old man blew out his cheeks. "Told him what he wanted to know, sure enough. But I never said I wouldn't tell nobody else."

"Tell what, Tom," Deborah pressed. "What were they after?"

Tom faced her, pain crying from his rheumy old eyes. He replied, "He was after you."

"I'm still not sure it was a good idea to bring that Givens woman along," Owen MacKenzie said when Whitehurst had rejoined him.

"I understand," Whitehurst agreed. He turned his back to the throng and allowed his smile to slip away. "But you should hear Cofield make a presentation."

"Not good?"

"Hopeless. He slips into this superman-scientist role and talks down to the world."

"Not the image we need here," the chairman agreed.

"Word is already out through the scientific community," Whitehurst went on. "I've been checking. This kind of news spreads like wildfire. Everybody who's anybody knows that Givens was behind the research. If we showed up here in public without her, we'd be tarred and feathered."

"What about this friend of hers, the guy from the FDA?"

"Cliff Devon. Nothing to worry about. He's barely a midlevel bureaucrat. Takes himself and his job far too seriously." Whitehurst permitted a glint of steel to show through. "When we pop the lid on this one, there won't be anything left of Devon but a greasy stain on the sidewalk."

Cliff took Rockville Pike southbound to where it became Wisconsin Avenue, and fought traffic the entire way. The little stretch of road that joined Wisconsin to Massachusetts was a snarling tangle that took a good twenty minutes to navigate. Cliff gave himself two pats on the back, one for leaving enough time for the Washington passage, and two for driving his Plymouth—the Jag tended to become surly in traffic. Cliff bided his time by replaying the Saturday evening he had spent with Blair.

For some reason, her defensive barriers still had not bothered him. He barely knew her, and yet had shown her a depth and honesty rare for him. Very rare.

After dinner they had taken a walk along the bay, then returned to sit on the porch. Blair's Aunt Sadie had long since gone to bed. They had sat in silence for a time, the rockers creaking a comfortable conversation for them. The night had soothed and caressed and invited warm intimacies.

After a time she had asked, "Do you like city living, Cliff?"

"It's where I need to be to do my job. If I had my choice, I think I'd rather be here."

That gave her pause. Then, "Do you love your work that much?"

"I feel like I'm doing something important. I feel like I'm good at it. As for the rest," he shrugged. "I've made peace with myself a long time ago. It's a shame that some others haven't."

"Like who, for instance?"

"Oh, my dad, for one. He's a surgeon. Top digger at a big hospital in Chicago. It was always expected that I'd follow in his footsteps. Then when I got to college I realized there was more to life than boning for grades. These days, most of the people who make it to med school basically live for that and nothing else. I felt like life had a lot of other things to offer—puttering around with the Jag, making friends, enjoying life."

Blair rewarded his honesty by reaching over and slipping her hand into his. Her fingers were cool, her touch as light as the breeze. "Was that tough for your father to accept?"

"Oh, Dad's okay," Cliff replied, achingly aware of her touch, yearning for more. "He just doesn't have room for anything else in his world besides medicine. My kid brother's just started his surgical residency. He has all the brains in the family. They get along great. But when I'm around, well, you can see both of them kind of floundering, trying to find something to talk about. Like, here's good old stumblebum Cliff. Let's be polite."

"Stop that."

"It's true, I tell you. Silence descends on the room, and they make these awful comments about the weather or something equally warm and congenial, until I feel like I'll explode if I stay there another minute. So I leave, and thirty seconds later they're deep in discussion, as though I had never even been there." He shook his head. "Yeah, going home is all laughs and good times for old Cliff."

"Family," Blair sighed to the night. "How can we love each other so much and still cause so much pain?"

Cliff turned. Streetlights gave her features a soft silver cast. He asked softly, "Who hurt you, Blair?"

There was a stiffening, a drawing away, before she forced herself to relax. The hand in his became cold. "Life," she said, her voice flat. She stood up abruptly, turned, and gazed down on him with eyes that saw nothing but what she refused to reveal. "I think it's time you were going, Cliff. Thank you for a lovely evening."

"Debs!" Seeing her seated in the wheelchair gave him a lance of worry. "How are you doing?"

"Not near as well as I will be when this is over," she replied. "But better now that you're here. Thanks for coming."

"No problem," he replied, and covered the upsurge of emotions by examining the hall. "Would you get a look at this circus."

Close to a hundred people swarmed the corridor outside the hearing rooms. Lobbyists buttonholed everyone in sight or stood in clusters and muttered among themselves. Journalists vied with one another to pressure incoming and outgoing congressmen and aides. The scene rang with self-importance. "It's easy to tell which ones are here to testify," Deborah said. "They're the ones wearing lost expressions and wishing they were somewhere else."

Cliff pointed to a group farther down the hall. "Who is that giving us the eye?"

"Don't point. That's my chairman."

"The chairman of Pharmacon is here?"

She looked up at him. "I agree. A month into phase two and they're already out in force. It's strange. All of this is strange."

Obtaining FDA approval for a new drug was a multiphase process. Including pretrial testing and development that had to take place before initial application, the procedure lasted well over five years.

After the initial analysis and synthesis, the new drug had to be tested in animals. A safe dosage for humans had to be worked out. Initial claims for benefits had to be developed and possible side effects—known as contraindications—established. And then a representative like Harvey Cofield would appear at the FDA offices, present reams of preliminary documents, and make the Investigational New Drug application. Only after the IND was approved could clinical trials on humans—and the actual FDA approval process—begin.

Phase one of the clinical trials usually involved between twenty and one hundred human subjects. This normally occurred over a three- to six-month period and concentrated upon safety. During this time, the medical doctor on the FDA team would conduct a safety review.

Phase two involved the first tests upon human subjects actually suffering from the ailment which the drug claimed to treat. This was where the detailed case studies began. Phase-two testing usually involved between one and three hundred patients and took something over one year. Phase three followed, with more than a thousand patients treated, and if the drug passed this hurdle it was approved.

On average, research and development and application for a new drug cost more than two hundred million dollars. For every drug that won FDA approval, nine were turned down. For the drugs that were approved, however, the payoff could be mind boggling.

Newly approved drugs had on average seven years left to run on their original patent. For those seven years, no other company was allowed to produce that drug, and prices could be set as high as the market would bear. For ground-breaking new medicine, the market could bear an enormous amount.

A new ulcer drug recorded first-year revenues of seven hundred million dollars. A new migraine drug cost seventy dollars for two doses and was expected to earn almost two billion dollars in the first eighteen months of its release. And so on.

Political and media pressure to accelerate FDA approval was commonly exerted, but usually not before phase-three testing had been underway for at least a year. Approval prior to this time was simply too dangerous.

Until a drug had been tested on a large number of patients over a substantial period, there was too much risk of something going wrong, of some unforeseen side effect appearing. No drug company could afford to take such a chance.

To have political pressure applied so early in the approval process was unheard of. Yet there was no other reason for Pharmacon to appear before the sub-committee.

Cliff asked, "Can we get together after this is over?"

"Doubtful. They've got plans to sweep us away someplace or another as soon as we're done." Deborah motioned him closer. "There's something I have to tell you." Swiftly she related the conversation with Tom.

Cliff grew more alarmed with each word. "Foreign industrial spies?"

"It sounds that way."

"Have you told the others?"

"I've tried. But right now they can't think any further than being the next act in line here." Out of the corner of her eye, Deborah saw a group of three congressmen exit the hearing room. She was scheduled to speak immediately after the morning break. Her heart rate accelerated. "I'll pin them down this afternoon and lay it out."

"You've got to be careful, Debs."

"Are you kidding? Our building is tighter than a bank vault."

"Yeah, but you don't live there all the time."

One of the congressmen, a handsome gray-haired man she recognized from somewhere, strode directly toward where Whitehurst and MacKenzie stood talking. Two aides were kept busy holding the journalists at bay. Whitehurst reached into his pocket and handed the congressman a note.

"Junior," Deborah asked, "who's that congressman over there talking with the suits?"

Cliff raised his head and snorted. "Larson. Congressman from Utah and head of the subcommittee you'll be addressing. He's no friend of ours. The FDA, I mean."

The congressman read the note, kept nodding as Whitehurst bent his ear with a whispered discourse. For once, the VP was not wearing his smile. "Why isn't he your friend?"

"Oh, his state contains a large number of vitamin manufacturers. Vitamins aren't covered by the FDA, and they're lobbying like crazy to keep it that way. Larson uses every chance he gets to toss grenades our way."

"That's right, I remember reading something about it."

The congressman said something, to which Whitehurst replied by pointing in Deborah's direction. She felt a chill rise as the three men started toward her. Larson called to an aide, who scampered over. The journalists saw the focus of their attention and realized there was someone potentially important in their midst.

"Looks like showtime, Junior. I'll call you when I get back to the hotel tonight."

"Debs—" Cliff was stopped by the descending swarm. They jammed around Deborah's wheelchair, completely blocking him out. Cameras flashed continually as the congressman bent over and shook Deborah's hand.

Cliff heard one journalist ask another in a whisper laced with whiskey and cynicism, "Who's the crip?"

"Dunno," came the muttered reply. "But if she brought Larson out of chambers, tomorrow she's probably gonna be news."

Despite her years of lecturing to classes far larger than this gathering, Deborah's opening comments were delivered in a voice so shaky she doubted anyone could understand her.

Nothing could have prepared her for the pressure she felt as she addressed the subcommittee. The congressmen sat on a raised dais in front of her, their semicircular desk sweeping out and around the witness table. Congressman Larson occupied the central seat. Behind them, aides sat, stood, wrote, came and went, leaned over and spoke into the ears of the congressmen. Behind Deborah rose tier after tier of seats, all of them occupied.

By the time she completed her overview of the drug and the initial clinical trial data, she felt her heart begin to descend from her throat. Congressman Larson smiled. "Thank you for your remarks, Dr. Givens. I wish all of our experts could be as brief and succinct in their testimony." He paused as the audience tittered appreciatively. "I am sure several of my colleagues will want to take advantage of your clarity." He looked to his left, nodded to a middle-aged congresswoman, and said, "The chair now yields to my distinguished colleague from Illinois."

"Dr. Givens," the congresswoman began, "I was wondering if I might ask you about some of the terms you used in your talk."

"Sure." Deborah found herself calming, steadying. She had spent most of her adult life dealing with students who did not understand.

"You mentioned that your compounds were naturally occurring, rather than biosynthetic, as though that were a problem. Did I understand you correctly, and if so, why is this an issue?"

"Biosynthetic drugs are manufactured in the laboratory," Deborah explained. "Naturally occurring drugs are derived from materials found in the physical world. Pharmaceutical companies prefer to work with biosynthetic drugs. Aspirin, for example, was discovered first in the natural world, then eventually a means was found to manufacture it in the lab."

"Why is that so important?"

"Because it's easier, and eventually cheaper. With naturally occurring drugs, we have to find methods of purification to remove any harmful substances in the final product. Then we have to prove that we will obtain the same pharmacological response every time."

"I beg your pardon?"

119

Deborah shifted to a lower mental gear. "We have to prove that the dose from this batch of plants will have exactly the same effect as the one from the next batch. We call it validation of the process, where every batch has the same purity and potency, time after time."

"I think I see," the congresswoman said, raising her half-moon eyeglass and inspecting a page of notes on the table before her. "One further question, please. You stated that you considered your product to be a possible alternative to monoclonal antibodies. Could you please elaborate?"

"Sure. Monoclonal antibodies are on the leading edge of antiviral research," Deborah said, warming to her discussion. "Mono means single; monoclonal means cloned from a single cell. Viruses themselves have DNA or RNA cores. Then they usually have protein shells surrounding this, but not always. They may have lipid layers. They may be round or square or triangular or octagonal. They are incredibly diverse. The molecular shape of these cores and exterior shells can usually be identified by a specific antibody. These identifiable shapes are called antigens. When we make a monoclonal antibody, we are fashioning a molecule that will go in, identify a specific antigen from a specific virus, and attach itself to it. Then the antibody is absorbed by the virus and destroys it."

The congresswoman was nodding and taking notes. Deborah felt more in her element. There was nothing that got her going quite like a student who truly wanted to learn. "In monoclonal work, every time a new virus is identified, a specific antibody is designed to combat that particular ailment. Specific to the point of designing new molecular chains and adapting genes inside the body's immune system to identify that new danger. But there are problems."

The congresswoman looked up from her note-taking. "The more specific you become, the greater the risk that something will do an end run."

"Exactly," Deborah agreed. "This is the problem with AIDS, and we think with a lot of other viruses. They adapt themselves to the body, and they *change*. So the immune system is taught by these new monoclonal antibodies to attack something that then masks itself by changing its molecular shape. And there is the additional problem of very severe contraindications, or possible adverse reactions when taken."

"And those are?"

"The majority of these new drugs have a slew of contra-indications," Deborah explained. "The list of cautions and warning statements included with their packaging may be several pages long. Interleukin-2, for example, is a drug known to actually kill about four percent of the people who take it. But this is the only known treatment for several terminal cancers. So the drug was licensed for limited use. The majority of these new monoclonal antibodies are very toxic in their own right. Thus the research on these new molecular shapes has been limited to the deadliest of diseases, where any progress is welcome, no matter how risky." She shook her head. "I decided to go in a different direction."

The congresswoman rewarded her with an approving look. "I am sorry I did not have you for freshman biology, Dr. Givens. I think I would have enjoyed it a great deal more than I did."

When the room quieted once more, Congressman Larson pointed with his gavel to the dais' opposite end and said, "The chair now recognizes the distinguished representative from Ohio."

"Dr. Givens," the florid-faced congressman boomed, "did I correctly hear you state that you do not know how your drug works?"

"That is correct."

"Forgive my ignorance, Dr. Givens, but doesn't that bother you? I mean, if I were to take a drug, I would most

121

certainly like to know *why*."

"Sometimes it's just not all that necessary to know how a particular result is achieved. That it works at all, and works well, is enough for the moment," Deborah replied. "For example, there are three new epilepsy drugs out—felbemate, camotrigine and gabapentin. We *think* the first blocks chemical-electrical brain signals, and we *think* the other two stimulate production of natural chemicals that calm brain activity. But we don't know. All we know is that they work incredibly well, and work for patients who have been unresponsive to previous treatment. For the moment, that is enough."

"And the same is true for your drug?"

"In a sense, yes. Great chasms exist between what is known and what is not known about the immune system. Even greater problems exist in identifying and attacking specific viruses. Perhaps by identifying these compounds that appear to strengthen the body against the viral attack, we will come to understand both better. In time, anyway."

"Thank you, Dr. Givens," Congressman Larson intervened. He glanced at the wall clock, then pulled the slip of paper from his pocket and said, "Before we recess for lunch, I would like to pose one question myself." He unfolded the paper and said, "Dr. Givens, in your opinion, has the FDA's ever-growing hunger for more and more paperwork hampered your company from delivering this most important new product to the sick and dying of our nation?"

Deborah did not know which startled her more—that the question was asked at all, or that it had been asked at the apparent request of Whitehurst. "Naturally, I would like to have our products released as swiftly as possible. But we are still in the very early stages—"

The gavel's rap was so unexpectedly loud that Deborah actually jumped. "Thank you, Dr. Givens, for a most erudite discussion. This hearing is now adjourned until two o'clock."

9

"None of this makes sense," Ralph Summers declared when Cliff finished describing the subcommittee hearing. "Why on earth would Larson begin baiting us on this one now?"

It was nine o'clock Friday morning. The three of them—Sandra, Cliff, and Summers—were seated in the small conference room adjoining the director's office. Sandra offered, "Maybe they wanted to start preparing the groundwork for a major assault."

"I don't see how," Cliff declared. "Pharmacon is at least a year away from starting phase-three testing. That makes it another two, maybe even three years before approval. By that time whatever happens now is going to be long forgotten."

Sandra responded to Cliff's observation with a smoldering gaze. Cliff offered a small smile, which inflamed her further. He wondered once more if he had made a mistake in not telling Summers the real reason behind Sandra's attitude.

Sandra had never been married. She claimed to like playing the field too much to settle down. And Sandra was proud of her ability with men. So proud, in fact, that she relished Mondays as the day to impress the girls in her office clique. Sandra liked to saunter into the offices after a weekend and respond to her friends' questions with exaggerated sighs and lots of eye rolling.

A certain type of man, Cliff was sure, would find Sandra at least challenging and possibly attractive. But not him. And that was the genesis of the problem.

During Cliff's first week at the office, Sandra had smilingly propositioned him. Cliff had responded politely. The second week, she had put it more bluntly. Cliff had held himself in check and given the same polite response.

The third time he had snapped back that he was not interested. Not then, not next week, not ever. The hostility had begun that same afternoon and never let up.

Cliff had often thought of going over Sandra's head and claiming sexual harassment, but was stopped by the utter foolishness of it. For one, who would believe him? A woman could claim it, sure; harassment charges were part of the modern-day office culture. But a guy?

He could just hear the cafeteria chatter now. Hey, why didn't he just go with the flow, take advantage of a good thing? Principles? Did he really say it was principles? Hey, let me borrow your dictionary, I got to see what this guy is talking about.

Ralph Summers remained bent over a notepad doodling, his brow furrowed, and missed the exchange. "No, I'd have to agree it is highly unlikely that they would open an attack this early. Unless, of course, they have been carrying on further tests we don't know about."

"Not a chance," Cliff said. "Debs would have told me. They've got clinical trials on a grand total of fifty-six patients."

"You're so close to this *friend*," Sandra sneered, twisting the last word, "that you can take her word on something like this?"

"Yes," Cliff replied calmly. "I am."

Summers raised his head, looked from one to the other, and started to say something, then simply shook his head and returned to his doodling. "How about a sideswipe? Are you working on anything controversial?"

"Nothing more than usual."

"Any contested holdups?"

Cliff mentally ran through his list of projects, decided, "Nothing that they could sensibly make an issue of."

124

"What about you, Sandra? Been anywhere close to the vitamin problem lately?"

"No," Sandra answered. "I leave it to Cliff to stick his nose where he doesn't belong."

Summers slapped down his pen. "Is there any reason why you two can't get along?"

"Not from my side," Cliff said.

"I prefer to spend my time working with professionals," Sandra snapped.

"All right, that's enough." Summers rose to his feet. "I'll have to pass this along upstairs, see if they can make anything of it. Are you talking with Dr. Givens anytime soon?"

"I was planning to go back down to North Carolina this weekend."

"Bad idea," Sandra threatened. "Very bad."

Cliff addressed his words to the director. "It seems to me that further contact at this point could only help. If we're going to stay on top of this, we need up-to-date information."

"I tend to agree," Summers replied.

Sandra slammed her notebook closed, gathered her papers, and stormed from the room.

His eyes on the door, Summers said, "You know, I can't help you if you won't talk to me about whatever it is that's going on here."

"I'll think about it," Cliff said weakly and left.

He walked the hall arguing with himself, only to come up time and again with the one undeniable fact. He was ashamed of the whole thing. And going public would only make it worse. Much worse.

Cliff was almost to his office before he realized he had forgotten to mention Tuesday's other curiosity. He debated going back, then shrugged and walked on.

As he had left the subcommittee hearing room after Deborah's presentation, a tall scrawny man with a rooster's comb of red hair had come up and declared,

"Hey, this is great, you just saved me a trip to Rockville."

"I'm sorry," Cliff said, searching the corridor for Deborah and seeing only strange faces milling about. "I don't—"

"Dr. Wendell Cooper," the man offered. "President of the Health and Medicine Advisory Council. And I believe you are Cliff Devon of the FDA." He stuck out his hand. "A great pleasure to meet you, Cliff."

"Likewise," he mumbled. Deborah was nowhere in sight. She must have left before he could escape through the crowd pushing for the chamber's single door.

"Yeah, I had planned a special trip up to Rockville this very week just to have the pleasure of making your acquaintance, and look what happens. Here, let me give you my card."

"Thanks," Cliff said. "I'm afraid I don't—"

"No problem. I already know who you are. Yeah, I got your name from a mutual friend. The infamous Tweedie."

Cliff looked up. "Horace Tweedie?"

"Hey, could there really be two guys with a name like that?" The man's laughter rang up and down the corridor. Attention turned their way. When their faces were not recognized, focus drifted elsewhere. "Anyway, we're a new advocacy group working with concerned citizens on health care related issues."

"Uh-huh." Since health care reform had surfaced as a hot topic, the number of lobbyists working the issue had exploded.

"Hey, I know what you're thinking. Listen, we're not like the others. No, really. We're mostly scientists. We've set up our own labs, and we're working on concerns that parallel your own."

An advocacy group that did medical research was a new one. "Where do you get your funding, from the AMA?"

"Sure, sure, we've got backing from every place under the sun," he replied cheerfully. "What I wanted to say was, if you ever run across something that really raises the red flag, we'd be happy to check it out for you. Confidentiality guaranteed, and no strings attached."

"The FDA does no research of its own," Cliff pointed out.

"Right. That's why we're not in conflict, see? We'd just like to be in on any major concerns that pop up."

"I don't think I've ever heard of the FDA working with an outside organization not actually connected to drug development."

"Great, great, we can call this a major breakthrough, then." The tall man stuck his hand out a second time. "Just remember to give me a call if anything happens to come up, okay?"

Cliff barely made it in the door before Madge said, "Call just came in for you. Line one."

"I'll take it in my office." He walked in, shrugged off his coat and tossed it in the general direction of a free chair, picked up the phone. "Devon."

"Isn't it great to have a friend to call," the voice on the other end said, "when the world starts falling apart?"

"Hey, Debs." He reached over and kicked the door closed. "Great timing. I needed a little cheering up."

"Then maybe I better call back later."

"Why, what's the matter?"

"Things are bad, Junior."

"How so?"

"'B' as in beastly, 'A' as in awful, 'D' as in disastrous. Real bad. Can you get down to Edenton?"

"I assume I should treat this as an emergency."

"I would say," Deborah said, "that just about sums it all up."

Cliff checked his calendar and said, "I've got a relatively clear day and plenty of leave coming. No reason I couldn't take off now."

"It would help a lot to have you around," she said.

"Then I'm on my way," Cliff replied.

"If you can get down before six, come straight to the lab. And Junior—"

"Yes?"

"If anybody up there asks where you're going," Deborah told him. "Lie."

"Too late," Cliff said. "I've already mentioned where I was headed."

"Then just come, okay? And hurry."

James Whitehurst strode into Harvey Cofield's outer office. Normally he took time for a verbal pass at Blair, something to the effect that the environment in his office was much more stimulating now that she was working here. Blair Collins was one trophy he had no intention of allowing Harvey Cofield to keep. But today all he said was, "He in?"

"All by his lonesome," Blair replied, not looking up from her console.

Whitehurst pushed through the door and said, "This friendship between Devon and Givens is growing very dangerous."

Cofield's eyes narrowed. "What are you talking about?"

"He's coming down here again today, for the third weekend in a row." Whitehurst flung himself down in a chair and scowled. "I didn't even hear it from her. I've just spoken to Devon's superior, a woman by the name of Sandra Walters. She's no happier about it than I am. Devon simply took a day's vacation. I checked with Givens. She confirmed he was expected here later this afternoon. She said she saw no need to inform us, since we had okayed his first visit. Did you know he had returned last weekend as well?"

"No." Cofield's eyes narrowed. This was all news, and dangerous news at that. Scientists were notorious for throwing roadblocks in the way of bringing new products to market. Their ears were deaf to the ticking of the profit clock. "Have you asked her why?"

"Yes," Whitehurst sniffed. "She said they were just two friends getting together and it had nothing to do with Devon's regulatory work."

"I don't believe that for an instant," Cofield snarled.

"Nor I." Whitehurst was on his feet again, pacing the carpeted expanse. He stopped abruptly. "On second thought, perhaps we should allow this visit to go ahead."

"But this is highly irregular," Cofield protested. "What if she passes over information that we don't want the FDA to have?"

"The time is almost ripe," Whitehurst replied. "Why not turn this to our advantage and strike now?"

There was no levity when Deborah met him at the entrance door to Pharmacon's lab. "Thank goodness you've arrived."

"What's the matter?"

"No time, no time." She led him through the first pair of automatic doors and said to the guard, "You remember Cliff Devon. He'll need another three-day pass."

"Sure, he's down okay. Have to ask you to go through the routine again, sir."

"No problem," Cliff said, sobered by Deborah's mood. He placed his hand on the scanner, repeated the voice identification sentence, accepted the card, and followed her into the hall. "What's the matter?"

"Somehow Whitehurst caught wind of your visit and insisted on this meeting," she replied, leading him urgently down the hall, her voice tight, "For both our sakes, whatever it is they say, answer yes."

"Cliff Devon!" James Whitehurst rose from the conference table and walked forward, smile and hand extended. "How great to see you again."

"Likewise," Cliff said, trying hard to match the man's false friendliness. "How are things?"

"Couldn't be better. Come on, have a seat right here. That's it. Get you anything?"

"I'm fine, thanks."

"Hey, that's swell. What say we get right down to business?"

"Fine."

"Splendid, splendid. Look, Cliff, we're growing concerned with the holdup over the echin drug approval." His gaze turned sorrowful. "We feel like we've gone out of our way to supply everything your people have requested, and yet we're not receiving very much in return."

"A great big zip," Harvey Cofield growled. "And it's getting under our skin. Seems to me like it's about time—"

"Harvey, please," Whitehurst soothed, "Devon here is on our side, I'm sure. Aren't you, son."

Cliff was far too baffled to be angry. He opened his mouth to ask, approval for what? Then he caught sight of Deborah's worried frown across the table, and changed his reply to, "I'd certainly like to be."

"Hey, didn't I tell you?" Whitehurst beamed at all and sundry. "Devon here is willing to play ball. And let me tell you, son, we don't forget our friends. Nossir, not us. Pharmacon always has room at the top for a bright young man in a hurry. Why, you just say the word and I'll have you flown up to New York to meet our chairman. He's looking for a new assistant right this minute."

"Just what exactly is it you need, Mr. Whitehurst?" Cliff asked.

Harvey Cofield barked, "An end to this bureaucratic stalling."

"But we've just received the first preliminary trial data," Cliff protested. "You can't be thinking—"

"We're under considerable pressure here, son," Whitehurst said around his semi-permanent smile, "and it's mounting every day. Between the press and these pressure groups representing the various ailments who want to start using our drug, why, it's a wonder I get any sleep at all."

"If you ask me," Cofield snapped, "it's time to go back up to Washington and light a few fires of our own."

Cliff decided they had the good-cop, bad-cop routine down perfectly. "But you're looking at two, maybe three years of testing before we can even think about granting full approval. Do you want to apply for a restricted license?"

"We want action," Cofield demanded.

"Exactly," Whitehurst soothed. "And we are delighted to give the FDA anything they require in order to have them act swiftly, aren't we?"

Cofield muttered something to the effect that there was something else he wanted to give them.

"But what we don't understand," Whitehurst went on, "is why a tentative approval can't be given while more clinical data is collected."

"You did it with AZT," Cofield snapped. "You can do it for us. And fast."

"AZT was a drug dealing with one limited group," Cliff pointed out, speaking as mildly as he knew how. "HIV-positive patients were faced with the prospect of either trying this drug or dying. Echiniacin, on the other hand, is a product that will potentially be used by millions of patients—"

"Exactly!" Cofield exploded, and slammed his fist on the table. "And it's nothing but you Washington bureaucrats sitting on your hands that's keeping us from getting our drug out there in the market!"

Cliff caught sight of Deborah's desperate look out of the corner of his eye. It was enough to check his immediate reaction. Instead he stood and said quietly, "I will check on this Monday."

"We can't ask for more than that, now, can we?" Whitehurst rose with him and Deborah, while Cofield remained seated. "Great to see you again, Cliff. Anything you need, you just have old Debs give me a call. And hey, have a great weekend, you hear?"

When the door was shut behind them, Deborah leaned her back on the wall and closed her eyes with a sigh.

"Are you all right?"

"I think so. Give me a minute."

"Can I get you something? A glass of water, maybe?"

She shook her head and pushed herself erect. "I want to show you my lab. With all the strangeness in the air around here, I don't know if I'll have another chance."

"What are you saying, Debs?"

"I don't know what they're up to," she replied. "They've sort of shut me out of things. But something's not right. They're making plans in there."

"To do what?"

"I don't know. That's what scares me."

He looked around the empty outer office. "Where's Blair?"

"Running for cover, if she's smart. Come on, let's get out of here."

"Hang on a second," Cliff said. He grabbed a pen and pad from the desk and wrote a swift note, suggesting plans for that evening. "Okay, let's go."

Entrance to the laboratory complex was completely automated. They took a second tunnel, this one lined with the clutter that to his mind had always meant scientists at work. Machines neatly stowed away beneath plastic dust covers. Computer printouts strung from girder to girder, decorated with caustic comments only a techie could understand. Opposing blackboards filled with violently scrawled mathematical arguments, punctuated with exclamation points and swirls and lightning bolts and a pause where the group left for beer. Cliff considered the hall a perfect example of what he called the First Law of Scientists—give them lab space the size of Arkansas, and within a week they would be spilling over the edges.

132

"I'm afraid my own lab arrangements aren't very impressive," Deborah said as they walked. "The only reason the suits let me chase down this lead in the first place was because I was on the way out. They got all oozy with fake sympathy when I told them about MS, but you could see the little adding machines at work behind their eyes. They took me off the research team I was heading and herded me into this little cubicle, a way station until their consciences would let them fire me. So I came up with this idea, and they did their bean-counting routine and decided since the numbers I was talking about were relatively tiny, they'd let me go out and play."

"For a while," Cliff said grimly.

"I figure I had maybe a year to come up with something," Deborah agreed. "Which in this business is nothing. I was just laying the groundwork, sort of going over the first trials, when I struck gold."

One at a time, they passed through yet another set of inch-thick glass doors and entered a miniature copy of the front enclosure—carpeted floors, walls, and ceilings, with another metal pillar at its center. Cliff passed his card through the slit running down one side, then set his right hand on the black surface. A scanner zittered, then a recessed screen lit and gave him the same sentence to read as he had said at the entrance. A ping, and the doors in front of him slid open.

When Deborah joined him on the other side, Cliff asked, "Whose idea was the security arrangement, anyway?"

"Dr. Strangelove," she replied. "Otherwise known as Harvey Cofield."

Deborah led him through a series of interconnecting halls whose glass walls displayed labs, each more spectacular than the last. Up a set of stairs, a pause to observe a lab that resembled command control center at NASA, more stairs, and at the crown of the lab globe was yet another door. As Deborah tapped a code into the electronic lock, Cliff asked, "What happens if you don't feel like scaling Mount Everest?"

"Oh, there's an elevator. But taking the stairs is a reminder to be thankful for the good days." She pushed open the door. "Welcome to my lair, said the spider to the fly."

Cliff entered a miniature chaos.

The only reason the cramped quarters did not feel as claustrophobic as a coffin was that every tiny room had a spectacular view of the surrounding countryside. There were five chambers in all, each separated by a wall of half fiberboard, half glass. "This was supposed to be files," Deborah said. "They got moved to the Tombs, and I was given their space. It was the bean counters' way of putting me as far as possible from the action without setting my lab in the parking lot."

The room they had entered contained four computer terminals, two tables piled to the roof with printouts, and a crawl space barely wide enough for Cliff to pass through sideways. The farthest terminal was occupied by a young man wearing tabi socks, Japanese house slippers, the bottom half of a very weary tux, and a surfer's T-shirt proclaiming the mysteries of tube riding.

"This is Kenny," Deborah said.

"Hi."

"Nice outfit," Cliff said.

"Kenny likes to dress up for work," Deborah explained.

"It's the only way I know of keeping the suits at bay," Kenny explained. "Otherwise I might catch the bean counter's disease, start staying up late worrying about numbers on a balance sheet."

"Kenny Gryffin manages my team of semi-house-broken computer techies," Deborah said.

"Yeah, even take them out on a leash a couple of times a day."

"The others put up with him because he's twice as fast as they are at the keyboard. They call him The Great Kensteennie."

"I have a degree in anthropology," Kenny announced proudly. "It makes me uniquely qualified to run a computer team for a drug firm."

"Any prevalent problems or issues?" Deborah asked Kenny. "Or can I take my guest on through with his limbs still intact?"

"Just mostly stuff of a general nature." Fingers tapped a computer keyboard at a speed faster than a drumroll. "This new data collation program is really user-surly."

"Oh my," Deborah said, her face grave.

"Yeah. The search routine is prehistoric. Installation hassles, compatibility problems, and the worst thing of all, it's a real bear to uninstall."

"Horrors," Deborah agreed. "How can you sleep nights?"

"Hey, who sleeps? I just plug myself in for an hour and re-juice." He pointed at a screen that had begun scrolling through graphs. "Watch and you'll see for yourself."

"I leave all such problems in your capable hands," Deborah assured him. She grasped Cliff by the arm. "Come along, Junior."

When they were into the next room he asked, "What was that all about?"

"Rule one of surviving in a modern lab," Deborah replied. "Never worry about what your computer techies say. Just toss in a bucket of new gadgets and software magazines every other day or so and keep their cages clean."

A miniature hall led them by a glass-enclosed jungle. "This is where we grow our test plants," she explained.

"It looks like they're about ready to take over," Cliff said. The plants were almost as tall as he was and jammed up hard to the glass.

"We amp up their growth patterns by using flicker lighting at night." Deborah frowned through the pane as though seeing the shrubs for the first time. "Maybe I better tell Cochise to give them a trim."

"Tell who?"

"In here, Junior. And be nice."

The next chamber was the lab, and occupying it was the biggest human Cliff had ever seen. The man was bent over a microscope. As they approached the man unfolded, then unfolded some more.

"Cliff, I'd like you to meet Cochise, my number one lab techie."

Cliff tried to match grips with a hand like a baseball mitt, and said, "Big man, big name."

The face creased into a ponderous smile. "One of those things I picked up along the way. Don't ask me how."

"Nicknames aren't meant to make sense," Cliff agreed. "Do they use you to keep order?"

The gut spilling over his fifty-inch waist resembled a buffalo about to give birth to a beer keg. "These techies don't have a muscle between 'em. Any of them get smart, Dr. Debs just gives them the toss herself."

Deborah said quietly, "I would like you two to be friends."

"Don't see why not," Cliff said agreeably. "We probably don't have a thing in common."

"Except Debs," Cochise said.

"Doggone right," Cliff allowed. "What's that line about the love of a good woman?"

"Don't ask me," Cochise rumbled. His eyes were dark and fathomless, his face folded down like a slumbering bulldog. "Wasn't much of either where I came from."

"Either what?" Deborah asked.

"Love or good women," Cliff translated, and decided he liked the big man.

"Cochise follows my instructions to the letter," Deborah informed him. "You'll have to spend some time around techies to learn how rare that is."

"Most techies are ready to give God advice about creation," Cochise agreed.

"His notes are meticulous," Deborah went on, "and he handles lab glass like a pro." She reached up and punched his arm. It was like attacking a tree limb. "With credentials like that, it gets easier to put up with that beautiful face."

"Heard a lot about you," Cochise said. "Good to have you around. Looks like storm clouds are gathering."

Deborah turned solemn. "Is this some kind of mystical Indian thing?"

Cochise gave his head a ponderous shake. "Gossip."

"Come on, Junior," Deborah said. "You can brace yourself with a jolt of lab coffee."

Cliff followed her into an office the size of a walk-in closet. As in the other rooms, the outer window curved up and over his head, revealing green fields and a cloud-speckled sky. He looked back through the glass half-wall and asked, "What's going on, Debs?"

"Oh, Cochise is preparing more doses. The root has to be ground, then pressed in that masher there. Then the juice is run through a series of increasingly tiny filters before we autoclave it and prepare test samples."

"I meant," Cliff replied, "what is going on with Pharmacon."

"I wish I knew," she said gravely. "I've effectively been sealed out of the decision-making process. And when I told them about Tom—you remember Tom, the old guy at the veterans hospital?"

"Of course."

"When I told them about the foreigner in the slick car bribing him, they sort of swallowed the information." She rubbed tired eyes. "They won't say what steps they're taking. Everything has suddenly become very hush-hush, at least as far as I'm concerned. And then yesterday they asked if I had clinical data on the original European drug. Which of course I did. Thousands and thousands of pages. They carted that off, and since then, nothing."

Cliff mulled that one over. "I don't understand."

"Me neither."

"You changed the molecular structure, isn't that what you told me?"

"For each of the compounds," she affirmed.

"Then why... " He shook his head. "I'm missing something."

"You and me both."

"So why did you ask me to agree with everything Whitehurst said? I gotta tell you, Debs, I was about a half step from exploding."

"I saw." She tried hard for a smile. "After the subcommittee hearing, the chairman of Pharmacon spent three seconds telling me I did a pretty fair job, then half an hour grilling me about you."

"Me?"

"Don't look so shocked. The FDA happens to figure very large in Pharmacon's future. As coordinator for the drug's approval process, you're man of the hour." The smile slipped away. "But since then, every time your name has come up, there's been these ominous rumblings. Nothing specific, but a lot of thunder over the horizon."

"Thunder comes with the job," Cliff said. "I'm used to it."

"Maybe you are," she replied. "But I've had the distinct impression that they were just waiting for a reason to forbid me to see you."

"They couldn't do that."

"They could make it a lot tougher for us to get together, and quite frankly I need you too much just now to want to worry about sneaking around behind Pharmacon's back." She sighed. "That's not all. Yesterday I was supposed to go out and check the plants for harvesting—we're almost out of the last batch, and we don't have enough in our little greenhouse to use with an expanded trial. I called Hank's farm, and his wife said I couldn't come."

"They were probably busy with something else.

Everybody has bad days." He drug up a smile of his own. "Even you, Debs."

"It didn't sound that way. When I pressed her, she said something about the breeze, then hung up on me."

Cliff had a sudden image of the farmer's raised face. "Maybe he *was* testing the wind that day, like I said."

"Yeah, okay, but why?" She lifted her purse and car keys from her desk. "Would you mind driving out there with me now?"

"In our scientific world, unsolved problems are the great equalizers," Deborah said as she drove toward the farm. "They reduce us all to ground zero. Only after the answer begins to emerge does the three-headed destroyer arise: greed, egoism, and ambition. Those three have done in more scientists than any disease on earth."

"Any other disease," Cliff countered.

Deborah rewarded him with a grateful look. "It's good to have you here, Junior. More than words can say."

Deborah turned onto the gritty side road and slammed on the brakes. She pressed her face to the front windshield and muttered, "What in the world?"

Across the road from Hank Aaron Jones' property lay the swathe of burned-out rubble. Beyond that stretched broad flowered fields as bright as a golden sea. And through the fields ran people. Hundreds and hundreds of shouting, dancing, laughing, singing people.

The neighbor's farmhouse was completely lost behind a great stretch of canvas and metal. Indian teepees. Fancy camping tents painted every color under the sun. Tall, medieval-shaped pavilions. Banners decorated with cryptic runes. Campers and buses sporting psychedelic murals of smiling rainbows and flower children and aliens floating toward earth on crystal spaceships.

The people dancing through the blooming rapeweed wore clothes as loose and flowing as their hair. Crowds gathered on great sweeps of bright blankets, lolling in the sun or reaching toward the sky and swaying to music provided by pipes and guitars and congas. At various points through the field, other groups whirled to music from boom boxes—everything from acid rock to new age. The cacophony washed over their jeep along with the constant ring of laughter. Wild, lilting laughter.

"It looks like a sixties rock festival, minus the bands," Cliff declared. "A real blast from the past."

"This day is definitely getting out of hand," Deborah said, and put the car into gear.

There was no sign of movement at the Jones farm. She pulled into the swept front yard, turned off the motor, and said, "That's funny."

"What is?"

She pointed to the black ash-strewn soil bordering the farmhouse. "Why would they burn down their rose bushes?" Deborah hesitated, looking up at the silent house, then walked up and knocked on the door.

A stringy woman walked onto the front stoop, pushed open the screen, said, "Miss Debs."

"Good afternoon, Mrs. Jones," Deborah said politely. "I was wondering if I could have a word with your husband."

"No you can't," she said, and crossed her arms across her chest. "He's laid up. Real sick."

"I'm sorry to hear that. I hope it's nothing serious."

She had the dried-up look of a woman reared on a hard life. "He'll get over it, God willing."

"I just spoke with him yesterday. He sounded fine to me."

"Everything was fine as fine could be," Mrs. Jones replied, her voice as taut as the veins in her neck, "until he had to go over and talk to that blasted neighbor of ours. I told him he oughtta wait and buy the land when this trouble's died down. But no, he's got to do it his time, his way. That man of mine's got a head as hard as the rock of Gibraltar."

The noise from across the road drifted on the still hot

air. "What is going on over there?"

"Trouble," the woman spat. "That neighbor of ours belongs in hell."

Deborah looked down at the ashes that scarred the otherwise neat yard. "I'm sorry about your roses. Did they become diseased?"

"You could say that. Cursed by an evil wind." The woman's eyes blazed. "Y'all will just have to see to yourselves today. I got my hands full, with a sick man and all. Just see you're off the land 'fore the sun sets and the wind picks up again."

When the door had slammed shut, Deborah turned wide eyes toward Cliff, who intoned, "Stranger and stranger."

Together they dug up root samples from three echin plants spaced well apart. The hot air was trapped by the bushes, now taller than a man. By the time they were finished, both were drenched in sweat.

Cliff carried the tools back to the barn, then joined Deborah in the jeep. "I could sure use something wet and cold."

"You and me both," she agreed, turning the air conditioner on full and starting down the long drive.

"Any idea what she was talking about up there?"

"I'm all out of ideas, Junior," Deborah replied, turning onto the farm road. "But that doesn't stop my mind from reaching."

They had scarcely driven a hundred feet before a shout called to them from the fields. Deborah halted at the sight of a young woman with flowing blonde tresses and a loose-fitting dress bounding across the scarred, burned-out stretch toward them. She was waving and laughing and calling, and she carried several stalks of blooming rapeweed.

Deborah rolled down her window as the woman approached. "Can I help you?"

"No," the girl half laughed, half sang. "Can I help *you*?" With that she thrust the rapeweed stalks into

141

Deborah's surprised hand, then spun around and raced back. Laughter rang in her wake.

Deborah looked at the golden blooms in her hand, then at Cliff. "Has the whole world gone crazy today?"

Cliff took the flowers from her hand. "Let's go home, Debs. Like you said, I'm all out of ideas."

Deborah drove up to the intersection with the county road and stopped. A sudden sense of lightheadedness hit her. Although it was not her usual warning sign, she reacted automatically. She pressed harder on the brakes, slid the car into park, and turned off the motor. A waking nightmare of hers had been to be struck by an abrupt attack when driving at high speed. She opened her mouth to ask Cliff to drive, when a sudden movement at the corner of her vision caused her to look up.

The stop sign had grown two arms and a pair of eyes and a grand smile, and it was waving her forward.

Beside her, Cliff let out a strangled cough. But she was suddenly too busy to pay any attention, for out of a clear blue sky it had begun to rain blossoms. Beautiful, delicate, golden, rapeweed blossoms.

Then the road turned to a living ribbon, a river of rainbow colors, and Deborah found herself suddenly swept away.

10

The following evening Cliff drove away from Deborah's feeling tired, jittery, frustrated, and horrifically hungover.

The night before, he and Deborah had remained trapped in the jeep for hours. The hallucinations had not relinquished their grip until long after night had fallen.

Deborah had come to first. When Cliff had finally focused on reality, she was wrapping the rapeweed blossoms in a plastic sample bag.

A flickering orange glow reflected in the windshield caused Cliff to turn around. Behind him, the rapeweed fields were bordered by numerous bonfires. Shadow figures danced weaving circles around the flames. Through his closed window came the shrill sound of fluting pipes.

He turned back when Deborah switched on the car's interior light and inspected the rapeweed stalks through the plastic shield. "What happened?"

Her brow was furrowed in tight concentration. "Do you want the layman's explanation or the scientific one?"

"Layman's. My mind's not quite up to speed."

"I think we've just had a glimpse of the psychedelic world view," she replied.

He sighed his acceptance. "And the scientific?"

"I don't know," she said flatly. "I wish I did."

Shrill laughter and wordless screams turned him back around. "It looks like a scene straight from my worst nightmare," he said.

"Not mine," Deborah replied, starting the car.

Cliff kept his attention fastened on the scene behind them. "What could be worse than this?"

Deborah drove them onto the main road. "To watch it spread."

Their visit to the sheriff's office had proven utterly futile. The only two patrol cars had been tied up with a bar-room brawl and a domestic disturbance, and the duty officer had not been ready to wake the sheriff over something like this. Deborah had then demanded where the nearest Highway Patrol office was located.

"Ma'am," the officer drawled, "you go spouting off your harebrained story to the Patrol this time of night, and them boys's liable to lock you up. Now why don't you two go on home and sleep it off?"

Calls to the Pharmacon hierarchy proved equally ineffective. Whitehurst and Cofield were both in Washington. No, their wives both stated flatly, they had specifically been told not to give out their number. This was Dr. Givens? What sort of emergency? Deborah bit down on her tongue and hung up. They drove in worried silence back to Deborah's house and tried to sleep.

The next morning, Cliff had risen to the sound of Deborah on the phone. He stumbled into the parlor as she hung up and said, "Blair doesn't know where the bean counters have holed up. Or why they went to Washington in the first place."

He poured himself a cup of coffee, thinking that he had forgotten to call Blair last night. "What do we do now?"

"Put on your clothes, and let's go try the sheriff's office again."

The sheriff was a lean, hard-eyed man with a deeply seamed face. He listened in silence to their descriptions of the night before, his expression giving nothing away. When they had finished, he said, "Been getting some complaints from Mrs. Jones across the road about the noise."

"Just noise?" Deborah asked.

"It's all the duty officer wrote down," the sheriff replied. "And that's all the call sheet is ever gonna state. Mrs. Jones is a good friend to us, and we respect her. But it's been a long hot summer, and there ain't nothing tougher on a woman than tending a big spread."

"She wasn't imagining things, Sheriff," Deborah said.

"Ma'am, this whole county is just as grateful as we can be for Pharmacon coming in and building this new plant," the sheriff replied. "But it don't give you any call to come bother busy people with things that don't amount to a hill of beans on a hot day."

"Just go out there," Deborah said. "Check it out."

"I got a patrol car swinging by Jude Taylor's farm twice a day already," he replied, his patience wearing thin. "Now, I'll be the first to admit that there's some bad blood between the Taylors and the Joneses. Don't ask me why, 'cause I don't know and don't want to know. The Joneses are farming some crops for you folks now, ain't they?"

"That's right," Deborah said worriedly.

"Well, I think it's right nice that you'd take up for folks that're helping you out. But that don't mean I'll put up with somebody wasting my time." He leaned back in his seat. "I seen it happen a hundred times. Them two farms are on the back side of beyond, ain't got another neighbor in three, four miles. That's one of the reasons why I let Jude carry on with this nonsense, that and knowing just how hard up the man is for cash. Now you'd think folks that're so far off the beaten track'd bend over backward to stay friends, wouldn't you. Nossir. Give 'em the tiniest little reason, they'll get mad, and they'll stay mad. That's a law of human nature, missy. Give folks like that a cause, and they'll nurse that grudge till kingdom come."

"I'll bet your cars all drive around with their windows rolled up and their air conditioners on," Deborah said.

145

"Just what do you expect my boys to do?" the sheriff asked, his exasperation growing. "It's a hundred degrees in the shade out there."

"The air conditioner would filter out the pollen," Deborah said, desperation tinting her voice.

"Ma'am, in case you haven't noticed, they're growing rapeweed out there, not marijuana." The sheriff rose from his chair. "Now Jude Taylor's got lawful permits for this hippie festival of his, I issued 'em myself. I ain't in favor of this sort of thing, but in times like these a man's got a right to earn himself a little extra cash. The permits'll run out in eight days. You go back and tell the Joneses they oughtta take a little vacation, go on down to the coast for a week if it bothers 'em that much."

"Eight days may be too late," Deborah pleaded.

"Y'all have just about used up my store of good will," the sheriff said, pointing at the door. "You better run on outta here before I get testy. Go on, now. Git."

Then, to top the whole mess off, he had argued with Debs.

They had returned from the sheriff's office to her home. The stress had begun to play on her, bringing out the fatigue syndrome, so Debs had retired to her wheelchair on the porch, letting Cliff see to sandwiches and Cokes. Over lunch she had tried to explain the process by which she and her team had altered the plant's molecular structure.

"The procedure centers," she told him, "on the restructuring of the plant's DNA in a plasmid solution, so that the cell is ordered to create a different compound than before." She paused to take the last bite of her sandwich. "It's the same basic process as genetic scientists use to strengthen a tomato's skin against insects or make apples grow bigger."

Cliff asked, "What was that word you just used, plasmid?"

"Plasmids are DNA that have been extracted from a cell." Deborah wiped mayonnaise from her upper lip. "We can create them now. Well, not actually create. We clone them. But we can rearrange the DNA before cloning to basically come up with any sequence we want. When we create plasmids and we cut the DNA sequence, we pull in additional DNA letters and form the sequence we plan to repeat."

Something began to niggle at him, a worry below the surface of conscious thought. "How do you cut something that small?"

"By chemical reaction. We run electrophoresis gels into the solution, which allows us to read the DNA structure using what is called a sequence analyzer—the full name is fluorescent detecting automated sequencing machine. This gives us a computer printout that looks a lot like the thin sheet of squiggles you get in analyzing sounds. After a while, you get so you can read it like a stockbroker reads his morning ticker tape."

"Maybe *you* can."

"When we've identified the section we want," Deborah continued, "we cut it with restriction enzymes. These cut the amino acid letters only at specific points, at the start and stop codons."

He passed a hand over his head, and made the sound of a jet taking off.

She smiled. "Don't feel bad, Junior. I meet scientists all the time who don't understand this stuff. There are a few of them wandering the halls of Pharmacon. That's what happened to Cofield, by the way. He just couldn't keep up."

"I was wondering why he was so bitter."

"Bitter and jealous. He's a hard man to work with."

"So you make these new genes. Then what?"

"Then we attach to it a promoter sequence, usually from a bacteria, since they're plentiful and easy to work with. We can set up DNA chains now to make the plant

147

produce more of a certain protein; we do that by adding the growth instruction to the protein producer instruction. So what I did was first change the protein producer code so that the new compounds included a marker molecule. Then I combined those with growth instructions."

"Wait a minute. You mean this promoter sequence is the same in bacteria as it is in humans?"

"Yes." She looked at him. "Is that a problem?"

"I'm not sure." He struggled to make sense of his worries. "So does a DNA genetic sequence mean the same in humans as in plants?"

She gave her head a decisive shake. "Extremely rare to never. It doesn't even work between species, like between roses and daffodils. There are only four DNA amino acid letters, but they can be arranged in an infinite number of variations, since there is no limit to the size of each word, or gene."

"But you just said the promoter was the same."

"Sure, but it's sort of like saying a period at the end of a sentence has the same meaning in different languages."

"Still, it could be possible, couldn't it?"

"I suppose so. Theoretically, yes. What are you getting at, Junior?"

"I don't know," he said slowly, wishing he himself understood the sense of rising unease. "Anyway, you were saying about attaching a promoter sequence."

"This new chain can be replicated through TAQ technology. Again, we're talking state of the art. But this synthesis is the key to the future."

"But how do you get it into the plant?"

Deborah shrugged. "Usual manner. We redesigned a viroid."

Cliff set down his glass. "You did what?"

"Don't look so alarmed. It happens all the time. It's a basic technique of genetic engineering."

"I can't believe you would do this."

"Calm down, Junior."

"You of all people, creating a virus."

"Viroid," she corrected.

"Viroid, virus, what's the difference?"

"Only about ten million molecules."

"Don't get technical on me. You always hide behind data that doesn't matter when you're trying to avoid something."

"I'm not avoiding a thing," she said defensively. The words were more clipped now, the tone terse. "I knew exactly what I was doing."

"But a virus, Debs. A virus is what's crippled you."

"Maybe a virus, remember? And if it is a virus, it's a very different one."

"You're so sure of that? What makes you so certain this one couldn't get out of control?"

"We changed the vector so that the virus could not replicate."

That slowed him down. "You can do that?"

"We were careful, Junior. We were more than careful. What we wanted was a means of inserting one series of genetic instructions inside the plants. We used a viroid, a virus without the external protein shell, as a sort of carrier for our commands. This particular viroid attaches itself to a plant's root systems."

"I know the word, viroid," Cliff said. "But I'm not sure I really understand what you just said."

"As far as we know, the viroid is the structural bridge between life and nonlife, between inert substance and living essence. By removing the viroid's ability to replicate itself—I won't even call it reproduction, because we're not sure if a viroid truly lives to reproduce or is simply a complex molecular structure that carries with it the ability to draw other molecules together, like a magnet does iron shavings—"

"You're getting technical on me again."

"Sorry." She sipped at her Coke. "By halting its ability to replicate, we both kept it from spreading and we held it in the realm of nonliving substances."

"So did this viroid of yours have a name?" he asked carefully.

"Delta," she replied. "We named it the Delta viroid."

"Delta is the symbol for change, isn't that right?"

"Very good, Junior," she replied. "You remember your lessons."

"Okay, so this Delta viroid was made. What then?"

"Well, first we changed the DNA structure of cells in an already existing echin plant," Deborah persisted. "I hope you're listening to me, Cliff."

"Of course I'm listening. If I wasn't listening to you I wouldn't be so worried."

"This means that the inserted genes are restricted to the plant we were actually working on. They can't be passed to future generations."

"You're sure?"

She nodded. "Then we mixed it in with the fertilizer and sprayed it onto the fields."

"Simple as that."

"Nothing about it was simple, Cliff. But it worked. That's the most important thing. It worked." She examined his worried features. "Why does this bother you so?"

"I don't know, I just feel like you've let loose the hand of chaos."

"The hand of chaos," she repeated, watching him. "And you say you're not a believing man."

"I don't know what I believe. I do know that you've created something too close to life for me to be comfortable with it. I just don't like this whole idea of shifting genes around. It gives me the creeps."

"Tough. It's the wave of the future, and it may prove to be the safest way to cure illness that man has ever discovered."

"How can you say that?" he cried. "We've just spent six

hours totally out of our skulls. Do you call that safe?"

"We don't know for sure the two things are connected," she snapped.

"Oh come on, Debs," he said, growing hot. "What, you think a field of rapeweed just happened to mutate all by itself and turn into a giant mental pyrotechnics clinic?"

Her voice tightened. "Right as we speak, there is a major project going on called the Human Genome Initiative. It is a worldwide scheme to isolate and identify every single human gene. We calculate that there should be about one hundred thousand of them."

"How utterly thrilling," he said sarcastically.

"Oh, pull yourself out of the last century," she bristled. "Try and think what this will mean. In ten years there will be a compendium available with the entire genetic makeup of the human body."

"You know what happens after that, don't you?"

"What?"

"Genetic selection to order. People will go visit some gene doctors to have their babies made up according to whim and taste. Not to mention prejudice."

"Why are you mister gloom and doom?" Her face was as angry as her tone. "Why don't you look at the good side? We'll be able to identify every single genetically linked disease and diffuse it before it even appears— Down's syndrome, certain forms of blindness and deformity, Alzheimer's, hundreds of problems that have plagued mankind down through the ages."

"And then what happens, Debs?" Cliff felt as though a weight of sorrow was settling upon his shoulders. "Do you kill all the babies who don't measure up?"

"Of course not," she snapped. "Don't talk crazy."

"But where do you draw the line? And who keeps the fad-conscious nuts from stopping a pregnancy just because they don't like a child's sex or hair color?"

"The alternative," she said, biting off the words, "if you'd just stop and think for a moment, is to alter the genetic coding before the fetus has grown to the point of being born ill or malformed."

"But I *am* thinking, Debs," he said quietly. "You're talking about altering life itself."

"Face facts, Junior. We do it every day. Every time you take some pill to ease an illness, you're altering the course of life."

"I don't like it," he said.

"Like it or not, you'd better get used to it," she said. His silence brought her to the boiling point. "Maybe you've got to see life from my perspective to understand."

"What's that got to do with anything?"

"It has everything to do with this. It's a lot easier for somebody healthy to philosophize about disease than somebody who is sick."

"That's not fair."

"Life isn't fair, Cliff." She took a breath. "Okay, let's make it personal. Let's say you get married and have a child. If your baby got a fever that could leave it blind for life, would you give it a pill if you knew that pill would cure it?"

"Of course."

"Sure you would. So what's the difference here, Cliff, except one of timing? The pill works on sicknesses that attack after the baby has been born. Genetic engineering fights ailments that could attack the fetus." Deborah took on a coaxing tone. "What if we discovered that MS had a genetic basis, some flaw that made the immune system unable to fight this disease? Would you condemn me to a lifetime of wheelchairs and growing debilitation because of some poorly defined principle?"

"Just because I can't put my concerns into the right scientific words doesn't make them any less real," he replied.

"Real? You want real?" She pounded a fist on the arm of her chair. "Take a seat in this, Junior. Try looking at the world from this perspective for a while. That's reality for me, and there are a lot of people out there suffering fates worse than this."

There was genuine pain in his eyes. "I'd give anything I could to see you well, Debs. Anything."

"So what about all those yet to be born? What about those who we *can* cure, if only this DNA technology is taken the next couple of steps? Are you going to condemn them?"

Cliff stepped onto Blair's front porch, the argument still raging in his mind. He would have passed right by Miss Sadie, had she not shifted in her rocker and said, "Now what on earth has your forehead all scrunched up like that, young man?"

Cliff started guiltily. "I'm sorry, I didn't see you."

"That's clear enough. What's got you all in a tangle?"

"A problem," Cliff said glumly. "And I just argued with a friend about it."

"Well, there's certainly no way on God's green earth to make a problem grow bigger than to argue over it. Are you involved in matters of science, young man?"

The question surprised him, coming from her. "In a way, yes ma'am."

"That's good. I don't hold to those hidebound folk who say we'd all be better off living in the past. The child of science is technology. Properly formed, the child grows up to be a useful part of our world. But twisted by haste and greed and blind ambition, the child grows up demented. Dangerous. A criminal that must either be confined or destroyed before it destroys us."

Cliff looked down on the old woman, mildly surprised at their discussion. "There's a lot of wisdom in what you say."

"The South is a good teacher, if you've a mind to learn. A small Southern town is a whole university in and of itself. You can major in the social graces, in country

153

culture, in heritage, in personal giving. Or, if you've a mind to, your studies can take a darker turn—gossip, spiteful slander, racism, unending bitterness."

Cliff's reply was stopped by Blair appearing at the screen door and saying coldly, "You said you would be coming by last night."

"I know," he said, and suddenly felt the burden of the past twenty-four hours settle on his shoulders like a weary blanket. "A lot has happened."

She stepped back and motioned for him to enter. When he was inside, she shut the second door to keep sound from passing onto the porch. "I waited for hours. You could at least have called."

"No," he replied. "I could not."

"I don't like it when men let me down, Cliff," she said. Her eyes were distant. Cold. Glacial. "It seems to be a serious ailment of the times, one I have suffered from too much and for far too long."

"Blair, let me explain."

"Why should I?" Her tone was not angry. Simply dismissive. "What would then keep you from doing it to me a second time? And a third? And a fourth?"

The smoldering coals of his anger ignited. "What are you looking for, Blair? You think maybe you could tell me that?"

"Somebody who knows how to spell *commitment*," she said, her face hot, "and who doesn't dive for cover at an incoming M word."

Cliff shook his head. "No you're not."

"And just what is that supposed to mean, mister?"

"Sure, you want it. But saying the words doesn't mean you're ready for them yourself."

Blair cocked two arms on her hips. "And just what makes you an expert?"

"Nothing but a pair of good eyes and an honest heart," he replied. "One that would like to talk about all those things but can't, because you won't let me."

"I think you've gone far enough."

"You want it almost as much as you're afraid of it," Cliff persisted. "Almost, but not quite. So now that somebody's come at you with something real, you run as fast as you can."

Her face a crimson flame, she pointed at the door. "Leave. Now."

"Why?" Cliff said, standing his ground. "So you can head back for the slick-talking guys? The ones you know you can handle?" He took a step closer. "The ones who don't care about the walls around your heart since they're not going to be there long enough to bother? Is what you want?"

Blair stepped forward and raised her hand to slap his face. Cliff stood and waited and tried not to flinch.

Blair checked herself at the last moment, lowered her hand, and said in a low shaky voice, "Just go. Please, just go."

"It's right there in front of you, staring you straight in the face," he said. "But you're so caught up in your fears you can't open your eyes and look."

Cliff turned and walked to the door. As he opened it he said, "Being the right person is just as important as finding the right person, Blair."

He walked across the porch and down the stairs and across the front lawn. The last thing he heard before slamming his car door was the soft steady creaking of Miss Sadie's rocker.

Cliff was halfway back to Deborah's house before his heart's aching emptiness doused the flames of his anger. He swung the car around and headed back to town. When he arrived at Blair's he walked up the stairs, nodded to Miss Sadie, and knocked on the door.

"She's gone," Miss Sadie announced, not pausing in her rocking.

"Where?"

"Just gone. Came out of that door about thirty seconds after you. Didn't say a word. Didn't have to. I imagine she's out somewhere walking off a full head of steam."

When Cliff started down the stairs, the old woman said, "Best let her be just now, young man. Let her listen to her heart before her head gets a chance to talk with you again."

Cliff hesitated, then nodded his acceptance. "Tell her," he stopped again, grateful that the night hid his sorrow. "You'll have to come up with something yourself. I'm all out of ideas."

"That is precisely the time to let your heart speak for you," Miss Sadie replied. "You just try and quieten down enough to hear what's going on down deep."

"All I can hear my heart say right now," Cliff confessed, "is that I just blew it big time."

The old lady humphed a single chuckle. "Young man, it is far easier to get a fishhook in than it is to get it out."

"What's that supposed to mean?"

Her voice carried humor through the dark. "Oh, it's wisdom you're after, is it?"

"I don't know. Maybe."

"I just repeat the expressions, young man. I don't interpret them." The rocker creaked with the contentment of having arrived at the years beyond passion. "My advice is for you to go out there and do the right thing. That's all the advice I'm good for."

Cliff mulled that one over, then asked, "Do you think I have a chance?"

The rocker silenced as the old lady leaned forward. "Young man, do I look like God to you?"

"Closer to Him than me."

"Well, now, just whose fault do you think that might be? If you want his help, go and ask. His ears are a good sight better than mine anyhow, I can tell you that for sure."

156

Cliff walked across the porch, bent over, and kissed her cheek.

"What on earth was that for?"

"Because you deserve it," he said, and stepped into the night.

11

The awakening dawn found Cliff moving as silently as he knew how. There was no sound from Deborah's bedroom, and he did not want to disturb her. He had thoughts he wished to work on alone, and the morning was too precious to share.

Cliff fixed himself a cup of coffee and took it out onto the porch. Pastel glimmers painted streaks of growing brightness across the sky. He sat in the swing and looked to the distant horizon of gold-flecked clouds. The bay was bathed in a blanket of peace, reflecting nothing but the mystery of all that lay ahead. Its calm enveloped him, distilling his thoughts into crystal clarity.

Gentle sounds carried an overwhelming force in the thin morning light. Young falcons cried like lost and lonely children. Jays shouted their approval of the day. Songbirds chorused from unseen perches. Waves chuckled as they lapped against the bulkhead.

The sun peeked orange and sleepy between pines across the bay, and a whiff of morning breeze brought a perfumed greeting from flowering trees. A pair of hummingbirds arrived like feathered lightning bolts to drink from the feeder, their wings making fragile thunder.

He remained wrapped in dawn's cocoon until he heard Deborah clattering in the kitchen. She stepped onto the porch, wearing a quilted robe and carrying a steaming mug, and offered him a sleepy hello. "How long have you been up?"

"I don't know," he replied softly, the morning's peace

too fragile to permit much speech. "Sorry about last night, Debs."

"Same here." She stepped behind the swing and gave his head a one-armed hug with the hand that did not hold her coffee. "You and your conscience are good for me, I suppose. But they can be a bitter pill at times."

"I don't mean to be," he said, and confessed, "I left here and had a fight with Blair."

"Sounds like you need help almost as much as I do." Deborah turned back toward the kitchen, saying, "Breakfast is do-it-yourself. When you're ready, we'll head in to church."

"A living church operates like a successful scientist," Deborah said, driving them toward town, "always working on the edge of possibility."

"I don't believe I'm hearing this."

"It's true. A church should always remain busy pushing out the edge of the balloon. Taking risks. Planting other churches. Organizing missions. Seeking new and unproven fields. The difference is, a church works for the sake of eternity."

Cliff inspected his friend. "You're really into this, aren't you?"

"I'm not perfect," Deborah replied. "And I don't wear angel's wings."

"Not yet," Cliff said quietly.

"But I'm learning that the distinction between right and wrong are immobile pillars in a good person's life. Greed or self-interest or ambition or scientific curiosity are not valid reasons for shifting the pillar of right a few feet to one side."

"So what are you telling me?"

"Some scientists turn away from God because He is not finite and can't be measured in a lab. But not most."

"No?"

"Not to my way of thinking. I believe most scientists turn from God because the idea of an omnipotent Being utterly beyond their control, beyond their mental prowess, is too threatening."

"I've always enjoyed these little impromptu lectures of yours," Cliff said.

"Pay attention, Junior. You might learn something. A lot of scientists consider themselves to be gods in all but name. They feel like the universe is theirs to manipulate, dissect, freeze, and rebuild when time and funding allow." She stopped at a light and turned to him. "And you know what makes them most uncomfortable of all?"

He shook his head, content to listen, absorb, play the role of student and friend.

"*Faith*. Values. Unchanging principles. Anything that sets limits on the power of their reason is seen as an enemy. Anything that they cannot prove by empirical method is a myth."

"So you're saying that no scientist believes in God?"

"Of course not, don't be silly. But a lot of my colleagues don't even have time for the concept. God simply does not fit into their mentality. They neither believe nor disbelieve. They give no time to genuine reflection on the possibility of God. They want the right to manipulate everything, no holds barred." She looked out toward the bright, shining day and smiled. "It's simple, when you think of it. They don't want to share the throne of knowledge."

The church was almost lost in a grove of elms that had been planted back when the church was young. Only the wooden steeple and red-brick front steps stood clear of the thicket. When Cliff left the car and walked around the elms, he found the church was built of whitewashed wooden shingles. The windows were lead-paned and hand-set and spoke of distant times and timeless beauty.

160

"This is really nice," Cliff declared.

"It's just another clapboard country church," she replied. "Oh, it's pretty in an old-timey sort of way. But the area around here is filled with so many old churches, I suppose most folks take about as much notice as they would of a beautiful tree."

"So why do you come here?"

She gave him her patented lopsided smile. "To reach out and touch the invisible." She started up the front steps. "Coming?"

Cliff's report on Monday did not elicit the response he had expected. Ralph Summers heard him out in gloomy silence. Sandra responded with her typical frigid anger.

"I'm afraid an indirect enquiry would be premature at this point," Summers replied when Cliff had finished.

"Premature!" He could scarcely believe his ears. "Ralph, maybe I didn't describe it very well, but that altered rapeweed is a menace."

"You described it perfectly," Summers said, avoiding Cliff's gaze by doodling on his pad.

"What if there are secondary alterations?" he pleaded, pushing for them to see. "What if there really is some genetic mutation that's spreading—"

"More likely he's had a wild weekend down there with his little friend," Sandra snapped. "And got in some kind of trouble, and now wants to cover his tracks. I'll get on the phone and see what the police have to say."

"Please, Sandra," Ralph sighed.

"I resent the accusation," Cliff said.

"Resent it all you like, buster," she snapped. "I've got your number."

"All right, that's enough," Summers said, raising his voice. "We've all got more important things to do than trade unfounded allegations."

"I agree," Cliff said.

"Then if you'll excuse me," Sandra said, slamming her notebook closed and rising to her feet. "I'll go see if I can get to the bottom of this." She marched to the door, paused, and flung back at them, "I can already tell you what I'll learn. That I was right. That Cliff made a serious error in going down to Edenton, and all this is just a crazy attempt to cover his tracks."

When the door had slammed shut, Summers said quietly, "There's a grain of truth in what she says."

"Ralph, I didn't go down and tie one on. This really happened."

"Not about that," he replied. "I spent this weekend trying to see if I could get a feel for what Larson was after."

It took a moment for Cliff to realize what he was talking about. "That subcommittee hearing seems a year ago."

"I wish it was," Ralph said, his head still bent over his pad. He was drawing a series of lightning bolts smashing down on three building-shaped letters—FDA. "Congressman Larson is intending to use the echin drug application as an example of how the FDA is abusing its authority, wasting millions of taxpayer dollars, and withholding a vital new drug from the public. I think I've got his words down fairly accurately."

Cliff was stunned. "That's crazy."

The director smiled humorlessly at his pad. "My exact response. Larson has been given a vast amount of clinical data, compiled in several European countries over more than twenty years, if my information is correct, which I think it is. The data indicates that the echin compounds are utterly without contra-indications."

Cliff was out of his chair. "But Debs has changed the molecular structure!"

"Sit down, son. I hate talking up to anyone except the President." When Cliff was again seated, Summers went on, "Based on what I heard, the only alteration was to

162

attach a marker molecule. Is that correct?"

"Yes."

"Well, according to my sources, Larson is going to point out that we have reams of data on the harmlessness of the antigens, since every monoclonal antibody utilizes them."

Cliff leaned back and ran frantic hands through his hair. "I don't believe I'm hearing this."

"It gets worse, I assure you." Summers laid down his pen and looked up. "Your trip down granted them the opportunity to formally accuse the FDA of foot dragging—that's what their little session with you was all about. This was one of Larson's conditions in going public. He wanted to have everything above board."

"They didn't say anything about all this," Cliff protested.

"They didn't have to," Summers said wearily. "All they needed was a chance to publicly rebuke us and give us what can later be called fair warning. Which they did. Thanks to you."

Cliff struggled to come to grips with the news. "And this new problem—"

"Maybe your friend can convince her superiors to look into it," Summers suggested. "But just stop for a moment and imagine what it would look like for the FDA to respond to this public enquiry by claiming that a drug which has been used by millions of Europeans for years suddenly is shown to turn roses and rapeweed into LSD. We'd be laughed out of Washington." Summers shook his head. "It's damage control time, son. You are hereby ordered to keep your head in the trenches. Which means no more trips down to Edenton."

"But Ralph—"

"That's it, Cliff. I'm sorry. Now get to work."

Cliff returned to his office and immediately put a call in to Deborah. She heard him out in silence, then said,

"They're not getting back from Washington until late this afternoon. I've got a meeting scheduled for tomorrow at ten, the earliest slot they had free. You sit tight until you've heard from me."

"I can't believe this is happening."

"I can." Deborah's voice was tight as a whip. "All the pieces are falling into place."

"What do you mean?"

"Leave it until tomorrow, Junior. I'll call you as soon as the meeting lets out."

To his sleep-filled mind, the phone's clamor sounded like Armageddon. Cliff fumbled on the side table, found the receiver only after knocking over his lamp and alarm clock. "This had better be good."

"Harvey Cofield is a worm in sheep's clothing," said a voice filled with recent tears.

"Blair?" Cliff searched and found the clock, forced his eyes to focus. Two-thirty. "What's the matter?"

"I have been ordered by his royal pain in the neck never to see you again."

He shook his head, hoping for a little clarity. "Harvey Cofield told you not to see me?"

"Upon pain of losing my job," she sniffed. "As though working for the pompous jerk were such a source of joy in my life."

"What did you tell him?"

"That he could keep his cotton-picking mitts out of my private life."

"That must have pleased him no end."

"I may be looking for new employment before long." She came very close to breaking down as she said, "Oh, Cliff, I'm such a klutz when it comes to affairs of the heart."

"But such a beautiful klutz," he said, his heart bounding joyfully.

"Have I botched things up totally and beyond repair?"

"I think they could be restored," he replied. "Given the proper ingredient."

Another sniff. "What's that?"

Cliff said softly, "Love."

12

"I've received a complete and total nix," Deborah proclaimed by telephone the next morning.

"That's impossible," Cliff replied.

"No," Deborah corrected. "That's Pharmacon. The suits couldn't care less about anything as ludicrous as our worries. That is the word Whitehurst used—ludicrous. He said I should restrict my activities to the lab and refrain from any more psychedelic accusations. He couldn't have cared less about Tom, either."

"Tom?"

"The old guy at the hospital, the one who was approached by the foreigner looking for industrial secrets."

"Oh, right."

"When I asked them about that, they looked smug and said it was all taken care of." Deborah sounded very worried. "That about sums up their whole attitude right now. Smug. Better watch out, Junior. It looks like they're getting ready to launch a broadside at the FDA." She paused, then added, "And to top it all off, I've been forbidden to see you, upon pain of corporate dismemberment."

"You and Blair both."

"Oh, you spoke with her?"

"Last night."

"Does this mean you two are back at being an item again?"

"I hope so."

"Well, at least there's a small ray of sunshine in this

otherwise gloomy day." Deborah sighed. "I've been racking my brains, Junior, but I'm coming up empty."

"What if we go to the press with all this?"

"With all what? We don't even have proof that there's a tie-in between the field with our plants and the one with the rapeweed. All we'd do right now is send a few journalists into psychedelic orbit and maybe have a hippie festival closed down. Not to mention alerting the suits to our willingness to go public."

She was silent a moment, then mused aloud, "No, we've got to wait until we've got the goods, then hit them where it counts. Which is a problem, because if I start any new study here, it's bound to get back to the Tombs."

"Hang on, I've got an idea." Cliff searched through his drawer and came up with the card handed to him at the subcommittee hearing. "Have you ever heard of a Dr. Wendell Cooper?"

"Not offhand."

"You'd remember him. He looks like a six-foot rooster. He's president of something called the Health and Medicine Advisory Council."

"Never heard of that, either."

"They've got their own lab, Debs. He offered to do drug analyses for us. For free. And confidentially."

"Go to an outside group?" She thought it over. "I don't like it. But again, I don't see what choice we have."

"I don't either."

"Let me call and talk to this guy, one scientist to another, and see what he has to offer."

"Good idea." Cliff read off the number.

"We'll need to collect some more samples in secret and get them up to you."

He checked his calendar. "I've got an air pocket tomorrow. I'll drive down after work today, take enough time to mend some fences with Blair, and give you a hand."

Deborah was feeling a little on the frail side, as she put

it, so she left Cliff in Cochise's capable hands. They drove and worked in silent accord. Cliff had no trouble with silence. It made for a welcome change from all the hot air filling the halls of federal bureaucracy.

It was close to midnight by the time they turned down the farm road. They spent a long moment watching the bonfires and listening to the shrill festivities, then drove on to the Jones farm, checked the wind direction, grabbed shovels and flashlights, and set off across the fields.

Digging up the echin plants was a time-consuming process. The big man carefully inspected each root in turn, trimmed off stalks and dirt, and handed them over for bagging. When they finally had enough, they walked back to Cochise's truck, dropped off their load, and stopped just beyond the psychedelic festival.

Deborah had been adamant about their preparations for the next stage. They did not know how the substance was ingested, she had told them, and could not afford taking any unnecessary risk. What if it could pass through membranes such as eyes or eardrums? What if it could enter through the skin? They had to go in prepared.

First came the foul-weather gear, including hats—the closest thing to an isolation suit she could come up with without being noticed. Then the silicon swimmers' earplugs. Then the insulated rubber gloves. Then tape around the openings at ankles, waists, necks, wrists—even taping the hats down around their heads. Then microfine masks covering mouth and nose. Vaseline over their faces. Goggles over the eyes. By the time they were done, Cliff was drenched in sweat. He followed Cochise across the stretch of scorched earth, his breath sounding like overworked bellows to his clogged ears.

The revelers showed no interest whatsoever in their approach.

They made their way within a dozen paces of one

bonfire encircled by two dozen dancing, shouting, laughing, gyrating people. Young people in various stages of undress. Gray-haired hippies caught by an earlier era, still adorned with headbands and beads and floppy hats and tie-dyed T-shirts. A score of musicians seated beyond the circle, piping and strumming and tapping out music.

Then a dark-haired girl danced over and grasped one of Cochise's gloved hands.

The big man turned and looked a silent question toward Cliff.

The girl tugged harder, trying to lead him toward the bonfire. Several of the others gestured for him to come.

Cochise gave a single shrug, walked over, and started a lumbering dance.

If Cliff had not been sweating so fiercely, more than likely he would have found the scene hilarious.

After two trips around the fire, Cochise broke loose from the girl's grasp, backed off, waved goodbye to all the folks, and motioned for Cliff to come along.

When they had filled several heavy-duty plastic refuse bags with the stalks, they returned to the truck, dumped the sacks into garbage containers, and taped the lids shut. Then they drove farther down the road, stopped again, and began a frantic sweaty stripping.

Toweling off his face, Cliff said, "I hope you enjoyed your little jig back there."

Cochise gave an enormous grin. "Probably thought I was just another friendly alien."

Once they were under way, Cliff said, "Mind if I ask you a question?"

"If I do," Cochise replied, "you'll find out soon enough."

"With all that build-up Debs gave you, I was just wondering. Why didn't you ever go in for higher training?"

Cochise was a while before replying, "My people come from down Wanchese way."

"Don't think I've ever heard of it."

"It's a small village near the coast. Just this side of the back of beyond."

"Brings to mind a sleepy land of marsh islands and anemic children," Cliff offered.

"Mosquitoes and snakes and not enough shade," Cochise agreed. "You been there?"

"Not yet. But I'd like to."

"Mostly made its living from clamming and fishing, until the sixties, anyway. By then the clambeds were giving out, and folks discovered there was a lot of money in drugs. Went into the importing business in a big way. I grew up chopping firewood for stills and hauling bales of marijuana dropped from low-flying planes. By the time I finished high school, most of my buddies were doing time. I got out the only way I knew how. I ran."

Cliff was silent for a time, then, "You're saying that you've come a long way already. I can understand that."

"Yeah, Debs said you were a smart one."

"She's a good lady."

"Debs is one of the finest people I know," Cochise agreed. "She's got a way of making sense out of a lot of stuff that before was just noise."

"You mean, like this religion thing?"

Cochise released his grin once more. "She's been after you too, has she?"

"Some. But it's like you say, somehow she does it without making me want to back off."

"Yeah, she's got me listening and thinking, I'll say that much. I ain't there yet, but if she keeps pushing, it's hard to say where I might wind up."

The sun was beginning to brush faint strokes on the horizon when they arrived back at Deborah's place. There was a note pinned to the door that read, "I've had a serious attack of the sleepies. If I'm disturbed I'll sic the cats on you, so be quiet. Blair called. She wants you both over for break-fast. She said anytime would be okay. I'll call you later."

When they arrived at Miss Sadie's, Cliff stepped from the truck and looked out over the bay. The town was as quiet as the sunrise and as loud as creation. Doves cooed and flew in peaceful pairs upon wings that whistled up the gathering light. A car passed slowly, apologetically, aware that its presence was alien to the moment. The air was hot and heavy with country odors.

He turned back to find Cochise watching him with fathomless dark eyes. Cliff said, "This is a million miles from what I'm used to, but somehow feels like home."

The big man nodded slowly, thoughtfully. The inspection continued a moment longer, then he asked, "This lady friend of yours much of a cook?"

"One way to find out."

Blair covered her shock at Cochise's size with a couple of rapid blinks. "I'm surprised I've missed seeing you up to now."

"I try to stay as far away from the suits as I can," Cochise rumbled. "They make me break out in hives."

"Well, pleased to meet you, I'm sure." She turned her attention to Cliff and her expression softened. "I'm certainly glad to see you again."

"Likewise." He put everything he could into his look, his smile, his hug. Her body felt so good close to his it was hard to let go.

But she eventually backed off, smiled once more especially for him, then turned and said, "Can I fix you some breakfast, Mr., ah, I'm sorry, I don't recall—"

"Cochise," he replied, ducking to enter the back door. "Been hearing it so long I sorta got used to it myself."

"All right," she said, trying not to be rattled by a man who loomed a full head and shoulders above her and outweighed her by at least two hundred pounds. "Why don't you two have a seat over there at the table?" She winced as the chair groaned loudly, but the legs held. "Now then. What would you gentlemen like for breakfast? I was thinking of some eggs and bacon."

"I could eat a few eggs, sure," Cochise rumbled. "Make for a change."

She paused with two eggs in one hand and the beater in the other. "A change?"

"From normal."

She turned full around. "And just what, may I ask, is your normal breakfast?"

He shrugged his massive shoulders. "Same as every other meal with my people."

"Your people. I see. And what might that be?"

"Sun-dried eel and corn fritters." From his back pocket Cochise pulled the makings for a hand-rolled cigarette. "Do you mind?"

Blair sort of shook herself. "Of course not. Use that saucer there for an ashtray. Did I hear you say eel?"

He nodded. "Deep-fried bloodworms and grits will do in a pinch."

She turned to Cliff and demanded, "Is that man making fun of me in my own kitchen?"

Cliff studied the big man, found himself understanding Cochise's need to flavor meeting this beautiful woman with his own brand of humor. "I'd always heard the tribes down east were partial to roadkill."

"Yeah," Cochise agreed, then licked and rolled the cigarette shut. "But only if they're ripe enough for us to find them by smell."

"Wait just one minute," Blair demanded.

"And bird-dropping soup, I heard that somewhere too," Cliff said.

Cochise grinned, showing far too much whitework to fit in one person's mouth. "Special occasions only."

"There are two men who in just about five seconds are

going to be wearing their breakfast instead of eating it," Blair snapped.

"Sorry," Cliff said, and let his own grin break through. He asked Cochise, "You think she'd hit like a man?"

Cochise gave her a frank inspection, said, "Naw, more like a truck, I figure."

"People who make fun of me in my kitchen tend not to get invited back," she said.

A scuffling in the hallway announced the arrival of someone else. "Blair? Do you have company in there?"

"Not for long," she said.

Miss Sadie came through the doorway, caught sight of Cochise, and stopped cold. "Good gracious sakes alive. How did you fit through the door?"

"Miss Sadie, this is Cochise," Cliff said. "Don't stand up, man, there hardly isn't room for us all in here as it is."

"Pleased to meet you, I'm sure. You can let out that lungful of smoke now. Your face is turning positively green. Don't worry, I've smelled a cigarette before." She inspected him more closely. "Are you an Indian?"

"Yes ma'am."

"And with manners. Well, that's nice. Where is your family from?"

"Down Wanchese way."

She nodded. "That is rough territory, from all the reports I've heard. I suppose your size served you well."

"It was enough to keep me alive and get me out of there," he agreed.

A glimmer of approval shone through. "And what are you doing now, may I ask?"

"Working in the Pharmacon labs."

"He's Deborah's assistant, Auntie."

"Why, of course, Deborah spoke of you the very first night she came by." She cocked her head to one side. "Yes, I can see how someone might think they had run into some serious trouble meeting you on a dark night. But Deborah spoke very highly of you. She said you are the most capable and intelligent assistant she has ever had."

Cochise busied himself by grinding his cigarette into the saucer.

"Well, I want you to feel free to stop by any time you are down this way."

"Thank you, ma'am," Cochise mumbled.

"Blair, dear, are you sure you're cooking enough eggs for two big men like this?"

"I'm cooking all we have."

"That will have to do, then." She turned toward Cliff. "And how are you this morning, young man?"

"Fine, thank you."

"We've been seeing quite a bit of you around here lately, haven't we?"

"Auntie," Blair warned.

"When I was your age, young man, a courtship would reach a point where—"

The spatula came down on the side of the frying pan with a bang. "All of a sudden the air is getting awfully stuffy in here."

"Just going, dear," she said mildly. Then to Cliff, "You must come by some time for another little chat, young man."

Blair gave the scrambled eggs a good working over and muttered something that sounded distinctly like, *over my dead body*. Cliff made do with a nod and a smile as the old lady patted his shoulder and shuffled from the room.

After breakfast they saw Cochise off to work, then took a walk down by the Edenton Bay. The water sparkled silver and beckoning in the morning sun. The breeze was just strong enough to keep the air from being sultry. The day smelled of water and dew-soaked grass and fresh beginnings.

"What made you decide to move down from Norfolk?"

174

"The job," Blair said, then stopped herself. "No, that is my automatic reply. It's true as far as it goes, I suppose. But that was the surface reason, not the reason behind why I started looking for the job in the first place."

Cliff felt more than heard the barriers coming down. He responded as best he could, by reaching over and taking her hand. Slender fingers responded with the lightest of pressure.

"It was too easy for me to lose my dreams in the big city," Blair said. "I became all wrapped up in things that didn't mean anything once the day was over."

There was such sorrow in her voice, he wanted to reach out, crush her to his chest, tell her it was all right now. All he said was, "I understand."

The pressure on his hand increased a fraction. "I suppose Norfolk is like any big city. It breeds a patter so polished it can blind you. No matter how hard I tried, I just couldn't hold on to my way. I forgot myself. I forgot what was important. All the ideals and all the things that made me who I was." She hesitated, then finished more quietly, "Or who I wanted to be."

They sat down at the end of the pier. Blair looked over the placid waters to where gulls made lazy circles over a pair of fishing boats, and told him, "You were right in what you said the other night. That's why I flew off the handle. It was hard to stand there and have someone see me so clearly."

Cliff said nothing, content to sit and bask in the warmth of a heart that was gradually opening for him.

She pulled off her shoes and swirled one toe in the cool water. "I left Norfolk because too much of the big city was rubbing off. Maybe a stronger-willed girl could have taken it, but I felt like I was just one step away from getting sucked down the tubes. I woke up one morning and realized I didn't like myself anymore. I hadn't been to church in I don't know how long. I drank too much. I punctuated my sentences with words that would have

175

gotten my mouth washed out with soap when I was a kid. My voice was becoming as hard as my eyes, and I was finding it tougher every day to remember all the reasons for saying no."

"You were raised in Norfolk?"

"A very different Norfolk. It was three completely different cities then—Norfolk, Portsmouth, and Virginia Beach. Now it's one giant urban sprawl, just melting into each other, joined by strips of fast-food restaurants and shopping malls. Most of the character I knew in my growing-up years has gone. What's replaced the traditional charm is certainly faster and glitzier, but an old-fashioned girl just doesn't have a home there anymore."

"Tell me about your family, Blair."

"They're good people. *Good* people. My older brother runs Pop's plumbing-supply shop and does a lot of work for the Navy. My baby brother is a guy who's been in love with machines since before he could walk. He could spend days talking about fixing up that car of yours. He's a specialist at repairing what they called CNC machines, those computer controlled tools that cost as much as some factories. He pulls in good money. Both my brothers are married and busy raising babies. My folks are in love with being grandparents."

"And what do they think of their beautiful girl of the family?"

She was too honest to deny her attractiveness. Instead she replied in a little-girl voice, "They love me and they hurt for me and they wish I was happy."

Blair turned to him, her look tainted with long-held sadness. "Who'd have thought it would be worth looking for lifelong love in a world that's gone crazy for Madonna?"

"You know what your problem is?" Cliff said. "You're too good for what modern times want to offer."

"So," Blair dredged up a smile. "You know any nice old-fashioned guys who're looking for a great deal on some slightly used goods?"

He nodded slowly. "Maybe you've already found one."

"Maybe so," she conceded, the smile vanishing. "Maybe that's what keeps me up at night, scared to death of being wrong one more time."

13

Sandra cornered Cliff outside his office just after lunch the next day. "What's this I hear about you taking more time off?"

"It was mine to do with as I please," he replied. After receiving Deborah's go-ahead, Cliff had taken the samples by the lobbyist's labs, and was now enormously glad to have them out of his hands.

"I just better not find out you've been down in Edenton again," she warned. "You come within a hundred miles of that place, and it'll cost you your job." She wheeled around and tap-tapped down the hallway.

Cliff sighed, started for his door, only to be hailed from the hall's opposite end. He turned to find an extremely nervous Horace Tweedie scurrying toward him. "Do you have a minute?"

"Sure, Horace, come on in."

"No, no, not in there. Let's just walk for a second, okay?"

Cliff allowed himself to be led down the corridor. The little man's forehead was beaded with perspiration. Cliff asked, "So how are things down in files?"

"Fine, fine." The little man checked the hall, then asked, "Have you been in contact with anyone strange recently?"

"Strange?" Cliff locked into gear. He lowered his voice. "Oh, you mean your friend Wendell. Sure, I saw him this morning. Gave him something to test at his labs."

Tweedie's eyes scrunched tighter. "Who?"

"Wendell Cooper. Head of the Health and Medicine Advisory Council. I think I've got that right. Like you said, a weird sort of character, but at least he's willing to help us." Cliff dropped his voice even further. "Just do me a favor, will you? Don't let anyone know around here. It's not really been approved by the higher-ups."

"But I don't know any Cooper," the little man whispered.

"Yeah, right," Cliff grinned. "Great idea."

"I'm not kidding," Tweedie hissed. "I don't know what you're talking about."

Cliff straightened in alarm. "Then who—"

"Look," Tweedie said, his voice hoarse with strain. "I gotta go."

Cliff grabbed for him. "No, wait a second, I—"

"I've got to go *now*." The little man pulled himself free. "You just watch your back, Devon. That's all I can tell you." He was already moving down the hall, picking up speed. "Watch your back."

Cliff was almost beside himself when he called Deborah that afternoon and announced, "I can't find him."

"Who?"

"Cooper. I guess that's his name. Now I don't even know if that's real."

"The guy at the lab agency? What's the matter?"

"I've just gotten back from his office. The people there don't know of any lab. And Tweedie's never even heard of him."

"Who's Tweedie?"

"The guy who introduced us. Supposedly. And now I just missed him."

"You're not making any sense, Junior."

"Hey, life isn't making much sense either."

"Slow down," Deborah intoned. "Take a deep breath."

Cliff did as he was told. "Okay."

"Are you all right now?"

"No. Definitely not. Something's going crazy around here."

"So start from the beginning and give it to me slow."

Cliff did so, though it cost him. "I called Cooper's office, and he wasn't there, and I asked to speak to his chief lab technician, and the receptionist said, the who? That got me going, let me tell you. So I drove out there. Which was a trial and a half, seeing as how the sky has decided to finally cave in." He looked out his rain-streaked window at a world gone dark and gray. It suited the way he felt to a T.

"Didn't you check out his lab?"

"Sure, I met him and discussed our problem." Cliff's free hand dragged continually through his hair. "He showed me around this incredible lab area, but you know, I was there after hours. That was when he set up our appointment. Said it would be easier for me, not drawing attention to myself if I came after work. So nobody was working in the labs. And when I brought the samples, he met me in a coffee shop halfway between here and there—I thought he was doing me a favor, helping me get back to the office as quickly as possible. Anyway, when I went out there this afternoon, it turns out the lab is one of these diagnostics groups that hires their services out, and Cooper's rented space from them because they have done a lot of work for him in the past. But it's not his lab, Debs. And they don't know anything about our samples."

There was a moment's silence, then the grim pronouncement, "We've been set up."

"Sounds that way to me," Cliff agreed, misery coalescing into a tight little ball at gut level.

"Not sounds," she corrected. "Is."

"I'm sorry, Debs."

"You and me both," she said. "I should have come up there and looked this thing over personally. But he sounded one hundred percent professional, knew the right words. He sounded so positive he could get to the bottom of this." She sighed. "Brother, did we ever get took."

"Who's behind this?"

"I wish I knew. You check around up there, see if you can find anything out. I'll do the same at this end."

Madge had one speed for work—first gear. Cliff did not complain. At least it wasn't reverse. She was as much a friend to him as she could be, after twenty-seven years of watching them come and watching them go. She did her work well, never needed to have anything explained twice, and never needed to redo. Madge held too much respect for her own time to make mistakes the first time around.

She was busy at her computer terminal when he walked from his office and announced, "They're gunning for me, Madge."

She did not even blink. "So I heard."

He was surprised but knew he shouldn't be. Madge was connected to the local grapevine at root level. "Yeah? And were you planning on sharing the news with me one of these days?"

She gave her hefty shoulders a simple shrug. "I didn't see how it would do you any good, so why bother you when you're so much in love?"

Cliff had to smile. "It shows, does it?"

Madge adjusted her cat's-eye glasses. "Who's the lucky lady, anyway?"

"Somebody I met down in Edenton."

"Gotta watch out for those small-town Southern girls," she warned. "Once they get their hooks in, they don't let go."

"In this case, I wouldn't mind," Cliff said. "So who's holding the weapons, Madge."

"Well, Sandra for one."

"Surprise, surprise," Cliff replied.

"Right. But she's got some kind of backers from outside the FDA. Somebody over on Capitol Hill, from what I hear."

"And Ralph hasn't said anything to back me up?"

"Sure he has. That's why you've lasted as long as you have."

Cliff felt a rush of relief. He liked Ralph and hoped the feeling was mutual. It helped to know the man had stood up for him.

"But Ralph is a political appointee," Madge reminded him. "He can only go so far before sticking his neck on the chopping block beside yours."

"How long before the ax falls?"

"Hard to say. Seems like things are in a holding pattern for the moment. Can't tell you why. Want me to check around?"

"If you wouldn't mind."

"I'll do it for you." Madge stood and shrugged on her coat. She seemed genuinely sad. "You're a good boy, Cliff. Maybe too good for the rough and tumble of bureaucratic life."

Cliff reached over and patted her hand. "You're not getting sentimental on me, are you?"

"Not me, honey," she said, collecting herself. "I've been around too long to waste a tear on the ways of this old world."

Horace Tweedie's frantic scampering was hampered by the heavy summer thundershower. Every third step or so, a sudden gust tried to wrench the umbrella from his grasp and sent bitter needles rushing against his body.

He never should have waited.

He knew it now. He could feel it in his bones. He should have taken the first big payment and scampered. But always the man had offered more. Bigger payouts. More cash. More freedom.

Now something in Devon's words left him terrified that the freedom was no more.

Another gust, fiercer than the others, almost blew him off his feet. Tweedie recovered, but in doing so he stepped off the curb and stumbled in the gutter. Water poured in a steady brown stream, ankle deep and treacherous and burdened by enough silt to form a viscous mud underneath. When Horace Tweedie righted himself, his shoe was sucked off by the mud.

Horace Tweedie shouted a curse at his fate, squatted, and stuck one arm down into the filthy water. As he fished around, another vicious gust powered through. First it blew his umbrella inside out, then wrenched it from his grasp. Horace let it go. He had to use both hands to free his shoe.

Water dripped down his glasses, turning them into liquid prisms. Horace pried his foot into the water-logged shoe and fumbled with his shoelaces. Then a gust blew the droplets from his glasses, and pushed his head up and over just far enough to see the car.

The car was moving far too slowly, even for this weather. And it was dark.

Horace squinted, wiped his spectacles with fingers that suddenly were shaking spastically, and saw, yes, it was a black Infiniti.

Thunder boomed around him, drowning out his high-pitched cry. Horace stood and started running, his laces still undone. The shoe sucked on and off and flop-flopped and finally slipped off entirely. This time Horace Tweedie did not even notice.

His glasses were fogged up now, coated with each gasping little breath as well as the rain. Which was why he did not see the car stop nor the aquiline featured man race up the empty sidewalk and seize him fiercely by the neck.

The iron grip dragged him back toward the waiting car. The man held Horace with one hand strong enough to crush his bones and opened the driver-side door. To Horace it looked like a looming maw of darkness. He struggled as hard as his fear-drenched body would allow.

"I wrote it all down!" His screams were almost lost to the din of lightning that streaked across the sky. "If I disappear it's all gonna come out! I got it all hidden safe!"

The stranger with the delicate aquiline features pushed him inside, then slid in behind him. A pistol with a silencer appeared in one hand as the other shifted the car into gear. "I am sure you will tell me all about it," he replied silkily. "In time."

14

"Thank you for being so patient, Ms. Walters. Congressman Larson will see you now."

Sandra Walters followed the chief secretary back into the congressman's inner sanctum and reflected that it might actually be happening.

The congressman had the telephone to his ear when she entered. Still, he bolted to his feet, shook her hand, waved her into a seat. "I've got to go now, Harry. Something mighty important just came in."

She permitted herself a small smile. Yes, the doors to real power might about be ready to open for her. Finally.

Congressman Larson set down the phone, swept around from behind his desk, and said, "Ms. Walters. What a wonderful surprise."

"I'm sorry to bother you like this, Congressman." One nervous hand rose to check her hair.

"Nonsense. Always have time for a beautiful young friend." He gave her his number one smile, showing off five thousand dollars' worth of capped teeth. He lowered himself into the chair beside her. "Now, what can I do for you?"

"I think I might have something of great importance for you," she said, barely able to keep her voice steady in her excitement. "Do you happen to recall what you said to me at our meeting two weeks ago?"

"Of course." He kept his chin cocked to smooth out the loose skin on his neck. "There is a very serious breach of public trust over at FDA. I have always been certain that some of the people working there must be aware of this, and chaffing under the restrictions placed upon them by those who insist on playing games with their power."

"That is exactly right," she agreed, trying hard to keep her eagerness under wraps.

"Naturally, my colleagues and I are seeking allies within the FDA, people who can be trusted to act in the public's best interest once our housecleaning begins."

"I'd certainly like to be counted on your team, Congressman," Sandra Walters replied, clenching one hand with the other. So close.

Larson examined her with a measuring gaze. "I thought I had identified such an ally in you, Ms. Walters."

"Congressman, just this morning I was given some potentially explosive information. It appears that one of my subordinates has gone against every FDA guideline and offered confidential information on a new drug to an outside laboratory."

Larson focused down tighter. "How did you learn of this?"

"I can't say," Sandra replied, which was literally the truth. The confidential caller had not given his name. He had simply passed on the information in a distinctly accented voice, then given the name of a person who could confirm it. Sandra had called the number of something called the Health and Medicine Advisory Council, whose director had cheerfully agreed that yes, Cliff Devon had delivered samples for inspection to him. Why, was something the matter? No, he was so sorry, he could not return the samples. They had unfortunately been stolen from the trunk of his car just the night before.

"No, of course, you must respect the confidentiality of your sources," Larson said, masking his disappointment well. "And just which drug are we speaking of here?"

"One up for a new drug application. One that I understand is of particular interest to you," Sandra said, letting the words roll deliciously off her tongue. "The echin drug."

"You were right to bring this to my attention," the congressman intoned, his voice taut.

"I couldn't let them just sweep another one under the rug," Sandra declared. "Which is exactly what they'd have done. Especially with this particular person. He's the apple of the director's eye, and he gets away with murder. As you can see."

The congressman's secretary chose that moment to knock, open the door, and announce, "Sir, you're due at the hearing in five minutes."

"Let them wait," he snapped, his gaze not shifting from Sandra's face. "And hold all calls."

When the door had closed once more, Larson shifted his chair closer, and said, "So tell me, my dear. What is this subordinate's name?"

Friday morning Deborah walked the halls of the veterans hospital, wrapped in a fog of frustration and futility. So many developments were screaming for urgent attention. She needed Pharmacon's equipment. She needed the backing of her superiors. She needed to be heard. But everywhere she turned she faced a stone wall.

And everything pointed toward her worst fears being confirmed.

Somehow there had been a transfer from one plant species to another. Which everyone involved in microbiology knew was impossible. Genetic material simply did not transfer.

Yet there was no other explanation.

She knew what should be done. The drug's clinical trials needed to be halted until a clear understanding was reached over exactly what was going on with the hallucinogenic characteristics of the neighboring rapeweed. But her warnings and pleas were simply being ignored.

Nobody at Pharmacon even wanted to listen. And Deborah knew why.

The smell of profit was strong in the air.

Deborah was so steeped in thought that when she stepped through the main doors, she blinked in the bright sunlight and for a moment wondered where she was.

Then she saw Tom.

"Stop!" The word was out of her mouth before she even realized she had spoken. Or before she fully understood what was happening.

Then her brain slipped into gear, and she began to run.

"You! I see you! I'm calling the police! Let him go!"

The man looked vaguely foreign, and possessed the strength of a supple steel cable. He glared her way and continued to drag the feebly protesting Tom toward the dark car waiting by the main gates.

Deborah spun around, flew back up the stairs, pushed open the main doors, and screamed at the top of her lungs, "*Cochise!*"

Then back down the stairs to follow the hustling dark-haired man in the light-colored suit as close as she dared. Her white coat hampered her legs. She tore it off and flung it to the ground. "You let him go ."

Behind her, the hospital's entrance doors slammed back against the wall with the sound of a firing howitzer. She heard the Cochise roar.

The man dragging Tom looked up and hesitated.

"I see you!" she shrilled, not caring how little sense the words made. "They'll track you down! Kidnapping is a federal offense! Let the man go!"

Features so finely sculpted they looked almost feminine drew back into a furious snarl. He shoved Tom toward her, wheeled about, and raced for the car.

Deborah ran forward and caught Tom as his legs faltered and began to give way. "I see you!" She screamed a third time, too caught up in the moment to wonder how smart it was to draw further attention toward herself.

The driver caught and held her in a look from dark, coldly fathomless eyes. Then the window powered up, and the car slid smoothly away.

"Take me on downtown," the old man puffed. "Gonna tell 'em everything I know."

"We need to get you back to bed," Deborah soothed, and allowed Cochise to take up the old man's weight.

"Been in bed. Been laying there too long, looking back at all the mistakes." Tom fastened rheumy eyes on Deborah. "It's time, Doc. Gotta start a new leaf while I still can. Take what's owed me, least for this one. That's all I could think of when he had me, how I'd left it for too late. Now the good Lord and you've done give me a chance. Well, this is one old fool who's not gonna let it slip by. Not again, anyhow."

Cochise knelt beside her, raised Tom to his feet with the ease of lifting a sack of feathers. "Everything's all right, old man."

"Take me on downtown, Doc," he repeated. "Gonna tell 'em all I know."

15

That Friday morning was a total wash for Cliff.

Conversations drifted off whenever he showed up. Appointments with colleagues became almost impossible to make. His name was on the lips of every gossip in the building. Madge could tell him that much, but little else, other than the fact that he was about to be erased and the bureaucratic herd instinct was shoving him out, pushing him to the edges, where the lions snarled and waited and hunted their prey.

Eventually the smirks and the almost audible snide remarks and the knowing looks became too much. Lunchtime he decided to call it quits for the day and head back down to Edenton.

Cliff cranked down the window of his Plymouth and took in great drafts of the humid summer air. At least out here he could breathe. He spent the drive down mulling over the Pharmacon mystery.

Prior to his departure, Ralph Summers had reported that Congressman Larson had scheduled a major news conference for Monday afternoon. He was going, according to scuttlebutt on Capitol Hill, to blow the FDA's lid into high-altitude orbit.

Cliff still had difficulty believing Pharmacon was going to use the European trial data as a basis for pushing the release of echiniacin. But what else could explain the things that were going on? And what would be the consequences if the genetically altered drug was rushed to market before adequate testing could be done?

Cliff shuddered. To take a series of compounds and

tinker with their molecular structure, then claim they were still basically the same, went against everything he felt was right and true. Such pressure to release the drug prematurely brought to his mind the biggest pharmaceutical nightmare in modern history.

Thalidomide.

In the early 1960s, thousands of pregnant women in Europe had had this sedative prescribed to alleviate morning sickness. The early tests had shown no side effects whatsoever. The American drug company and the U.S. press had gone into fits of hand-wringing despair over the FDA's refusal to accept the European clinical studies. The press had accused the FDA of distrusting the nation's closest allies. The FDA had pointed out that none of the tests had actually been carried out on pregnant women.

Then disaster had struck.

Thousands and thousands of European babies had been born horribly deformed—armless or legless or both. Eventually it had been proven beyond the slightest doubt that the single cause was this supposedly tried and true drug.

Cliff had studied the thalidomide scandal very carefully during his first year with the FDA. He kept a file of clippings in his bottom drawer. They were never shown to anyone; they were for him alone. He kept them as a reminder of the responsibility he carried and the reason for responding to political posturings and journalistic pressure and corporate greed with caution and courage.

Now he was being cut off, hamstrung, and ignored. But the memory of his psychedelic hammering still lingered. He did not need scientific proof. He did not care that it was supposedly impossible to transplant altered genes from one species to another. His gut instinct told him that the genetically altered viroid was responsible for what he had experienced down there in Edenton.

And he was going to prove it. Then he was going to go public, stop this blind stampede for profit before more people got hurt.

He had to do it, no matter the cost.

But he had a feeling the cost might be staggering.

Cliff stopped at a service station on the outskirts of Edenton and called the Pharmacon facility. Deborah was still up at the Norfolk Veterans Hospital, he was told, and Blair had left for the day. He drove straight to Blair's house.

Before he was even out of the car, Miss Sadie called down, "She's just back from work, young man, but she's gone to the store for me. Shouldn't be more than a country minute. Come up and keep an old lady company, if you don't mind settling for second best."

"That's one thing I'd never call you," he said, climbing the front stairs. "Not ever."

"Well, you're very kind. Take this rocker here beside me. Would you care for something cool to drink?"

"No thanks, I'm fine." Her hand continued to raise in greeting to every passing car as he settled in. Cliff asked, "Do you really know everybody driving by?"

"Of course not, don't talk silly. My eyes are so bad I can scarcely make out the folks standing right in front of me."

"Then why—"

"Now you just stop and use that head of yours for something besides holding up your hat. How do you think a friend might feel if they passed and waved and I didn't wave back?" She started rocking once more. "Safest thing is to wave at everybody."

Cliff began pushing himself back and forth. The rocker's gentle reply was a comforting urge to let it go, settle back, relax, step away from the stress and the worry and the unanswered questions. "Sure is nice here."

"Don't let these pretty facades fool you, young man. If

a body's got a mind to be miserable, a small town doesn't offer a bit more shelter than anywhere else." She pointed down the street, toward a three-storied Victorian mansion of perhaps fifteen bedrooms. "One old woman lives in there with seven dogs as her only company."

"Must get awful hollow around dark."

"I would surely think so. Of course, there's no escaping the tremors of loneliness if a body manages to tack on enough years." She began rocking once more. "That house next to it but one used to be my aunt's house. In all of my growing-up years, I hated that house. But it looks so different now, I've come to love it, at least a little bit."

"Why did you hate it?"

"It was the town's funeral parlor as well as their home. My uncle was the town mortician. The front parlor was where they held the services before everybody gathered in the church."

"That's a pretty good reason."

"When I was a little girl, I always felt like there was somebody just out of sight, watching whatever I did." She suppressed a very genteel shudder. "My granddaddy was laid out in that front window, my daddy and my momma as well. Got too many memories of that front room to ever sit comfortable in there."

"Do you have any family left?"

"Just Blair. My folks both died young. Husband too."

"I'm sorry."

"Still and all," she went on, "I think I've been fairly lucky. Mama and Daddy raised me well. I had most of what a girl could ask for—a happy home, nice clothes, good friends, a family that loved me. In this big world, that's saying a lot."

"Sure is."

"Even when they left me, they made sure I was well taken care of. Didn't either one of them depart until I married Harry. That was a good man, Harry Atkins. As sweet a man as God ever set on this earth. The good Lord didn't see fit to let us have children before He called Harry home. That's about the biggest bone I've got to pick with Him when I arrive. Even then, I was allowed to have my Blair come and see me through my waning days."

Cliff hesitated, then asked, "Can you keep a secret?"

She gave the single-note laugh of the very old. "Young man, around these parts a secret is something you only tell to one person at a time."

"You don't strike me as a gossip."

"Small towns have a different way of dealing with the world. To a lot of folks around here, gossip is just another name for a telephone ministry."

"Maybe I better keep this one to myself, then."

"Oh, go ahead and speak your piece. You're fit to burst as it is." She reached over and patted his arm. "Think of it as a kindness to a lonely old lady, and remember that no good deed will go unpunished."

He looked at her askance. "Are you sure you've got that right?"

"Wise as doves and harmless as serpents," she replied. "That's the way to survive in a small town."

Cliff confessed, "I think I'm falling in love with your niece."

She inspected him carefully, then asked, "Are you going to take her away from me, young man?"

"I don't know," Cliff said truthfully. "I've been thinking I'd be happier living around here than in D.C., but I don't know what I could do. Of course, the way things are moving just now, I don't know how much longer I'll have my job in Washington. A lot has been going on. If I lose it," Cliff took a breath. "Well, maybe this would be a good place to put down roots."

"An honest answer, sure enough. And a good one. Well, I shall keep you in my prayers."

"Thank you," he said quietly.

"You're welcome." She nodded at a form that was hurrying through the gathering dusk toward them. "Now my nose tells me there's another somebody who needs to hear what you've just told me."

"Cliff!" There was genuine pleasure in Blair's voice. "What are you doing here?"

"Waiting for you." And then he saw her rush up the stairs and set down her bags and laugh when one spilled before she tumbled into his arms. He knew then, with the softness of her yielding to him and her hair spilling over his face and her fragrance filling his mind, he knew that somehow it was going to be all right.

"Last September, one of the world's largest pharmaceutical companies reported pretax earnings for the financial year of 2.5 billion dollars on sales of 7.4 billion dollars—a thirty-four percent profit level during the world's worst economic downturn since the Great Depression. Our per capita expenditure on health care is ten times what other Western nations are paying. Does that sound reasonable to you?"

"No," she answered quietly, her gaze unwavering.

"Not to me either. The United States medical-industrial complex is so big it would qualify for membership in the G-7, which means that we spend more money on medical care than some of these other top seven countries even *make*." He shook his head. "Something's wrong with this picture."

They sat on the front porch, coffee at their elbows, hands touching, sharing the night. After dinner Miss Sadie had smiled and said the night was meant for those younger than she. They had shared a shy look and not urged her to stay.

Lightning bugs illuminated the darkness, fairy lights that danced to the music of night breeze through pines. Their flickering ballet accentuated the heat and the humidity. The incense of honeysuckle and freshly watered roses invited him to sit, relax, and savor a quiet country evening.

Blair pulled from him the worries which had driven him south, listening with a quiet intensity that made the memories come alive. Perhaps it was another gift of a Southern upbringing, Cliff reflected as he spoke, this ability to listen and share in more than the words.

Blair asked, "So do you see a lot of this sort of injustice in your work?"

He laughed. "Are you really sure you want to get me started on this?"

"Did I just uncover a raw nerve?"

"You could say that."

"Oh goody." She reached over and stroked the hairs on his arm. "So tell me what it is that ruffles your feathers."

He sighed and struggled to focus beyond her touch. "Pharmaceutical companies are running ads on television, saying how all they really want to do is find the cure for whatever ails you. At the same time, their industry body is lobbying Washington, warning how devastating it would be to have price controls on drugs. We are professionally responsible companies, they say. We can police ourselves just fine, thank you."

"I take it you disagree."

"Here's one case from a hundred. I know because I try to keep track of the worst examples of profit gouging in the drug industry. There's this salve used for people who suffer from skin viruses like shingles and cold sores. It doesn't cure the illness, just suppresses symptoms. Which means that patients have to buy more of the stuff every time there's an outbreak. The ointment appeared about eight years ago, and it cost twenty-five dollars for a tube about half the size of my little finger."

"Wow, that's pretty steep."

"Wait, it gets better. Since then, the price of this stuff has risen at *twenty times* the rate of inflation. To make it worse, the company's British operation successfully lobbied to have it declared an over-the-counter drug in England. Doctors over there were reluctant to prescribe it, both because of the price and because less expensive salves did almost as well. The company decided they could sell more by lowering the price and advertising directly to the public. So overnight the price dropped to *one-third* what it cost in the United States. Now in a couple of years the patent is going to run out here, and what do you think will happen?"

"Others will start producing it," she said, "and the price will drop like a stone."

That gave him pause. "You're a quick study."

"There's more in this pretty head than just a pretty head," she replied. "Tell me more."

"Okay, here's one closer to home. A company here in North Carolina recently went to court, trying to extend the patent on its ulcer drug. What they did was, they took the original formula for this stuff, and they shifted around a couple of molecules. They then went up to the patent office and said, Ta-da, lookee here, we've got a whole new drug. Somehow they got those jokers to swallow it, and so they've wound up with a new patent, one that doesn't run out until the year 2002. The original patent would have expired in 1995. Which means they get another seven years to charge whatever the market will bear."

"Which is a lot, right?"

"Enough for them to make over two billion dollars a year from this drug."

Blair hummed an impressed note.

"Another company, one that makes generic drugs, has taken them to court, claiming that the pharmaceutical giant is trying to pull a fast one. If they win, you'll see the price of the ulcer drug plummet."

"We're talking about people's lives here," Blair said, sensing his concern.

"The drug companies are big businesses," Cliff replied. "They're out chasing the almighty dollar as hard as they can, just like any other business. And all that hokum they're throwing at the people on television is nothing but advertising copy."

She stood up and pulled him to his feet. "Mind taking me for a walk?"

"Of course not."

They crossed the street and took the sidewalk lining the bayside. A warm breeze caressed their faces, pushing fat, silver-white clouds across a star-streaked sky. Blair moved up close to him, sliding her arm around his waist. Her body felt lithe and beckoning against his.

"Okay," she sighed. "Let's hear it."

"Hear what?"

"All this is a little too good to be true. The looks, the car, the attitude, it's too much. I need to hear about a few warts to balance out the picture."

"I don't have any."

"Not wart warts," she replied. "Habit warts. Thought warts. Things that you hide from the people you want to impress."

Cliff mulled that one over.

"Well?"

"I don't want to tell you."

"Of course you don't. That doesn't have a thing to do with it." She pulled far enough away to be able to look up at his face. "You don't smoke, I take it."

"No, never have."

"Chew tobacco? I must warn you, there is positively nothing that would make me less inclined to offer my mouth for a kiss."

He shook his head. "Tootsie Rolls."

"I beg your pardon?"

"I need something for my mouth to fiddle with when I'm working. I keep a bag of Tootsie Rolls and a jar of peanut butter in my desk drawer. Extra chunky."

"And you just happened upon this," she delicately chose the words, "this remarkable combination."

"No, it took a while. I tried all kinds of stuff. But this really works."

"I'm sure it must."

"See, you unwrap the Tootsie Roll, then dig up this big gob of peanut butter and suck it off with some of the chocolate. Then, when the taste's back to all chocolate, you jam it back in for another load. Once you get the hang of it, you can make a Tootsie Roll last for hours."

"How perfectly fascinating."

Cliff turned toward her. As though of its own accord his hand rose from his side to touch her face, trace a finger's line across a soft cheek, around full lips, down to the delicately sculpted chin. Which he raised. Still he hesitated, drawn by the wells of loneliness, of hurting and the fear of being hurt again, of open yearning in those jade-green eyes.

Then he bent and kissed her, for a long time, for an instant, for a moment when the world began and ended in the span of a kiss.

Gently she drew her face from his, returned for another tiny taste, then laid her head on his shoulder.

And the night breeze sang a gentle melody to match the sound of her sigh.

16

Owen MacKenzie, Pharmacon's chairman, was greeted at the Washington airport Saturday morning by one of Congressman Larson's fresh-faced aides, who announced, "He's vanished."

"Who has?"

"The FDA man we're supposed to be accusing of mishandling confidential information. We can't find him."

"Well, he's bound to show up. How are the other things moving?"

The aide scampered alongside him, trying to match the chairman's lunging strides. "The congressman wishes to tell you that everything else is proceeding according to plan, sir."

"Well, that's good. The news conference still on?"

"Yessir. But this Devon, we—"

"There's bound to be a hitch every now and then in something this big. Got to learn to move with the punches."

The aide was finding it hard to talk and keep up and draw breath. "But sir, it may be that Devon is down at your North Carolina facility."

MacKenzie swung around. "What's that you say?"

"His friend, Dr. Deborah Givens, yesterday went to the police in Norfolk and claimed that an industrial spy had tried to kidnap one of her patients from the veterans hospital. That's why Mr. Whitehurst isn't here. We heard about this early today, and he left immediately to try and straighten things out. It also appears that Dr. Givens is still trying to draw attention to this accusation of possible hidden dangers from the echin drug."

"I've heard about all I want over this psychedelic nonsense," the chairman snapped. "Some kind of New Age flower child stuck a load of flowers in her car window, isn't that right?"

"Yessir, something to that effect."

"So what's to have kept them from spraying some junk on those posies, you know, one of those designer drugs?" The chairman was growing red in the face. "This is just like a scientist. The minute somebody starts talking profit, they dig their heads in the dirt, afraid of being contaminated." Angrily he shifted his briefcase to his other hand, making an arc that almost took off the aide's left hip. "So what does this have to do with the Devon kid?"

"That's what worries us, sir. We don't know."

"The sooner that blasted troublemaker's got the feel of asphalt under his britches, the better off we'll all be. And I've about had it up to my hind teeth with this scientist of mine. You got a number where I can reach Whitehurst?"

"Yessir." The aide dug a slip from his pocket. "He asked you to call—"

Owen MacKenzie jerked the slip from the aide's hand, wheeled around and stomped down the corridor. "Come on, I've got to get to a phone."

Luis de Cunhor had never known a fury as great as that moment's. Not from the humiliation of hearing his family whine and complain at never being given the wealth they deserved. Not from having to spend four endless years slaving away in a country he loathed and a language he detested, to earn a degree and a key to his own advancement. Not from waiting and sweating while his grandmother's aged sister, a crone with one foot in the grave, approached her own eldest son, Fernando de Cunhor, the Padron, and begged him to give Luis a chance.

No, nothing approached the frustration and fury he knew just then.

Just when he should have been basking in the praise of his Padron, when he should have been preparing for the receipt of his long-awaited reward, when the gates to his own office and power and wealth should have been opening, here he was. Stuck in an old rental boat stinking of fishbait and gasoline, tied to a stump rising from a fetid marshland, swatting at mosquitoes, waiting for a cursed doctor to return home.

The loose tongue at the FDA had been taken care of. The government's enquiry was set to explode at any moment. Samples of the genetically altered root had been obtained. The fake lobbyist Wendell Cooper had wisely decided to take a long vacation in Switzerland.

Luis had carefully used the FDA coordinator's desire for more research and his ongoing battles with the Walters woman. From what Tweedie had told him, the coordinator was a typically innocent and trusting American named Devon, a name that sounded like tasteless white cheese and probably fit the man perfectly. Devon's career had then been set up and shot down like the pigeon he was.

But this, this infuriating turn of twisted fate had to happen now.

Luis kicked angrily at one filth-encrusted gunnel. Who would have ever thought that the old man at the veterans hospital could be such a problem? Not to mention that cursed woman doctor. Luis planned to do away with her need for a wheelchair. Permanently. And the old man at the veterans hospital was not long for this earth.

Fernando de Cunhor had been his childhood idol. The Padron's story was told by all the family with envy and pride—the man who rose against all odds to become owner of Brazil's third largest pharmaceutical company. Rumors of illegal doings followed him like shadows and were whispered by people who feared him too much to speak them aloud. Luis had listened to them all, drinking in the tales made more dramatic with repeated telling, knowing that one day the world would grant him too the glorious mantle of fearful respect.

And now this.

He shifted to ease the gun's jamming presence in his waistband. The sudden movement caused the boat to rock. Luis grabbed the seat, steadied himself, then noticed how the scummy water in the boat's bottom had stained his ivory-colored shoes. He cursed the fate that had dragged him here, and he willed the doctor to hurry home.

He would not fail the Padron.

Luis stiffened and glanced over to his right. Something had shifted the plants bordering the bulkhead. Yes, there it was.

As stealthily as the unstable boat permitted, he reached for his gun.

But the plants did not move again.

"Whitehurst? This is Owen MacKenzie."

"Mr. MacKenzie, good of you to call. I think I've managed—"

"Stow it," the chairman barked. "Listen up. We've got us a problem here, mister. I want you to get rid of it."

There was a long pause, then, "I'm not sure I understand."

"You want to see the inside of the boardroom, don't you? Well, here's your chance. Get rid of the problem."

"You mean—"

"I mean get rid of it." MacKenzie looked over to where the aide stood, pretending not to be trying to hear. He swung his bulk around so that he was facing the swirling airport scene and lowered his voice. "These doggone shenanigans have got to stop."

"But Dr. Givens—"

"That Givens gal is just like any other scientist. Get

'em within ten feet of a good idea and they'll do their dead-level best to mess it up. But Givens is only half of the problem."

"You mean Devon."

"That's right, I mean that FDA snit. Word is he's down there again, sticking his nose where it doesn't belong." Owen MacKenzie bore down hard. "Now do you or do you not understand what I'm saying to you?"

Whitehurst picked his words as carefully as walking through a mine field. "And if I am able to eradicate this problem—"

"You do what's necessary," the chairman barked, "and I'll get you on the board. Simple as that. Owen Mac-Kenzie is a man of his word. That's something you can bank on."

"I'll, ah, need some help."

"Right. Got a pen?"

"Yes."

"Hang on." Owen MacKenzie pulled out his pocket diary and thumbed to the telephone directory. He had collected quite a few odd contacts and odder memories along his scramble to the top. "Okay, write this down." He gave him the number. "Ask for Chico. Tell him Frankie sends his regards, and spell out what you need."

"Chico," Whitehurst repeated, his voice faint.

"Right. Now get out there and do what's necessary, Director Whitehurst."

"You should have called," Deborah said for the dozenth time.

"I tried a couple of times before we sat down for dinner," Cliff replied. They were returning to her house Saturday morning from the supermarket. "When I didn't get an answer, I just went ahead and booked myself into the guesthouse. It's not a problem, Debs."

"Yes it is. I don't like you spending good money for a room. I'm going to have a key cut for you this afternoon, and then you can come and go as you please."

The offer silenced him. Then, "Thank you, Debs, that means a lot."

She shrugged it off. "It looks like you're going to be spending a lot of time down here. I don't want you racking up any more hotel bills during your courtship."

Courtship. It sounded so formal, yet it fit the place and the woman. Blair. He could scarcely think her name without feeling his heart take wings. "Where were you, anyway?"

"After the police got all the details of Tom's kidnap attempt and finally let us go, I decided I'd had enough of this. I went to see a friend who teaches at the university in Norfolk. He's agreed to make some room in his lab, as long as we can be through before the summer break ends."

"That's great, Debs."

Her hand made a see-saw motion in the air between them. "Good and not so good. Warren is not all that great shakes at research, which means I'll basically have to do everything myself to get usable results. And what's worse, he is a real publicity hound. I had to spill the beans about what was going on here. Or at least what I think is going on. If it turns out to be true, Warren is going to go as public as a skyrocket. That's not just stretching the boundaries of ethical conduct as far as Pharmacon is concerned. I've snapped them like I was playing with rubber bands."

"Hey, but look at how they've treated you."

"Two wrongs don't make a right, Junior. That's one lesson you should have learned by now." She squinted through the windshield at the old black man who was walking down the middle of the road, waving at them. "What on earth is Reuben up to?"

She pulled up beside the old man, stopped, and rolled down her window. "Good morning, Reuben. What's the matter?"

"Morning, Miss Debs. Probably ain't nothing," he replied. "Just seemed a trifle strange to these old eyes, is all."

"What did?"

"There's a feller out fishing in front of your house. 'Cept he ain't got no fishing gear. And he ain't dressed like no fisherman I've ever seen, and I've seen a lot of 'em in my time."

Deborah cut off her motor, her face suddenly pinched. "Did you get a look at him?"

"Made a point of it, yes ma'am. Don't look like nobody from around here. Black hair all slicked back, skin kinda dark. Got on a fancy suit, dirty white color. Nice shirt, tie, the works. Just sitting there, watching your house like he was up to no good."

Deborah started the motor. "Climb in, Reuben. You mind if we go use your telephone?"

"'Course not. Who you done got mad at you, Miss Debs?"

"That's the problem," she replied, putting the car in gear. "I don't know."

"Don't tell me this is gonna become a regular habit with you." The sheriff squinted out over the empty waters of Edenton Bay. "I don't take partial to being called up and told to drive all the way out here just so I can admire the view."

"Is that what you think this is?" Deborah struggled hard to keep her voice under control. "Just a hoax?"

"Right now I don't know what to think," the sheriff said. "What I *know* is that there ain't no boat out there tied to any cypress stump carrying no foreign spy in a fancy silk suit."

"I don't know if it's silk."

"Well, soon as you do, missy, you be sure and let me know. Danged if it won't be keeping me up nights 'till you call."

"You don't believe Reuben either, then, I take it."

"Shoot, I've known Reuben since I was knee-high to a grasshopper. That man's older than Santa Claus, you know that? I hope my eyes are half as good as his if I ever get to be his age." The sheriff kicked at a loose clod. "I just can't believe you'd try to railroad a fine old gentleman like that into your wild schemes."

"Wasn't like that, Sheriff," Reuben said, his gaze direct. "Nossir. Wasn't like that at all. I's the one saw that feller out there in the boat. Told Miss Debs just like she say. Tha's why she calls you like she did."

The sheriff turned and stared out over the placid waters. "I'm still waiting to hear how you're gonna tie this to the hippie gathering over at the Taylor farm."

"I don't know anything about that," Deborah replied. "But now that you mention it, I imagine there is a connection somewhere."

"I knew it," the sheriff told the bay. "Sure as I'm standing here, I knew that one was coming. Saw it a mile off."

"What about the attempted kidnapping up in Norfolk," Deborah demanded. "Are you going to shrug that one off too?"

"Yeah, I'm aiming to give those folks up in Norfolk a call just as soon as I get back to the office. 'Fore I do, though, lemme make sure I got it all straight. This alleged kidnapping was of an old geezer from a veterans hospital, who claims he was on the take for handing information over to a foreign spy, now, is that right?"

"I know it seems far-fetched, Officer, but I assure—"

"Wait, now, it gets better. The only other witness to this alleged kidnapping was a big Injun feller on your payroll, who just happened to be strolling by."

"He wasn't strolling by," Deborah snapped. "I called for him."

"Right, 'scuse me, I got that part down wrong. Now

what did you say his name was again?"

"John Windover," Deborah replied grimly.

"No ma'am, I'm referring to the name that everybody knows him by, according to you."

"Cochise."

The sheriff broke out a leathery grin. "I been raised on fish-camp tales, but man, if this story don't take the cake, I don't know what does."

Deborah asked in a soft voice, "So who is it that's got you on their payroll, Sheriff?"

The face snapped down tight. "I'll forget I ever heard that, ma'am. On account of if I don't I'd be tempted to break one of my own rules, which is to never strike a lady, which all of a sudden I'm not so sure you are." He stared at her hard. "Now, if you'll excuse me, *ma'am*, there's a world of other items out there just waiting for my attention. And if this phantom of yours happens to come rowing by again, why, don't you hesitate to call on your friendly neighborhood sheriff's office."

Deborah watched him stomp back to his car, then said to the pines and the wind and the surrounding day, "I just goofed up big time."

Reuben hummed a two-tone agreement. "Don't believe I'd have said what you said like you said it. Not in a million years."

"My temper got ahead of me."

"That's the time I find it best to haul back on them reins and shut my mouth up real tight."

"Sounds like good advice to me," Cliff said, speaking for the first time since the sheriff's arrival.

"Yeah, it's seen me through a lotta trials and a lotta years," Reuben replied. "'Course, them reins do start to chafe sometime. Yes ma'am, they surely do."

"I guess I can't count on him to come back anytime soon," Deborah said to the empty road.

"Well, now," Reuben said, "I'd say if you was to call

him tonight, that sheriff, he might get here 'long about Christmas time. Give or take a month."

Cliff looked across the road at the ever-growing collection of tents. "From this distance it looks like the world gypsy congress."

Deborah stripped off the rest of her protective gear and followed his gaze. Aging flower children strolled through the golden fields of rapeweed. Younger people clustered and danced and raced through the dying rays of another day. Groups of musicians played a variety of instruments, their sounds drifting over the distance like some cacophonous alien tongue. The atmosphere was surreal, timeless, unnatural.

"Four more days," she said.

"Do you think the effect might spread before they shut it all down?"

Deborah kept looking out over the fields. "I don't think so. I hope that's my head talking, and not just my heart. But no, I don't think so. The viroid cannot replicate, as I said."

"You think that's what happened? The wind carried the fertilizer and the viroid into the rapeweed fields?"

"It's the only thing that makes any sense. The altered genetic sequences were taken into the rapeweed root system and had an effect on the pollen."

"But what happens if the pollen spreads its effect into the next generation of plants?" Cliff pressed.

"Then we're lost," Deborah said simply. "But I don't think, no, that's not strong enough. I am ninety-nine point ninety-nine percent certain that it is impossible. The basic tenet of using nonreplicating genetic instructions means that we are affecting only one generation at a time." She swung open her door. "Come on, Junior. You've scared me enough for one night."

"Where to?" he asked, climbing aboard. "Norfolk?"

"Not tonight. I'll drive up tomorrow when I'm fresh. Do you mind if I stop by the lab on the way home and just check for messages? I haven't been by since Thursday."

"Go ahead," he replied, not yet ready to let the matter drop. "So exactly how do you make up this new genetic sequence anyway? The other day you said something about it, what did you call it, tack technology?"

"T-A-Q," she corrected, spelling it out. She rewarded him with her lopsided grin. "That's what I like about you, Junior. Never afraid to face up to the vast reaches of your own ignorance."

"You don't have to sound so pleased."

"Okay." She put the car in gear. "We've got to go back to the farthest reaches of time for this one. All the way back to 1985, when the world of microbiology was completely turned on its axis. The dust still hasn't settled. That year, they discovered something called PCR, or preliminary chain reaction. This change made it possible to manipulate DNA and grow new chains. Not in months or years, but in hours." She stopped at the intersection and used two hands to form a coil in the air. "DNA is a double-helix, spiraling up sort of like a twisted ladder. Anybody who has taken high-school biology knows this. But what isn't so well known is that DNA is not stable. Under certain conditions, like high heat, it falls apart, sort of like a zipper being opened."

Deborah turned onto the main road and drove toward the sunset. "There are enzymes called DNA polymerazes, which attach themselves to certain DNA sequences. This has been known for a long time. It's one of the body's basic building processes, enzymes reacting to certain amino acids, forming proteins and disposing of others. But the problem was, the same high heat that opened up the DNA protein also destroyed the enzyme."

Cliff turned his attention from the road, watching his friend, enjoying as ever the shared thrill of her scientific world. The longer she spoke, the more excited she grew. Her mind focused with diamond-fired intensity on frontiers a scarce molecule wide.

"In 1985, though, some researchers isolated what are called TAQ enzymes from thermofile bacteria. These are organisms able to live in superheated conditions, like around the undersea volcanoes at the ocean floor. These TAQ enzymes remained intact even at heats that unzipped the DNA. This was really important, Junior. *Really* important. You have to open up the DNA chain to get at any particular gene. But you have to have some chemical hand ready to reach down and pluck out the gene when it becomes freed. And presto, the TAQ enzymes could be chemically programed to do just that."

Cliff watched and saw as her face lost its aged look, her eyes their weary cast. She lived for the challenge of this work, he knew. She *lived* for it.

"So the DNA was split up under the high heat, and the TAQ enzyme pulled out the specified gene," she continued. "And now you have the really big surprise, the explosive payoff. When the solution was cooled down, what happened but this isolated gene joined with free-floating amino acids left in the solution and *grew another helix*. After that, it became almost a continual chain reaction. Heat it up, the helixes unzip. Cool it down, more amino acids are gathered and more helixes are formed. Over and over and over, each new helix a perfect copy of the gene you wanted to isolate and use. Doubling every few minutes. Very simple, very powerful."

"Humulun," Cliff said.

The sudden shift startled her. "What?"

"I was trying to remember where I had heard of that technology before. I didn't handle the application, but I remember somebody telling me it was going to be the wave of the future."

"Oh. Sure." She glanced into her rearview mirror, signaled, turned. "DNA-engineered insulin. Humulun is the trade name, right?"

Cliff nodded. "Lilly makes it."

"Right. I've read the literature." She frowned at the

211

rearview mirror, slowed, speeded up again. "What is that clown doing?"

"What's the matter, Debs?"

"Nothing, probably just a little jumpy."

The next turning came. She took it, her attention now split between what was behind her and the road in front. "Humulun is almost identical to what the healthy human pancreas produces. Before, they would buy hog and cattle pancreases from slaughterhouses and extract insulin. There were a lot of people with bad reactions to this alien substance. Almost all the contraindications have been eradicated with this new product. Genetically manipulated E coli bacteria were the growth medium. I personally think..." Deborah stopped, her attention caught by whatever it was she saw behind them.

Cliff swiveled around. "What's the matter?"

"I'm not sure," she said worriedly. "Those headlights have stayed glued to my bumper through the past three turnings." She shot him a glance. "Is your seat belt on?"

"Yes."

"Then hang on."

17

They were rammed at the worst possible point on the highway—a sharp curve alongside the intersection of two deep-water canals.

Had they been in any other automobile, they would have skidded down the ravine and plunged into the canal. But the Cherokee was big and heavy and sat on massive broad-grip tires. It slewed hard at the slamming, threw sparks high into the night, but clung gamely to the road. Cliff had a brief glance into the dark depths, a fleeting vision of descending into a watery grave. But the jeep held, and Deborah fought the bucking wheel like a pro. As soon as the Cherokee rocked back onto all four tires, she floored the accelerator and raced for safety.

The big dark car roared along behind them, fighting for another chance. But Deborah did not offer one.

She took the Pharmacon parking lot entrance-ramp so hard all four tires left the road. The dark car behind them squealed and swerved, slamming brakes and blowing up a cloud of burning rubber, and then produced a second cloud as the engine roared and the tires slewed around before the car powered away.

Her first words, when she was able to speak again, were, "Did you get the license plate?"

"Are you kidding?" Cliff puffed, swallowed, struggled to get enough air into his lungs. "I still don't know if it was a car or some kind of black killer bug."

"It was a sedan. An Infiniti, I'm pretty sure."

"You drove like that and still had a chance to see what kind of car was behind us?"

But she was already reaching for her door. "I think I've seen it before."

Cliff followed her through the first set of bulletproof doors on rubbery legs. The guard was plastered to his outside window. He turned and hit the communications button. "What was *that*?"

"Call the police," Deborah said, still gasping for breath. "Tell him a black Infiniti just tried to ram me off the road. I think I know who it was."

"Have to be the sheriff's office," the guard replied, reaching for the phone. "We're outside the city limits here."

Deborah groaned softly.

"Dr. Givens?"

"What about the highway patrol?"

"We've got strict instructions to report everything directly to the sheriff," the guard replied. "They can get awful sticky about jurisdiction."

Deborah hesitated, then said, "I guess it couldn't hurt."

"Right." The guard started dialing.

Deborah turned to Cliff. "Okay if I leave you here for a minute while I check my messages? I can't let you come up without going through the whole rigmarole again."

The guard broke in. "You're Mr. Devon, aren't you, sir?"

"That's right."

"I can't let him come in anyway, Dr. Givens," the guard said apologetically. "Strict instructions from Mr. Whitehurst. Sorry."

Deborah gave Cliff an angry look. "Bean counters at work."

"There's been four or five messages for you, though."

Deborah turned back to the guard. "For me?"

"No ma'am, at least, nothing since I came on." He pointed at Cliff. "The messages were for him. All from a man called Summers, I think, wait, I've got them here.

214

Yeah, that's right. Ralph Summers. He wants you to call as soon as you can. I can pass you a mobile phone, if you like."

"Cliff, good of you to call back. Sorry to disturb you over the weekend. Sandra said I'd probably find you there."

"Ralph, I know you told me not to come down, but I can explain—"

"Too late for that, I'm afraid." The man's voice was unusually somber. "Cliff, did you pass on samples of a drug under review to an outside laboratory?"

"Not of the drug itself," Cliff replied, his blood going cold. "Of the roots used for manufacturing the extract, and of some other plants. You see—"

"Close enough." The director released a long sigh. "I hate to do this, especially over the weekend and on the phone, but there's no choice, really. I'm afraid we're going to have to let you go."

The chill of dread turned to ice. "What?"

"You know as well as I do how many policies you have flouted with this action. Probably better than I do for that matter."

"But, Ralph, there are serious dangers—"

"Just hear me out. I know your concerns, and believe me, if I had my druthers, I would let you pursue them. But things have moved beyond that point. Far beyond it, I'm afraid. Word has been leaked to Congressman Larson about your actions. He plans to use it as additional fuel in the news conference he has called for Monday. You can imagine what that's going to sound like. An FDA employee breaches the trust of the pharmaceutical company, while at the same time we continue to drag our heels over accepting European clinical trial data and refusing to release this new wonder drug," Ralph paused, then went on, "I shudder to think what the newspapers are going to make of this."

Cliff let his legs go limp, and fell onto the leather bench. "I understand," he said dully.

"Believe me, son, it pains me to have to do this. But I don't have any choice in the matter. Our only hope at this point is to stay one step ahead of them and issue a press release of our own. First thing Monday morning we are going to do just that. How our own internal investigation turned up this matter, and how you were immediately released. I've been trying to reach you all day, wanting you to hear it from me first and not read it in the paper."

"You've always treated me right, Ralph," Cliff said, his heart thudding slow and heavy in his ears. "I'm really sorry about all this."

"Not near as sorry as I am." He sounded as though he truly meant the words. "I've always had the greatest respect for you, I really have."

"Could I ask a favor?"

"Of course you can."

Cliff did a swift run-through of the fears they had, of the kidnap attempt on Tom, of the stranger in the boat, and now of the ramming. "We still don't know exactly what's going on or who's behind it, but all this makes us increasingly certain we're onto something big."

"If this had come from anybody but you," Ralph said, "I'd have told them to roll over and go back to sleep."

"This is real, Ralph. I can see the mangled fender on Deborah's jeep from where I'm sitting. The local sheriff thinks she's crazy. Could you maybe try to light a couple of fires up in Washington?"

"Not immediately," he replied. "I'm going to have my hands full for the next few days. Damage control. I've got to try and garner support for the FDA over on Capitol Hill. But I'll have somebody spread the word now, and then work on it myself once things have settled down here."

"Thanks, Ralph. I appreciate it."

"Listen to this guy. Thanking me for giving him the ax. Where will you be in the meantime?"

"I guess I'll hang around here. Deborah's been given lab space up at UVA's Norfolk campus. I'll probably play gofer, save her the wear and tear."

"Let me hear if you come up with anything definite, all right?"

"Sure, Ralph."

There was another long sigh. "Take care of yourself, Cliff."

"I'll try."

"And stay in touch."

Cliff switched off the phone, raised his head to where Deborah stood in the doorway watching him. "I've been canned."

"So I gather." She walked over and sat down beside him. "I'm so very, very sorry, Cliff. It's all my fault."

"No it's not."

"If I hadn't dragged you into this mess, none of it would have happened."

"Well, it's too late for all that. I'm here and I'm in it." He dredged up a small smile. "Way up over my head, from the sounds of things."

"We'll figure something out." She reached over and mussed his hair. "Cute hunk like you shouldn't have any trouble finding work. I could always use another techie myself, but the way things are right now, that might be the quickest hire and fire of your life."

"Thanks, Debs. I appreciate that."

Deborah rose to her feet. "Come on, let's go home. Things always look better in the light of a new day."

When they were almost to the outer doors, the guard said, "Dr. Givens?"

"Yes?"

"The sheriff said to tell you that he would drop everything and rush right over. He asked for you to wait right here until he arrived."

217

"He didn't give you an idea how long he would be, did he?"

"He just said directly. That's all. He'd be over directly."

Deborah turned back to the door. "If he ever shows up, tell him he'll find me home in bed."

Cliff dug in his heels. "Are you sure that's safe, going back to your place?"

"Safe as anywhere else around here, and I'm too beat to look any farther."

She tugged him forward. "I'll stop by Reuben's and ask him to have a look around. Come on, Junior. You look as tired as I feel."

Ralph Summers sat staring at the phone. In his entire career, he had never been forced to do anything that felt as wrong as firing Devon.

Try as he might, he could find no other alternative. Still, in this case, political expediency was not going to help him feel any better. No matter how necessary the move might have been, in his heart Summers knew the FDA had just lost a very good man.

And no matter how crazy it sounded, Summers was positive that Devon's concerns were not completely unfounded. Misguided perhaps, but nonetheless real.

Trying to hold his shaky alliance of congressional support was going to occupy him completely over the coming few days. He would have to give this to someone else.

Summers mulled it over, then grinned without humor and reached for the phone. He searched his directory and found Sandra Walters' home number. Yes, it would serve her right. Let her lose a weekend over this. He did not know exactly how, but he was positive her hand had been in this somewhere. Good. She could reap a little of the benefits now.

Summers sat and listened to the phone ring and

thought again about Devon. He sighed. It did not look like he was going to get much sleep tonight.

As soon as they pulled away, the guard checked his clipboard and placed the call. When it was answered, he said, "Mr. Whitehurst? It's Jack, sir. You said to call if either one of them showed up. Yessir. Both of them together. Nossir, of course not, I didn't let him in. No, she just checked her messages and went home. Yessir, that's what she said, home to bed. But maybe you ought to know, sir, there was a problem... hello? Mr. Whitehurst?"

The guard stood there a moment, phone in hand, wondering. Then he shook his head and put the phone back down. Best not to get involved. What he didn't know couldn't hurt him.

Cliff was awakened by the sounds of gunfire and baying hounds.

He leapt out of what was the customary side of his bed at home, or at least tried to, and slammed square into a wall.

He rocked back prone, holding his forehead and moaning. Deborah came rushing in. "What was that? Are you all right?"

"Fine," he groaned, and struggled to his feet.

A voice called from the darkness outside, "Miss Debs?"

"Reuben? Is that you?"

"Yes ma'am. It's safe for y'all to come on out now. They's gone."

Deborah turned on the outside lights, wrapped her robe around her, unlocked her screen door, and walked down the porch steps. "Who is?"

"Whoever it was sneaking up on you." Reuben hefted the shotgun in his hand. "Sicked ol' Wilbur on 'em and fired a coupla bursts in the sky, them two was off like turpentined cats."

"Did you see who it was?"

"No ma'am, not me." He motioned to the grinning girl and boy half-hidden by night shadows. "You remember my two biggest gran'kids."

"Of course I do. Good evening, Amy, Stanley. What on earth are you two doing up so late?"

"Guarding your house," Amy replied proudly. "I saw 'em good. Both of 'em."

"Couldn't keep her in bed with a rope," Reuben grumbled. "Ever since you helped with her mama's illness, that little gal won't stop going on about you."

"They was white," the girl offered. "Weren't no foreigner like Granddaddy saw."

Deborah shot a baffled look toward Cliff. "You're sure?"

"Sure as sure can be," Amy replied.

"I was there too," the boy added. "She right. One of 'em, he had gray hair, the other was real blond."

"You were that close?"

"Close enough to hear what they was saying," Amy replied.

"That little gal is gonna be the death of me," Reuben moaned. "I thought I could last the night, but danged if my eyes didn't start dropping like they was tied to weights. I go back for my son-in-law, but he's working nights this week, and by the time I get my daughter up, them gran'kids is just raring to go. Had their clothes on and was out the door faster'n greased lightning."

"I stayed down low and watched 'em," Amy took up the tale. "Stan went back for Granddaddy."

"Bringing Wilbur was my idea," the boy announced. "That ol' hound was harder to wake up than Granddaddy."

"Did you really hear what they said?" Deborah demanded.

"Yes ma'am, surely did. They was whispering, but I could still hear 'em clear as day. One of 'em say, Be sure and get 'em both. The other say, What if he ain't here?

The first one say, He's here. I know that for a fact. Your job is to find him. The woman too. Get 'em both."

Deborah looked at a wide-eyed Cliff. "They're after you too? What for?"

"Miss Debs, we do surely love having you for a neighbor," Reuben said. "But with all them comings and goings, I do believe you'd be better off sleeping somewhere else for a spell."

"Thank you all very much for your help," Deborah said solemnly. "Reuben, I'm sure it will be safe for you all to go home now. We'll be moving in the morning. I'll stop by on my way out and thank you again." She turned and started up the stairs, leaning heavily on the railing as she climbed.

Cliff asked, "What are we going to do?"

"Try and find Cochise," she replied, walking slowly down the porch. "Then get some sleep. I'm too tired to think much beyond that."

18

Cochise waited in the loaded truck while Cliff gave Deborah a goodbye hug. "Take care of yourself."

"Listen to the man. He's been set up, fired, sideswiped, shot at, and now he's going to go off to goodness knows where, and he's telling me to take care." She forced up a weak smile. "Did you get through to Blair?"

Cliff nodded. "She said you were right. No reason for us both to be walking around making targets of ourselves."

"Blair is a good woman with a level head. You should keep hold of that one."

"I'm trying." The protest slipped through once more. "Debs, don't you think—"

"No I don't, and we've been through this a dozen times. There's nothing you can do for me in the lab. If you go stay at Blair's it would only endanger her and Miss Sadie. So you go lay low for a couple of days and let me see if I can come up with something strong enough for us to take public."

"It makes sense," he admitted, wishing it were otherwise.

"When I went over to thank Reuben and his family this morning, I told them about our troubles. I decided it was the least I could do after his family helped out. You know what he said?"

"I can't imagine."

"He told me that we'll always be moving against the world's flow. He called it a fact of life for anybody trying to follow a higher calling."

Cliff mulled that one over. "Sounds like a wise man."

She patted his arm. "Go on, now. I'll take care. And I'll be working on this just as hard as I know how."

"The lady's right," Cochise said over the noise of the truck's heavy-duty muffler. "Easier to keep her mind on the problem knowing you're somewhere safe."

"Then why doesn't that make me feel any better?" Cliff replied.

Cochise grinned. "Because you're her friend."

Their way took them out of town and over the Highway 17 bridge leading east toward the Outer Banks. The road was speckled with signs for beachfront hotels, gas stations, and tourist shops.

Cochise pointed at a fast-food joint they passed. "You know what they're serving in there? A breakfast burrito. Can you imagine? I mean, a body gets up, shaves and showers and puts on deodorant, gets all dressed up, right? After all that, some fool's gonna say, hey, what I need now is a mess of beans and onions and chili peppers for breakfast."

Cliff watched as they turned off onto a side road that appeared to run forever down an endless green tunnel. He asked, "Mind telling me where we are?"

"Oh, this is a real interesting sorta region for nature buffs. For borders we got ahead of us the Albemarle Sound. On the other sides are the Little Alligator River, the Big Alligator River, and the Dismal Swamp."

"This is a joke, right?"

Cochise shook his head. He pulled his makings from his pocket and deftly began rolling a cigarette with his free hand. "Naw, this is what they mean when they say you're going where you don't want to go unless you know how to get out."

"So where are you taking me?"

There was an enormous display of teeth. "You just settle back, hoss. What you don't know won't scare you."

They followed back roads farther and farther into marshy land, empty of all human life save the occasional logging truck. Eventually Cochise pulled into a lay-by bordered by three tumbledown wooden shacks. He extracted a key ring from the glove compartment, walked over, and opened the center shed. Inside were five neatly stacked canoes. He motioned for Cliff to come join him.

The canoe they chose was of simple green fiberglass with aluminum railing. Two paddles rested on the gunnels, but strapped to the stern was a four-horsepower outboard. A pair of cushions rested on folding legless chairs.

"What?" Cliff joked, carrying one end toward the landing. "No hollowed-out tree trunk?"

"Sears offers a guarantee," Cochise replied, lowering his end into the water. "Trees don't."

They loaded the supplies, then Cochise steadied the canoe while Cliff settled in the front. The big man lightly stepped in, keeping his weight low and in the center. Then they pushed off. With two deft strokes Cochise had them out in deep water. The little motor fired at first pull.

They continued on through dark green waters for a good half hour. The river broadened to where the far banks were lost behind morning mists. Cochise selected one broad channel, puttered up there a ways, then cut the motor.

"Best if we go in quiet from here. Mind paddling a while?"

"Not as long as you tell me what to do."

"The front paddler's job in easy waters is to give power," Cochise told him. "You leave the steering to me, and switch sides whenever your arm gets tired."

Cliff pulled out his paddle, fitted it to his hands, started what he hoped was a pace he could keep up for a while. "Is this something all you Indians do?"

That earned him an appreciative snort. "I started coming out here to sober up. Had to do something to occupy my hands and keep me out of sniffing distance of bars."

"You used to drink?"

"Yeah, drinking was a full-time job with me for a while. I liked to think there wasn't anything a couple slugs of whiskey couldn't put in better perspective."

"What changed your mind?"

"Mornings," Cochise replied. "Early light is a hard thing for an honest man to face with a hangover. I decided I either had to learn to lie to myself better or stop drinking."

Cliff paused to wipe at the sweat gathering on his face. "I can't imagine what it would be like to drink all the time. One night is enough to bring me close to death's door."

"Full-time drinking takes skill and practice, just like any profession," Cochise replied. "Means memorizing all the stages of being drunk. There's nine of them, ten if you're an Indian living in a trailer park, which I was at the time." The paddle kept up its rhythmic strokes. "Yeah, I got all sorts of fuzzy memories from those times. Hour-long arguments over what makes a better rope, hemp or nylon. Watching my waitress turn from woman into angel. Trying to get my money back from a tattoo parlor 'cause I don't know any woman named Sheila." Another stroke. "Yeah, just look at all those good times I've left behind."

"You make it sound as inviting as a fifty-mile hike."

"We'll take this next left turning," Cochise directed. "Quiet now."

They paddled up a water-floored hall lined with cypress and flowering reeds. The creek was so narrow Cliff could touch either bank with his paddle, but so deep he could not probe the bottom. Ten soft, quiet strokes and his world became endless shades of green. The sky was gone, the air stifling.

Fifteen minutes further on, Cochise banked the canoe

at the base of a mammoth cypress. The dense brush had been cut back and the earth stamped down. A scooped-out depression was lined with ashes from earlier fires. From low branches hung four knotted mosquito nets and balled-up hammocks.

"You'll camp here," Cochise said quietly, stepping into the knee-deep water and pulling the canoe up onto dry land.

"All the comforts of home," Cliff said.

"If anybody shows up, show your hands. Speak respectfully. Mention my name as soon as you can."

"Who's going to come?"

"Probably nobody. Almost all the ones who used this place are still in jail."

Cliff stopped, one leg in and one out of the canoe. "For what?"

"Just stay cool and talk respectfully. And mention my name. You should be okay."

The unloading went too swiftly. Cliff looked around at what was to be his home and asked, "What do I do if you don't show up?"

Cochise pointed at a leaf-strewn path and said, "Highway 17 is five miles down that way. Just stay on the path, and don't try it at night. But don't worry. You've got three days' supplies here easy. I'll be back before then."

"But—"

"I'll be back," Cochise said, walking toward the canoe. "This isn't the kind of place for spending time on the ifs and buts of life. Too many voices start coming at you out of the dark. Just hang in there and keep a cool head."

Cliff held the canoe as the big man climbed back in. When Cochise was balanced, Cliff maintained his grip. "Debs might have been right."

"She often is."

"I meant about us maybe being friends."

Cochise met his gaze. "I'd like to think so." He lifted the paddle in salute. "Three days tops."

"I wish I knew what you were up to," Deborah said.

"You've got enough to keep even your head busy," Cochise replied.

She nodded, still unhappy with the idea of his going off on his own. "Promise me you won't do anything crazy."

"Stop worrying so," the big man replied. "You'll only make yourself sick."

"No time for that now," she agreed.

"This time it's out of your hands," he said. "So just let it go."

"I trust you," she decided solemnly. "That's what friends are for, isn't it? So I can let go."

"Ain't nobody can do the work waiting in there but you. So get in there and get busy."

She touched his arm and said, "Thank you, friend."

Cochise watched her climb the stairs and enter the Norfolk university lab, his face as impassive as a stone mask. When the steps were empty of everything but her absence, he went around to his truck, got in, and drove away.

Cochise drove back into North Carolina, taking it slow. There was nothing for him to do until it grew closer to sunset but wait, and the road had always been a steady companion. It stretched out in front of him, as clear and straight as he wished his thoughts could be. He stroked the place where Deborah had touched his hand. He could still feel her fingers, hear her words, see her face. Friend.

Cochise had received his name during the lifetime spent in bars. He had kept it as a reminder of what he once had been and could easily be again. His name was a way of always hearing the threat of weakness, of backsliding, of defeat.

He had come very close to the edge, filling his body and mind with enough poisons to destroy a smaller man.

And it had almost wrecked him. But he had stopped. One booze-soaked dawn, Cochise had woken up cradling a bottle in another nameless alley. He had sat up, and just as he raised the amber fluid to his lips, he *saw*.

He had heard about this from other alcoholics, people who had approached the abyss and found the sudden strength to turn away. Why it came to him as it did, when it did, he never questioned. It was enough that it came, and in its coming granted him a freedom he had never thought possible.

In that rubble-strewn alley, there had come to him a moment of crystal clarity.

Deborah was the first to put words to the experience. For that matter, she was the first he had trusted enough to tell of it at all. She had listened to him recount his tale with a focused intensity that was all her own. Her listening was an honor, a treasure, one that still baffled him. That she would care so much to have listened so well, and then to have answered from the heart, was a mystery that touched him deep. Very deep.

Cochise was not a man of words. Deborah's ability to describe his moment of vision as a gift from God left him valuing her ability to explain almost as much as he did the experience itself.

It was in her faith that he found the clearest memory of his own invisible gift. It was in her words that he found the gift's greatest meaning. So he prayed, as she asked. But he did not tell her that many of his prayers were for her.

And now there was Cliff, a man whom Deborah held with such affection that it shone from her eyes whenever she spoke his name. Yet it was the affection of a sister for a younger brother, or the affection between friends. Cochise had never known friendship with a woman until he met Deborah, never even dreamed that such friendship was possible. And here it was, shared not just with him, but with another who had been there before him. He wondered at times why he felt no jealousy for this other friend, wondered at his own willingness to accept her request for them also to become friends.

But he did, both because it was Deborah who did the asking, and because Cliff also valued her friendship and tried to be worthy of it. Such a man was rare.

And now, because of these friends, he was laying aside the ingrained habits of a lifetime. He was becoming *involved*.

That, too, was a considerable mystery.

Cliff awoke to the sweaty heat of a sultry summer afternoon. He glanced at his watch and groaned. Only one thirty. He would never have believed that time could move so slowly. The day was only half over, and it had already lasted several weeks.

He struggled upright and slid from the hammock. He pulled off the mosquito netting and grabbed for his shirt. Despite spraying himself every hour, the little suckers had taken a liking to him that was distinctly one-sided.

Something jangled at the very back recesses of his brain. A hint of a dream. Some trace of a secret whispered while he had slept. Cliff felt a distinct unease tugging at his mind and decided maybe a coffee would help him think.

He lit the Coleman stove, poured water from a canteen, and set the pot on the flame. He sat and waited and looked around.

Katydids sang their serenade to the heat and the sun and the still-flowing waters. Butterflies flitted between cypress trees blanketed with Spanish moss. Eagles and egrets circled in the patch of sky above his clearing, a sky of endless, aching blue. His ears rang from the accustomed noises of men and cities that were no longer there.

When the water boiled, he mixed in coffee crystals and condensed milk, turned off the stove, then went to the water's edge and hunkered down. Somewhere beyond the creek's nearest bend a fish splashed. The noise was a clashing cymbal in his quiet world.

He sipped, breathed loudly just to hear himself, sipped again.

Deborah. The worry had something to do with her. But why? She was up in Norfolk, safely stowed away in a university lab. Nobody knew she was there but him and Cochise.He stopped in mid-sip. He had told Ralph on the phone. Yes. He remembered it now. Ralph had asked what he would be doing, and he had told him. But what was the matter with that? Ralph was trustworthy.

Cliff was suddenly on his feet without realizing he had stood up. Sandra. He did not know why, but his mind screamed danger at the thought. Sandra. Ralph had spoken to her earlier; he had obtained the Pharmacon number and the advice to seek him there. Sandra. Ralph had said he was going to be too busy to take care of Cliff's request to look into these Edenton problems himself. What if he gave the duty to her?

Who else would she tell?

Cliff dumped his coffee, gathered his scattered belongings into his shoulder bag, scribbled a note in case Cochise returned early, and started down the path.

Cochise pulled his truck up behind Blair's car, cut off the engine, and walked over. "This the place?"

"Just up around this next corner." She looked up at him. "Are you sure you want to do this alone?"

"What, you figure this little fellow's gonna give me a hard time?" Cochise grinned down at her. "You be sure and keep your window rolled up tight, missy. Gotta be one of us with a head clear enough to drive."

"If it goes according to plan," she amended.

"It's a good idea," Cochise replied. "Best I've heard. You just stay well back, so if anything does go wrong, our buddy up ahead won't have anybody to blame but me."

"And Debs," she added worriedly. "He's going to immediately assume she had something to do with it."

"From the sounds of things, Debs is already up to her neck in hot water. Another coupla drops won't make much difference."

Blair nodded. "That's what I thought. I really wanted to do something to help out."

He patted the top of her car. "It's a good idea, and I'm right glad you trusted me with it."

"You be careful," she replied.

"Hunker down low when you see me coming back," Cochise said, and started back for his truck. "In case he decides to come quiet. Which I doubt, given everything I've heard about this turkey."

Harvey Cofield was as furious as he had ever been in his entire life.

He spent his Sunday afternoon as he did almost every week, mowing his lawn with his top-of-the-line Toro riding mower, then pulling his big Merc 500 SEL from the garage and getting out his bag of cloths and waxes and sprays and chrome polish. His house was quieter than usual. His wife had become fed up with his tirades against fate and Whitehurst and the Pharmacon board and had gone to see her sister. Good riddance.

Whitehurst. Thinking the name had him polishing with maniacal frenzy, rubbing hard enough to threaten the paint. The man had ordered him, *ordered* him, to stay behind in this podunk town. When it was he, Harvey Cofield, who was the company's director of research, personally responsible, in a way, for discovering the drug in the first place. So while Whitehurst schmoozed with the board and the other bigwigs in Washington, he, Harvey Cofield, was imprisoned down here in the middle of nowhere.

It was an outrage.

To rub salt in the open wound, Whitehurst had phoned

that morning. The man had sounded like a loon. He had claimed to be in Norfolk, and he wanted Cofield to check up on some nonsense about Givens and her sidekick, that character from the FDA. Cofield had given as good as he got, asking how the weather was up on Capitol Hill, saying he'd be simply delighted to help out, soon as he himself got back from being wined and dined with the bigwigs. Whitehurst had breathed heavy for a couple of seconds, then slammed down the phone. No question about it, the guy was coming unglued.

Cofield was so wrapped up in his own rage he did not hear the newcomer walk up, did not notice anything until a voice two octaves below double-bass rumbled, "How's it going, Doc?"

He spun around, and the sight was so startling he backed up until he was jammed up tight against the car door. At first he thought a tree had moved in on his driveway. Then the man shifted so that the sun was not in Harvey's eyes, and he could see it was Deborah's assistant. That Indian. The one with the funny nickname. "Cochise! You almost gave me a heart attack, sneaking up on me like that."

"Sorry about that," the big man said. "Awful quiet around here."

"My wife's away." Cofield had to squint to see Cochise's face. He hated how the man stood so close, forcing him to look up, accenting how much bigger he was than Cofield. "Look, could you back up a little? You're crowding my personal space."

"Right." The man did not move. "Wasn't sure we'd find you home. How come you're not up in Washington?"

"I wasn't—" Cofield shut it off. "What kind of question is that? My comings and goings are none of your business."

"You know, my pappy used to say there wasn't much of anything a good dose of a two-by-four wouldn't cure." The Indian lifted his head, squinted, and searched the empty sky. "Yessir, good length of two-by-four is a country boy's best friend. Why, it'll even cure a mule of a case of the stubborns." He hefted an invisible baseball bat. "All you got to do is apply it judiciously between the mule's eyes."

Cochise dropped his arms and stared down on the little man. "Way I see it, we got two ways to handle this. The easy way, and the hard way."

Cofield rammed the polishing rag into Cochise's chest, trying to push him away. It was like trying to shift a house. "You better watch your step, mister, or you're gonna wind up in all kinds of trouble."

"The hard way. Shoulda known." Cochise raised one mallet-sized fist and cold-cocked the doctor on one temple. Cofield crumpled like a puppet. Cochise swung him up easily with one arm and started for the truck, said softly to the slumbering man, "Time to get a move on, Doc. We got us a rendezvous with destiny."

19

When Harvey Cofield came to, he thought at first he was still dreaming. Which was understandable, considering that his hands appeared tied to the safety strap of a truck being driven by a giant, hairless bear. But the thundering of his head helped clear his vision, and he eventually realized he had been kidnapped by Deborah Givens' lab technician. When he could shape the words, he asked, "Where are you taking me?"

"Not far," the Indian replied, not turning from the road. "How's the head?"

"Hurts."

"Got some aspirin in the glove box. Lemme make this turn and I'll fish you out a couple." He swung them onto a small side road, stopped, reached over. "Sorry about all this inconvenience, Doc, but it ain't been all that easy to get you suits to see reason."

"What are you talking about?" Harvey Cofield watched the Indian pluck two tablets from a tin, slip them between Harvey's lips, then hold a canteen up for him to drink. Harvey took in too much water, had it shoot up his nose; he snorted, choked, almost lost the aspirin down his windpipe.

"Slow down, Doc. Ain't in that much of a hurry."

The second time went better. When he had drunk his fill, he gasped, "You can have my car, take it, I'll report it stolen, I won't say—"

"Calm down, Doc. It ain't nothing like that. You're not being kidnapped."

Harvey Cofield glanced at his wrists, which were

expertly tied with nonslip nylon cord. "I'm not?"

"Well, not like you think. This is an act of pure desperation." He put the truck back into gear and started off. "I was told a lot of other stuff I was supposed to say, but I forgot most of it. Sorry."

"Who told you? Deborah Givens? She's in on this?"

"Naw, not really. She'd have blown her stack if I'd told her about this, so I didn't."

Harvey Cofield tucked his head down and wiped his sweating face with his shoulder. He watched the Indian turn off onto an even smaller country lane, one lined by nothing but forest and fields. His gut clenched with the thought that this was it, the end, the final journey. "Hey, look, I'm a reasonable man. If Debs wants something, why doesn't she just ask?"

"She did. But like I said, she's not in on this."

"More lab space, machinery, her own executive office, more staff..." Harvey realized he was babbling, didn't care, just couldn't see beyond the thought that the end was drawing near. "Anything. I'll get her the world on a string. Just look, let me go, okay? I've got a lot left I need to do."

His tone rose a full octave as Cochise pulled off the road, turned the truck around, parked, and cut off the motor. "I'm a rich man, well, not rich rich, but not bad off—look, whatever she's paying you, I'll make it better."

Cochise climbed from the cab, shut his door, walked around, opened the passenger's side, and stepped back as Cofield tried to connect with a kick. "Enough of that." The big man did not seem the least bit put out. "This is all gonna be over soon."

"No, look, stop, don't."

Cochise released Cofield from the strap but kept his hands tied. The big man plucked Cofield from the cab and set him down on the pavement, one massive hand keeping an iron grip on his upper arm. "Walk."

"I'll double it," Cofield said, half walking, half letting himself be dragged down the road. "Whatever it is she's paying, I'll double. No, triple. There's a safe in my closet behind a false wall. Full of stuff. Cash, jewelry, my wife's crazy for jewelry. Fortune in there. Bonds. Take it all. It's yours. Just please, don't, no, I don't—"

Cochise stopped and shook the smaller man so hard his teeth rattled. "Will you just stop?" When he was sure Cofield was listening, he went on, "All we're gonna do is go up around this bend, walk one time through this field, go back to the car, and wait a while."

Harvey Cofield found himself hard put not to snuffle. If the Indian hadn't held him up he would have collapsed into a weak little puddle on the empty road. Where was a cop when he needed one? "Please, Mister Cochise, I never meant you any—"

"Listen up, Doc. You remember the warnings Debs kept trying to tell you folks about?" He shook the little man, gentler this time. "Remember? The rapeweed? Remember her trying to get you folks to come out and see for yourself?"

A single ray of hope split the night of terror in Harvey Cofield's mind. "Rapeweed?"

"The rapeweed, Doc. It changed. Remember Debs telling you that?"

The ray of light and hope and safety grew stronger. "That's all this is about? Rapeweed?"

Cochise turned and dragged the little man on down the road. "Let's go, Doc. You'll see for yourself what it's about soon enough."

He shuffled on alongside Cochise. Off the road, across the burned-out rubble, into the golden rapeweed. Joining hundreds and hundreds of other people, nobody paying any attention to the giant Indian dragging a man with his hands tied in front of him. Harvey Cofield's mind had trouble taking it all in, the scene was so bizarre. Musicians playing stuff he had never heard of before, never imagined as music, but who knew what kids liked these days? Except they weren't all kids. A lot of older people, dancing and racing and laughing and just walking around, eyes wide open but not really focusing on anything he could see. People shouting sounds at the sky, as though talking with invisible beings in some alien tongue. A forest of tents and campers and flags and more people out beyond the fields.

"Okay, that's enough." Cochise led Harvey Cofield back out of the rapeweed, across the burned expanse, onto the road, hurrying now, hustling toward the truck.

Despite himself, Harvey Cofield was curious. "What's going on back there?"

"No time, no time." Cochise was almost running. "Pick it up, Doc, we gotta get back to the truck before it hits."

"What hits?" He was puffing hard, trying to keep up with the Indian's long strides.

"Debs doesn't know how long it takes to grab hold." The Indian grunted as they rounded the curve and the truck came into view. "You feel anything yet?"

"Feel?" Harvey Cofield chuffed, his lungs working overtime. Getting hit on the head, kidnapped, dragged through a field, now running back to a truck. And the Indian wanted to know how he felt?

Cochise flung open the passenger door, pushed and shoved Harvey inside, started to retie his wrists to the strap, when suddenly his stare went all distant. "Uh-oh."

Cofield watched in utter astonishment as the Indian let his wrists go free, slammed the passenger door, and staggered around the truck as though trying to run through quicksand. Cochise pulled open his own door, sprawled in, reached, fumbled and managed to close his door. His breath came in deep moaning grunts. Harvey Cofield opened his mouth to ask what the heck was going on, when suddenly his eyes started seeing colors he didn't even know existed.

Then his whole world took a very sharp turning to the left.

20

Luis de Cunhor leaned one elbow on the sill, all four of the car's windows open to catch the cool sea breeze. He read and reread the slip of paper, then searched the map, neither his eyes nor his mind truly focusing on the matter at hand.

He examined the paper once more, trying to see beyond the handwritten words to the implications of what he was reading. His mind came up blank.

The message had been passed on by the secretary of the scientist on their payroll, the man now touring the Alps. The message itself was perfectly clear. It simply said, "The woman doctor is in Norfolk, at the University of Virginia lab."

What was baffling was that the message had come from the Padron.

The *Padron*.

Luis turned the page over, as though underneath might be written how the Padron, seated behind his desk four thousand miles away in Sao Paulo, had come to know where the woman doctor was located.

Or how he had come to know of the woman doctor at all.

Still, orders were orders, especially if they came from the Padron. Luis checked the map once more and drove on. Indeed, the Padron was a remarkable man.

Cliff took the Norfolk streets like an Indy racer headed for the checkered flag.

The only car Hertz had available was a full-sized Buick

at some astronomical cost per day. He slid his credit card over without protest, figuring that it couldn't put him much further in the hole than he already was. The clerk showed a little hesitation, which was understandable, seeing as how he was about to lease a twenty-five-thousand-dollar car to a guy dressed mostly in leaves and dirt and sweat. But the card appeared okay, and the driver's license showed a normal guy in a suit, and Cliff came up with a semi-believable story about being in a rush on a construction job, so he passed the keys over with the papers. Cliff was out the door before the clerk could ask if he needed a map.

The path of Cochise's had proven to be the five longest miles in Cliff's entire life.

The forest had shut out all hint of breeze. The air had been so humid and fetid with rotting brush that each breath was a desperate search for oxygen. He had arrived at the highway covered in the results of having tripped over five or six or maybe seven roots—he had lost count. On legs that had long since gone rubbery, he had walked to the dead center of the highway and stood there with arms over his head. Hit me or give me a lift, he had thought as the truck roared up with bellowing horn, it's your choice.

When the truck pulled over and stopped, Cliff had gone around to the side, looked up at the round-eyed driver, and said as calmly as his shaking chest would allow, "You wouldn't believe me if I told you the truth, and I'm too tired to lie."

"Brother, anybody hard up enough to try and stop a truck with his bare hands deserves a lift," the driver told him. "Climb on in."

The truck had headed north, away from Edenton and his car. Cliff had let himself be dropped off at the Norfolk airport, but not before he had thanked the driver and his partner with solemn handshakes and promises to write and let them know how it all ended up.

Cliff pulled the car up to the curb, stopped another pedestrian, asked for directions a third time, offered hasty thanks, and roared away. The University of Virginia's Norfolk campus was a patchwork of buildings spread out over a couple of square miles, with bits and pieces of city life in between. The lab buildings were close to the teaching hospital, that much he had learned from the cop who had given the first set of directions, but only after a cautious inspection of his papers and license.

Cliff turned the corner, breathed a great gasp of relief when he saw the hospital directly in front of him, then cut it off when he spotted the dark car in front of the red-brick lab building. Cliff squinted, decided that yes, it was definitely an Infiniti. Black. As the car angled to pull into a parking lot, he saw the mangled front bumper. And lo and behold, through the open windows he saw an aquiline-featured foreigner dressed in a cream-colored suit and a very nasty scowl.

With a war cry that would have made Cochise's ancestors proud, Cliff slammed his foot down on the gas pedal. The big V-8 roared. Tires squealed and burned a neat patch of smoking rubber as Cliff raced the final thirty yards, shouting a wordless scream the entire way.

He hit the Infiniti with a force that rocked it clear off the two nearside tires.

Cliff backed up, stopped to catch his breath and inspect the results. Through the open window he saw a dark-haired man slumped over the steering wheel. Blood seeped from a cut on his forehead.

Cliff looked around, expecting to hear shouts and sirens and racing feet.

Nothing. Nobody on the streets, no heads from windows, no flashing lights. Amazing. Definitely his lucky day.

Cliff put the Buick into drive, listened as the engine replied with some sounds that had absolutely not been there a minute ago, and drove around the block to find a parking space of his own.

He got out, locked the door, and inspected a hood that now lurched upward and slightly to the left. He then turned and started toward the cluster of buildings, wondering which one contained the labs.

Deborah dropped her stylus and eased the ache in her shoulders. With the movement came the warning knell. Was it the first? She stopped, held her breath, and did her internal checklist. She could not recall. She had been too wrapped up in her work to notice. Fatigue rolled over her in waves. Bad.

Her table was strewn with DNA spectroscope readouts and her own calculations. At any other time she would have reveled in the challenge of mathematical biology, but not now.

There was no longer any room for doubt. Her restructured viroid was not a respecter of species. The instructions that had carried it into the root system of one plant had taken it to the pollen of another. A remarkable feat, one that would excite the entire scientific world.

A pity it had to be discovered this way.

The recombinant DNA affected the rapeweed pollen in a way that produced a hallucinogen. It had to be one based upon a complex amino acid chain, one that had the ability to flow through the blood-brain barrier intact. She scanned the long sheets spread out before her, reading them as easily as a composer did a musical score. The signals were there. The supposedly harmless marker molecule connected with the pollen molecular structure in such a way as to send any human who came into contact with it to the far side of the moon.

There were two big unanswered questions. First, was this effect to be found in every flowering plant, or just rapeweed? She hoped for the latter, but the scarred patch of ground before the Jones' home, where rose-bushes once had flourished, was there to haunt her every time she shut her eyes.

But it was the second question that really brought out the nightmares: Did the recombinant pollen DNA have the power to self-replicate? Were they going to find an ever-expanding harvest of hallucinogenic plants? Deborah did not think so. The impossibility of self-replication was one of the basic tenets upon which modern microbiology was founded.

Yet a lab-restructured viroid that was no respecter of species was also totally, utterly new. And this shadow of doubt left her more frightened than she had been since the first dark nights of her impending illness.

Her colleague Warren chose that moment to enter the room. "How's it going, Debs?"

"All right." Deborah pushed back her chair. She had to go lie down. Suddenly the act of rising seemed a daunting task. She glanced at her watch. Almost five. Eight hours without a break. Very bad.

Warren moved to the lab's far corner and busied himself over the coffee machine. "Hey, you'll never guess who I saw sitting in a car outside the lab."

"Who?" She made it to her feet by pressing up with both arms. Then she realized she had left her wheelchair in the jeep. She had felt so good that morning she had seen no need to bring it up. Very, very bad.

"James Whitehurst." Warren stirred in a spoonful of sugar. "At least I think it was him."

Deborah stood frozen to the spot. "Whitehurst of Pharmacon?"

"Are there two? I met him at a conference a while back. Sent him my curriculum vitae, thought maybe I could get a step up in the world. Never heard back from him. That's why I didn't go over and say hello. Wonder what he wants." Warren took a noisy sip. "I'm pretty sure it was him."

Whitehurst. Deborah felt faint tremors run through her limbs. Everything was falling into place. The man who had stalked her house had gray hair. Of course.

Whitehurst saw the Echin drug breakthrough as his key to the boardroom. He would do anything to hold on to that.

Anything.

Deborah started for the door, her feet shuffling noisily across the floor. "Could you give me a hand, Warren?"

His back was to her. "Sure thing, Debs, just let me make a quick call, okay?"

"Warren," she said, then stopped. He was already on the phone. She reached for the door.

She had to find a place to hide.

James Whitehurst tried to look at it like a trip to the dentist, painful but unavoidable. Down deep, however, he found the whole affair utterly despicable.

Having to deal with riffraff such as this man beside him, a dead-eyed lout with white-blond hair and pupils of palest blue, one shade away from a true albino. A gun for hire. To be forced to stoop to such things. Whitehurst climbed the laboratory stairs, fighting down his anger at Owen MacKenzie, at Pharmacon, at fate, but not at Givens. No, that anger he wanted to let burn like a white-hot flame. It was the only way he could keep going. And he had to. Doing what lay ahead was his only way to get what he deserved. Though it left him sweaty palmed and queasy, Whitehurst kept climbing the stairs. At least he wouldn't be the one to pull the trigger.

Whitehurst stopped before the door the receptionist had directed him to, and motioned for his heavy-lidded companion to wait. He raised his hand to knock on the door, when a soft moan sounded from farther down the corridor.

It was worse this time than it ever had been before. The warning tingle in her head had grown to an angry buzz, sort of a cross between a berserk electric razor and a beehive on the rampage.

Then the socks appeared on her ankles.

That was how somebody in the support group had described it. Deborah had only gone three times before tiring of all the pain and anger and fear. Maybe it helped the others to lay it all out over and over and over around the room, but not her. She had enough trouble dealing with her own distress, much less that of two dozen others.

The socks. The socks started unrolling up her legs, like somebody was dipping her limbs in novocaine. She stumbled over to the side wall and let herself slip down to the floor. Already she had lost her feet.

It was up above her knees now, and at midthigh the new fear emerged. What if it didn't stop? What if it kept creeping right on up, farther and farther to her neckline? She knew it was a possibility. She even knew the name for it. Chronic progressive, it was called. The form of disease that turned a living, breathing, feeling, shouting, lusting human being into a prisoner, trapped inside a body that no longer moved upon command. Sometimes for a night, sometimes for a lifetime.

Deborah breathed a soft moan, almost delirious with relief when the numbness stopped and held, claiming only her legs.

Then she heard the footsteps walk toward her, and she held her breath. But the footsteps continued their quiet careful approach.

Until two pairs of legs came into view.

21

"It's too quiet," Cochise announced.

"Quiet's fine with me," Cliff replied, climbing the stairs beside him. "Quiet's great."

Cliff had been halfway across the broad lawn when a blaring horn had turned him around. Blair had flung her car into a free space, waved him over, grinned from ear to ear when Cliff's jaw hit his chest at the sight of Cofield sitting there beside her.

Cochise had untangled himself from the backseat and swiftly explained how the research director had been persuaded to see the light. Cofield had just sat there, still shaky from the experience and afraid the three-headed purple people eater was going to swoop down again and carry him off for good.

But Cliff had managed to give almost as good as he got. He had taken Blair and Cochise by the mangled Infiniti, shown off his handiwork, bragged a little over how not everybody could have done such a job—see that, hit him dead center, look at how that door's bent, it almost makes it halfway across the front seat. Cochise had asked, if Cliff had done such a great job, then where was the guy. Cliff had replied by pointing at the hospital and suggesting that a stroll through the emergency room might reveal a foreigner with a leaky head.

Then they had sent Blair back to baby-sit their semi-reformed research director and gone off to find Deborah Givens.

Cochise stopped him with an upraised arm the size of a tree branch. "This place is quiet like before a big storm."

But Cliff was still too high from his meeting with the Infiniti to care. "I got it now. This is another Indian thing, right?"

Cochise shook his head, his eyes staring hard up ahead, as though trying to see around corners. "I just got the feeling this place is waiting for an explosion to go off."

"So let's go see," Cliff said, climbing the final stairs. "What lab did she say, two-oh-one, is that right?"

They stopped before the door and knocked. A muffled voice answered from inside. Cliff opened the door, shook his head as Cochise hung back, scanning the hall. "Afternoon. Is Dr. Givens around?"

"Just stepped out." The guy made more noise sipping from his cup than Cliff would have thought possible. "You from Pharmacon?"

"Sort of. Do you know where she went?"

"She'll be back. Can't have gone far, her purse is still here." Another slurp. "I thought you were probably from her lab. I saw James Whitehurst down there a minute ago, didn't I?"

The pieces fell into place with an almost audible click-click-click. "What?"

"Whitehurst. Did you come up with him?"

"Whitehurst is here?" Cliff wheeled around, ready to shout for Cochise, when a scream floated up through the open window.

The big man blew into the room, scaring the guy at the desk so badly he poured coffee down his lab coat. Cochise held one woman's shoe in his hand. He pushed Cliff away from the window, craned, searched, pointed, shouted, "There!"

Cliff left the room a half step behind Cochise, caught up with him on the stairs by jumping the banister's curve, led by two strides when he slammed through the front doors. He took all eight entrance stairs in one bound, spotted Blair pointing across the lawn to where Deborah was being bundled toward a car, and roared.

Whitehurst thrust his face within inches of hers. "Take a last long look at the real world, Doctor. The one you scientists never get around to understanding."

The blond guy carried her with the ease of one whose muscles did not bulge. Her hands were tied, her mouth stuffed with Whitehurst's handkerchief. They had taken the stairs with caution, Whitehurst up ahead to make sure the coast was clear. But it was summer, and the weekend, and the place was almost deserted. They scampered under the receptionist's window and through the doors, made another check, then hustled across the lawn.

But the need for speed did not stop Whitehurst from railing at her. "I can buy brains like you on every street corner," he rasped. "All I have to do is snap my fingers and say the magic words, sterile lab, and they're mine. You all are."

The blond man was more frightening because of his silence. His eyes scattered everywhere, checking in all directions, watching for the first sign of danger, paying Whitehurst's tirade no mind at all as he hustled her across the lawn.

"You people hide in your ultraclean little rooms because you're terrified of real life." Whitehurst's words tumbled out in the effort of trying to speak and jog at the same time. "There's a basic rule of real life you never bothered to learn, doctor scientist lady. You take care of business. You do whatever works. You deal with what's there. And if anybody gets in your line of fire, hey, there aren't any white flags in the real world."

He stopped by the car and caught his breath and fumbled for his keys. "So you can just kiss—"

"Heellllp!" The scream was so high as to sound disembodied. "Clifff ! Cochiiisse! Poolllliiice!"

Whitehurst whirled about, and was shocked into a

moment's stillness by the sight of Blair Collins jumping up and down and pointing in their direction.

The roar behind them galvanized the blond man into action even before the sound had registered in Deborah's ears. He slammed her into Whitehurst so fast and so hard it knocked them both to the ground. Then he turned and made two blades of his hands.

Cliff saw the man turn and crouch and raise his hands like he knew what he was doing. But Cliff was too fired up with too much anger to stop. He put his head down and charged.

But the man was no longer there.

Then Cliff was flying through the air, his right arm flailing at an uncertain angle.

And then he hit. Hard.

"That's one of them!" Whitehurst's voice was almost incoherent. "Do it!"

The blond hair was a white frame for eyes that held no expression, no feeling, no concern whatsoever as they appeared over him, the fist cocked back for the final blow. Then the blond man simply disappeared.

There was a moment of shouting and feet scuffling and a whanging sound of something being rammed repeatedly into the side of a car. Then a pair of figures were suddenly laid out beside him, resembling a pile of wadded up clothes more than James Whitehurst and a blond thug.

Then the sky was replaced by a very big man, who puffed, "That sure was dumb."

Cliff tried to rise, found his arm wasn't responding to orders. "I think I'm hurt."

"Did you study to get that dumb, or does it come natural?"

The pain hit him then. "I think I'm hurt bad."

"Serves you right."

The Indian was replaced by a very pale Blair, who

cradled his face in two very cool hands and asked, "Where does it hurt?"

"Everywhere, but mostly my arm."

She ran fingers over his neck and spine, then turned to Cochise and said, "Lift him gently, and let's get him over to the hospital."

"Let me bind up the riffraff here." Cochise picked up Whitehurst and the blond man by one heel each, and dragged them off across the lawn.

Cliff swiveled his head, found Deborah leaning up against the side of the car. "You okay?"

"Never been better." She looked from one to another and said, "I'm not going to try and thank any of you."

Cliff managed a smile. "Oh, go ahead."

Then the Indian was back, sliding his hands under him, scooping him up. And with the motion came the pain, a great roaring wave of it that came crashing down on his head, blacking out all light, all sound, all thought.

22

Deborah found herself unable to pay attention to what the minister was saying.

Sunlight played through the old church's side windows, making golden pillars in which dust motes danced and flickered like tiny angels. The minister's words washed over and through her, lighting her up inside, even though she was unable to focus, concentrate, use her special talent to delve and seek and understand. No, today the effort was too great, her happiness too strong. It was enough to sit and rest and be home.

The news conference had blown away like smoke in the wind, along with Congressman Larson's noisy threats. Ralph Summers had moved into high gear after they had found him late Sunday evening, sat him down, and gone through the entire story. Harvey Cofield had contributed little except confirmation that yes, the rapeweed pollen had been genetically altered, and yes, he did agree with Deborah's assessment that the cause was the recombinant DNA, and yes, Whitehurst and an accomplice were in custody in Norfolk. The calls and discussions had carried on long into the night, while Deborah dozed in Summers' guestroom.

Monday afternoon Cliff had found himself not only reinstated, but promoted. His victory was sweetened by the news that his former boss, Sandra Walters, had been placed on administrative leave pending an investigation of her role in the affair.

Cliff's new title was to be Assistant Director for Consumer Affairs, but first he was to complete a temporary assignment as the FDA onsite controller at Pharmacon's Edenton facility. He had traveled back down to Edenton with Deborah and Cochise and Blair, a very bemused young man. What's the matter? Deborah had demanded during the journey, isn't this what you want? Cliff had replied with a shrug and the words, I suppose so. Deborah had grinned and said, better watch out, Junior, or you might get what you wish for.

The condition of her legs had not improved. From time to time there had been occasional tingles, enough to have her holding her breath and hoping that the feeling was about to return. But nothing more. Yet. Deborah was nothing if not determined. She had refused to give in to the dark despair of resignation.

Ralph Summers' renewed backing had been sufficient to obtain a court order, and on Tuesday the sheriff's department and the Highway Patrol had mounted a raid and cleared out the hippie camp. The court order had stipulated that all law enforcement officers were to wear protective gear and take every possible caution. Still two of the officers had been dumb enough to pluck off their masks and wipe at sweat; the result had been enough to sober up all of their company. The camp had been deserted by midnight.

Wednesday the fields had been doused with kerosene, set alight, then bulldozed under—all but a dozen bags of samples. Deborah had then stopped by the Jones homestead. She had explained what had happened, apologized, and promised that they would be compensated for all their troubles. She had left them both troubled and relieved.

Thursday the first series of tests came back. The entire lab resources of Pharmacon were now at her disposal, and things moved faster than even she would have thought possible. Friday the initial results were confirmed. The genetically altered pollen was not regenerative. The hallucinogenic effect was restricted to that generation of plants and could not spread beyond plants actually brought into contact with the altered viroid.

With that verdict, Deborah had felt as though a thousand-pound load had been lifted from her shoulders. She had slept through the entire night for the first time in a week and awakened with the feeling that there might really be light at the end of the tunnel.

She had deliberated about what to do personally, and had finally come to the decision that she would stay at Pharmacon. The drug remained a good one—great, in fact. Anything that could assist the body in fighting off viral infection was a major step forward.

Even Harvey Cofield had asked her to stay, and had promised her everything except his own job.

The key now was to find a way to produce the compound synthetically, so that there was no possibility of further harm to the environment. Deborah sat and reflected on the peace that filled the little church and corrected herself. No, that was just the external key.

The internal key proved harder to grasp, yet equally vital. But she began to get a glimpse of it now, sitting here in her wheelchair, drawn up in the aisle beside Cochise.

The big man looked uncomfortable in the way of one not accustomed to wearing a tie. But he had remained by her side throughout the entire period, silent and solid and always ready for her to draw from his incredible strength. In those long and tiring days, Deborah had grown very close to the quiet man and his steady ways.

Beyond Cochise sat Blair and Cliff, the pair so wrapped up in their newfound love that the rest of the world might as well disappear. Her gaze returned to Cochise. The man loomed tall and utterly still, his brow furrowed with concentration as he listened to the sermon. Deborah felt a flood of tenderness wash over her. She reached over and settled her hand into one of his.

The big man started, utterly surprised by the action. He glanced down at her fingers, then his dark eyes turned toward her face. He studied her a long moment. Deborah did not flinch. There was no need. She held his gaze and let her heart show through her eyes.

A tension flowed out of the big man, one there so long she did not truly recognize it until she watched it dissolve. His features relaxed, then relaxed some more. Eyes the color of agate looked at her with such tenderness she felt as though her heart was going to burst. He swallowed her fingers within a grasp as gentle as his gaze.

Deborah turned back toward the front, her world complete.

Yes, the internal key. She as a scientist was tapping into creation, she saw that now. It was her gift, this ability to fathom some of the depths of the invisible universe. But she was also human, finite, fallible. She had to take care, great care, greater care than ever as she launched herself farther and farther into the unknown. She had to ask for help and guidance at every step.

The realization that she had both understood and accepted the responsibility filled her with such a feeling of lightness and well-being that for a moment she lost contact with where she was. Then the service was over, and Cliff was standing and stepping behind her chair and reaching for the handles to steer her out. But the intimate peace and power stayed with her, and strengthened, then strengthened even more.

Deborah reached a hand over her shoulder and stopped him. "Thank you, dear friend," she said, rising to her feet. "But I think I will walk."

Epilogue

Owen MacKenzie stood at the reception room's solitary window and stared out over the sprawl of Sao Paulo. His face gave nothing away as he silently decided, this place is the eyesore capital of the globe.

The sound of a door opening spun him around. The slender man with the bandaged head said, "Mr. de Cunhor will see you now."

"It's about time," Owen MacKenzie growled, reaching for his case. "I've been cooling my heels out here for almost an hour."

The young man did not reply, merely stood by with eyes downcast. He seemed strangely subdued, this man. Probably still bothered by whatever it was knocked him upside the head.

As Owen passed, he gave the man a closer inspection. The bandage fit him like a turban, covering the entire top of his skull and fitting down over one ear. One eye was swollen shut. Yessir, whoever did that got in a couple of good ones.

Fernando de Cunhor played it hard and tight and tough, because that was what was expected. But both men knew the deal was done long before Owen MacKenzie arrived in Sao Paulo. In truth, all had been set in motion even before MacKenzie had supplied information on the Givens woman's whereabouts. Fernando de Cunhor's rigid negotiating tactics were as much show as MacKenzie's anger over being made to wait. Show and not show. A weaker man would have been eaten alive, but not Owen MacKenzie. This American had proven himself to be a survivor. He knew when to cut his losses and retreat, to return and fight another day.

Yes. With such a man Fernando de Cunhor could definitely be partners.

So for him, this time, the cold ruthlessness was merely show. And a warning. And Owen MacKenzie's seething rage was nothing more than a reply that he understood, that he accepted the challenge.

When the details were hammered out and the terms settled, both men relaxed as much as they could while still in the presence of a former adversary. Fernando de Cunhor sent Luis for an aperitif. Owen MacKenzie refused the liquor, but lit up a Havana cigar. The two men eyed each other with the calculating gaze of respectful enmity.

Owen MacKenzie asked, "How long before your men have the process up and running?"

When Luis had translated, Fernando de Cunhor replied in Portuguese. He understood English perfectly but preferred to use translators whenever dealing with foreigners. It permitted him an additional moment to think, and often allowed him to take advantage of slipups when the others became tired. "They say they can have the solution ready for spraying on the plants within three months. But you know scientists."

"Yeah," Owen MacKenzie growled. "I know scientists. Real well."

"How long do you think it will be before the synthesization process is worked out?"

Owen shrugged. "Coupla years, then maybe another couple before the FDA approval process is completed. You won't have any of that kinda trouble down here, I take it."

"No, poor countries such as my own cannot afford to waste time on disputing fine points of biochemistry when tens of thousands die every day from viral-related illnesses."

"Now that's the kind of sense I'd like to see more of in my country."

Fernando de Cunhor listened to Luis's fluid translation and thought, what a waste. A fine young man with great potential, but flawed. Miserably flawed. And a failure. Fernando de Cunhor could not permit failure, especially not one as public as this.

No. Luis would not be with him long. A pity. He had such great hopes for the boy. But no matter. Because Luis was family, his departure would not be as public as his error. Instead, he would be kept here and treated well, so close to the Padron that none could think to accuse him of wrongdoing when the accident happened.

Look at the young man, all subdued and sorrowful, as though being apologetic would affect the outcome one iota. No, Luis was history. It was only a matter of time.

De Cunhor turned his attention back to the American. "Speaking of scientists, what of the woman, the trouble-maker?"

"Yeah, she is that all right. But she's also in the spotlight, and she's got as good a chance as any of getting the synthesis process off the ground. We'll make good money in the rest of the world with your production here, but to crack the American market we've got to sanitize things. So the scientist lady is gonna be staying with us at Pharmacon." Owen MacKenzie puffed hard on his cigar, until the tip burned ruby red. Then he released a great cloud of smoke and the words, "For a while."